Here are what reviewers are saying about

A Deeper Cut by Sheri Wren Haymore

"Sheri Wren Haymore has spun another murder mystery in A Deeper Cut—too compelling to be put down until the last word is read . . . Haymore's writing teases with clues of expressions and strong characterization that quickly creates images in the reader's mind. The story lines evolve, the protagonists mature and their decisions become more realistic. As with her novel A Higher Voice, the villain does not turn out to be the reader's first assumption!"

—**Barbara Norman**, Editor for Yadkin Valley Living Magazine

"Haymore has written a book that is part Nicholas Sparks and part James Patterson. Set on the coast at Beaufort with the angst of young love and a serial killer on the loose, this book held my attention with characters that are believable and at the same time surprising. I strongly recommend this book to anyone who wants to curl up with a good book on a cold winter's night or to lie on the beach for a good summer read."

—**Tom Perry**, author and owner of Laurel Hill Publishing, LLC

"AMAZING! Well crafted! Deeply defined characters! FABULOUS! Those are just a few things to say about this book. Ms Haymore has continued on her journey of magnificent writing. You'll enjoy the mystery and intrigue of this book! It starts out a little slowly but builds in a way that will catch you off guard. One of my favorite parts of the book is the simple goodbye at the end. It's powerful and breathtaking. GET this book! I am a fan for life of Sheri Wren Haymore!!"

—**Melanie Adkins**, reviewer for "Have You Heard Reviews"

A DEEPER CUT

A Novel

Sheri Wren Haymore

A DEEPER CUT

Cover and interior design by Ted Ruybal.

Manufactured in the United States of America.

For more information, please contact:

Wisdom House Books
www.wisdomhousebooks.com

Paperback:
ISBN 13: 978-0-9891821-1-9
ISBN 10: 0-9891821-1-8

LCCN: 2013919011

FIC031000 FICTION / Thrillers / General

1 2 3 4 5 6 7 8 9 10

DISCLAIMER:

Beaufort, NC, is a real place, which I happen to love. Every character in the story is fictional, and I've taken liberties with lots of details, including the landscape and most especially, the investigation. The landscape of the heart as described in the story, however, is quite true.

DEDICATION

To clarity in thinking
and the people who keep me focused:
Clyde, Carrie & Erik

CONTENTS

ACKNOWLEDGEMENTS

There are so many people who have encouraged me, and kept me going, and helped me see past my small world to the reality that my stories have a place in the larger scheme of things. This page won't hold the wealth of names, but my heart carries them all. And so I say thank you to—

My parents, Al and Ruth; my sisters, Pat and Meg, and my other sister Kathy, for tireless advocacy.

My MASH 72 friends, for showing up; and especially Melissa and Jan, for shoving me into the spotlight.

The whole congregation of PGBC, for unexpected enthusiasm.

My Cooking Gang, for keeping it real.

Darrell, my son from another mother, who can clear my thoughts with a single word.

Every single one of my Golden Girls, who show up with hugs, lift up with prayers, make me laugh, and keep me young.

And finally, to all at Wisdom House Books: Ted, for turning out yet another beautiful book; Susie, for insightful editing; Sara, for background effort; and Clara, for making magic happen with resourcefulness beyond my ken—my heartfelt thanks!

ONE

He sat on a bench on a balmy spring day and sharpened his knife. Nobody paid any attention. People walked right by him on Beaufort's wooden boardwalk, inspecting the yachts in their moorings, taking in the calm morning blue of the inland water. Overhead, a gull shrilled a question, and another one answered. Close by, somebody hosed down a yacht, the sound of water spraying the only ambitious noise on the waterfront.

He could make out snatches of conversation as people strolled by. A kid, excited: "Hey, look. That boat's from Jamaica. How did it get to North Carolina?" A woman, with anticipation: "Ooh, this place has grouper sandwich! Let's eat here for lunch." A man, quite seriously: "The tide's going out."

Actually, the tide had just turned and was coming back in. He knew this because he knew the water. Smiling to himself, he returned the knife to its sheath. People may not have noticed his knife today, but very soon, all of Beaufort would fear it.

A couple strolled by, and he watched them closely. The young woman was quite beautiful, and he could tell by the lift of her chin and the sway of her hips that she enjoyed the stares she was drawing. The white gauzy skirt she was wearing flowed seductively in the breeze, and she dangled a wide-brimmed blue hat in one hand.

The young man sauntered along, one hand in his pocket, the other lightly brushing his companion's back. To the casual observer, the young man might appear nonchalant, unaffected by the glances from other folks on the waterfront. But the man with the knife was far from casual. He could read a cocky swagger in the square of the young man's shoulders. He knew to the minute what time the couple had arrived in Beaufort the previous evening, and he even knew the young man's name: Hunter Kittrell.

Just then, a kitten, perhaps lured by the odor of frying burgers that drifted from the closest restaurant, danced around his legs, bumping him, begging attention. When he picked it up, it purred. *Perfect timing. A Kittrell and a kitten in the same breath.* He decided to call himself "The Cat."

❋ ❋ ❋

Unaware of the man's stare, the young couple continued on their way, and soon they were seated on the dining porch of a waterfront restaurant. While Hunter Kittrell tucked into his burger and fries, the young woman returned the stares of passersby, her gaze enticing, her smile bemused. When she noticed a heavyset woman hovering just off the porch, she set the blue hat on her head at a deliberately precarious angle, the brim nearly hiding her face.

"Miss Singer? May I have your autograph?" asked the heavyset woman as she tried to peer around the hat brim to see the young woman's face.

"Of course. And what is your name?"

"Carol."

"So nice to meet you, Carol. It isn't often that I get the chance to meet my public." And "Miss Singer" scribbled a bold, illegible script on a paper napkin and extended it by delicate fingertips to Carol.

"You don't know what this means, Miss Singer. I'll treasure this always." Carol continued to hover expectantly, clutching the napkin with one hand and twisting the hem of her Beaufort souvenir T-shirt with the other.

"Do," the young woman said, and she pulled the brim of the hat lower, shutting out the woman. She reached a manicured hand to grasp the arm of her companion. "Hunter, please forgive the interruption." Her voice was practiced, lacking accent. "You were saying you were caught in a storm?"

"Mmm." The young man's voice was bored, but his gray eyes were not.

"How awful that must have been for you," she said in exaggerated horror.

"Not nearly as awful as you are, Babe," Hunter answered, his voice low, his eyes amused. "Miki, you keep me in awe."

"Shh. I'm Vanessa Singer today, and my fans think I am the goddess of Hollywood." She gave him a sly, wicked smile. Sensing

3

other patrons staring, she said loudly, "This place is boring. Let's motor on down the waterway," and abruptly she stood, leaving half-eaten sandwiches for the gulls or the startled waiter, whichever arrived first.

Hunter flourished a twenty and drowned it carelessly in his glass of water. "I'm right behind you, Vanessa. Just where you want me." A few steps and they were off the dining porch and on the boardwalk, gliding toward the yacht slips, the spring breeze billowing Vanessa's skirt around her legs.

A subtle tip of the hat and a wink brought a middle-aged fellow scrambling off the porch. "Vanessa! Wait! Miss Singer!" He cut them off on the walk, more out-of-breath than the distance warranted. "I thought that was you, and I told my wife . . ." He stopped, anxious. The blue eyes he sought were staring at the water; all she was offering him was her profile.

"Miss Singer will be delighted to give you an autograph," Hunter said easily. "She's quite worn out by the cruise. You understand."

"Oh, of course," he said, not questioning why a cruise would tire a body, and after fumbling, produced a wadded dollar bill from the depths of his pockets. "Make it to Bob and Vena. That's my wife, over there."

Miki gave a delicate fingertip wave in the direction of the porch, scribbled across George's face and left the bill and pen in Bob's hand without a word. A few more steps and she was off the boardwalk, down the ramp, past the "Boat Owners Only" sign, followed by the obliging Hunter.

"Thanks! We loved your last film!" shouted Bob.

"My fans always have the last word," Miki said smoothly and passed through a gate and down a narrow dock. Now they were hidden by a Hatteras cruiser from the stares of the tourists. The yacht's owner raised an eyebrow and a highball glass in their direction and went back to his charts.

"The lovely Vanessa was last seen lunching in Beaufort on her way to West Palm and points beyond," Miki announced, giving the hat to the wind and the skirt to the bowsprit of the yacht before slipping into the salty water.

"Damn, Miki," was all Hunter said as he followed her.

Hunter and Miki hooted with laughter as they purchased a shirred gauze skirt to go over Miki's soaked bodysuit, attracting stares of another kind. With her blonde hair down and streaming water, she looked like the college kid she was, her vivid blue eyes drawing attention away from the classic bone structure so like Vanessa Singer's.

"I always knew I could pull that off, ever since seeing her in *Final Darkness*. How do you like me as a thirty-year-old movie star?"

"Thirty," he repeated. "That's, like, a decade away. What I've gotta do in this decade is graduate and find a job."

He squeaked down the sidewalk beside her in soggy sneakers, hands in his pockets to hold his damp shorts away from his legs.

She stopped and stared up at him. He was good-looking in an easy sort of way—watchful eyes beneath sandy brown hair, strong jaw, full lips. He had a man's high, square forehead and a confident lift to his chin, and yet he appeared boyish, as if his youthful features still waited to be chiseled handsome by life. When she saw his familiar careless smile, she moved on, saying, "For a minute there, I thought you were serious."

"Maybe I am. You are an expensive hobby, Miki."

"I thought your rich uncle died and left you a bazillion dollars or something."

"My rich uncle left me *something*. I have to get my broke self through college before I can find out what it is, and it may not turn out to be money. I've told you that a hundred times. Don't you listen?"

"Yeah, I listen. But get real, Hunter. Rich dead uncles don't make a big deal about leaving somebody a couch. You're getting big money in two years, no doubt about it."

"A couch?" Hunter sputtered in laughter. "Does this mean you'll leave me for a guy with a fat billfold if it turns out to be a couch?"

She cut her eyes sideways at him and swayed closer as she walked, her long skirt brushing his bare leg. "Maybe the couch will be stuffed with money."

When he smiled his slow smile, she hooked her arm through his and walked with her head against his shoulder. "You know, I could use a couch," he said.

Actually, he did need a sofa. Hunter climbed the steps to his garage apartment later that night and surveyed the room's sparse furnishings. He could also use a table and some chairs and maybe a lamp. He did have a bed and a lovely stained-glass window and some smaller windows overlooking Beaufort's Taylor's Creek.

Although Hunter didn't often think about it, he was sitting on high-dollar real estate with nowhere to sit.

All that mattered to Hunter was that it was summer break and he was at his Granny Jen's. He crossed the room to stand beside the open windows and look out. Taylor's Creek formed a deep channel between the Beaufort waterfront and a grassy sand bank populated by wild ponies and assorted shore birds. The shoal protected Beaufort from the winds of the open sound; still, on a May night like this, Hunter could catch a nice breeze through his windows and smell the salt air from the Atlantic Ocean beyond.

His Granny Jen would have been mortified had she known the sorry state of the apartment over her garage. No longer able to climb the narrow staircase easily, it had probably been five years since she had seen the room. At that time, the apartment had still been furnished amply with family heirlooms. It was still cluttered about the corners with assorted circa 1960s fishing gear, croquet and badminton sets, and the like, but the heirlooms had slyly vanished, their disappearance coinciding with the visits of certain cousins. All that remained was a hideous Victorian headboard, a reasonably comfortable mattress, and an overlooked dining chest housing a few bits of china. Hunter could have tea in heirloom cups, if he took the notion, so long as he didn't wish to sit at a table.

Hunter wasn't complaining. Having a place to sit was optional. Having Miki along was a bonus. From the time he was four years old, he had left his home in Raleigh to spend the summer with his granny, and he had continued this practice through three years as an architectural student at UNC-Charlotte. Hunter had carefully explained to Miki that Granny Jen had only one strictly enforced rule: Miki must stay in her designated bed. Miki had laughed in his face, but when she came face-to-face with Granny Jen and the scrutiny of those wise old eyes, she had hauled her bags to the room beside Granny Jen's bedroom without another word.

Hunter slipped into the bed and bounced a bit to hear its familiar squeak. He was at Granny Jen's. Maybe Miki wasn't in his arms, but she was with him. This should be the best summer yet.

At two a.m., Hunter awoke to darkness, a rush of air, a thump on the hardwood floor. The sheet was tangled around his legs, and he kicked it to the floor just as the overhead light jarred him to a sitting position.

"Where is all my furniture?" he heard his grandmother's voice say.

"What?" He had been locked in a dream with Miki's eager body straining against his, and he scrambled to cover himself, sweating and confused, squinting in the light.

His grandmother crossed the room heavily and sat on the edge of the bed, breathing hard.

"Granny Jen, what are you doing?" he asked, his voice thick with sleep.

"I must apologize to you, Hunter." Holding her cane, Granny Jen leaned her head on her hands and drew more breaths. Her white hair, usually held in a dignified twist at the back of her neck, hung in loose strands to her shoulders. "I heard your young friend go out the back door, and I intended to stop that foolishness." She looked around. "I see now she didn't come up here, which seems even more foolish. Where is my furniture?"

"I don't know. People keep helping themselves, you know?"

"Shoot. People are determined to get my stuff whether I die or not." She tapped the floor with her cane and breathed easier. "So, where did she go?"

"Don't know," Hunter said, falling back on the bed.

"Why didn't she come up here?"

"Granny Jen!"

"Hunter."

"Why do you just assume that we, you know, she and I . . ."

"Hunter."

"Aargh!" He wrestled his pillow and sat up again. "Okay. You win. It's because it's your house. I told her we couldn't sleep together all summer because it's your house."

She chuckled. "You must have wanted to come here pretty badly."

"Yeah. I did." Crossing his arms over his chest, he cocked his head and said, "You could change the rules a little, Granny Jen. Make it easier on all of us."

"That charming smile won't always work on your old Granny. Where did she go?"

"Don't know."

"A young girl like that can't roam the streets at night. It's plain dangerous."

"Oh, Miki can look after herself."

"You act as if you don't care."

He shrugged. "It's not like we're engaged or anything. She can go out."

"Go out? At two in the morning?" She regarded him a long minute with unfailing gray eyes until he bounced the bed to break the gaze. "Hunter, you have become careless about many things."

A grunt escaped him. "Do you want me to go look for her or something?"

Granny Jen continued to stare at him as she pushed herself up by the cane and reflexively smoothed her satin robe. "Hunter, would you like to know what the Lord has told me about you?"

"Not really," he mumbled.

"Among other things, he has promised that you will do something worthwhile."

While she was speaking, Hunter had been rummaging among the clothes within arm's reach on the floor, and he now produced a pair of drawstring pants. "Do you need help down the stairs?" he asked, pulling the pants on over his boxers.

"Just go down ahead of me in case I fall." She observed him as he stood up, sandy hair tousled, under-drawers sticking out above the pants. "Want to know a joke?" she asked. "That dining chest there is worth more than all the junk they've hauled out of here."

"No kidding." He scratched his chest and yawned.

"Somebody way back in my grandfather's family built it. Probably had no plans to go by; I've never seen another one like it. You can tell it's hand-planed. Imagine a man taking the time from the everyday grind of feeding his family to design and build a piece like that."

"Mmm. Maybe his wife built it. Sanded it during the two o'clock feedings."

"I like how you think, Hunter." She tapped her cane on the floor, indicating she was ready to go. "Somebody back then took the time to build something lasting. Worthwhile. Think about it."

They descended the steps slowly, with difficulty. He let her walk across the yard alone but did not take his eyes from her until she was safely on the back stoop. She turned and said quietly, "I'm too old for this nonsense, Hunter."

"I know, Granny Jen. You have my word as a Southern gentleman I'll live a totally clean life for the next three months."

"Good enough." She turned toward the door, hesitated, then said without looking at him, "And check into that insulting odor coming from Miki's room for me, would you?"

He watched her go into the house and started off across the lawn. When he reached the street, he looked in the direction of the town docks for a moment, sighed, and headed straight across toward the water, cursing softly when he stepped on a sharp rock. The hangouts along the historic waterfront had been closed since midnight. Miki had probably found a private party. Or maybe she would be heading home in a few minutes. Hunter sat on the family pier. Across the water, ponies could be heard munching on the tough grass. Water slapped the dock in rhythmic splashes, soothing, mesmerizing. Dawn found him lying face-down on the pier, a life jacket from his uncle's skiff his only pillow.

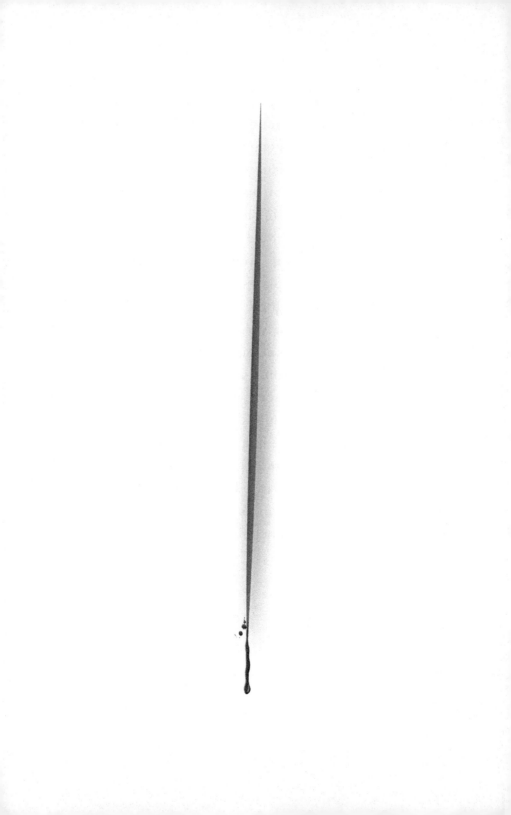

TWO

Grayson Tucker looked over his notes and tried not to choke on his gravy biscuit. A small-town police chief like himself didn't get too many murders, particularly not a professional job like this one, and especially not one involving a transient. His people stabbed each other from time to time in the heat of anger, as people everywhere might do, but murder to a stranger was unsettling. The man had been found dead in the stateroom of his yacht right in its slip on the historic Beaufort waterfront. A knife wrenched into his windpipe and sliced through the carotid artery had taken him out, probably in his sleep, for he was lying in his blood-soaked bed. There was evidence of female companionship at some point in the evening. The knife was not found. It was the man's cat mewling continually through the raised hatch that finally led dockside neighbors to look inside and call the dock-master, who called Grayson.

The victim had a drug record in Florida, but a preliminary search had turned up no drugs or cash. Perhaps he was clean. Or perhaps the killer had been thorough in his own search. The entire scenario was giving Grayson heartburn as he downed his breakfast. The implications for the future peace of his simple town were sickening.

Grayson washed the greasy biscuit down with stale coffee and pushed back from the table. The victim's closest neighbors had promised to stick around for a couple of days, but he couldn't hold all the boats in the harbor indefinitely. He had to get moving if he was going to interview every person on the water who might have seen or heard anything in the wee hours of the morning. And he would need every one of his officers' help. There would be no parking tickets written today.

☀ ☀ ☀

The murder made front-page news, and Hunter faced his first afternoon at work bombarded by tourists who were hungry for waterfront gossip. Hunter had worked as a deckhand aboard the ketch, *Pirate's Lady*, for several summers, sailing day tours and moonlight cruises around the waterway. As deckhand, he also served as steward and tour guide, and as he went about his duties in his noncommittal manner, which the passengers interpreted as easygoing, he was met at every turn with questions. If a white-legged fellow in baggy shorts wanted gore, he invented gore and declared it was straight from the harbor master. If two pretty young things confessed fear among giggles and rolling eyes, he

feigned fear himself and vowed to see them home, even though
they were staying at the beach forty minutes away and he had a
dinner cruise in an hour. Altogether, the job provided him some
amount of entertainment and wages, plus a bit of tan to boot.

When he got off at nine o'clock, Miki was waiting, having finished her afternoon shift working in a tourist information booth
on the waterfront. She stood with her back to the water, leaning
against the boardwalk rail, the breeze playing her long skirt sensu-
ally around her legs. With a shawl wrapped around her arms and
a wide, beaded belt around her waist, she looked like a funky rich
lady who had just stepped off one of the yachts. *Funky and bored*,
he thought, as he came closer. She turned her head away from him
just then and seemed to speak to an arrogantly handsome fortyish
man who stood a few feet away from her, foot on the rail, looking
out at the water. The man moved at that moment, came alongside
her, spoke a few words without looking at her, then walked on.
Hunter brushed past him as he approached Miki.

"Aah, the sailor home from the sea!" she declared when she
saw him.

"Bored?" he asked.

"No. I was imagining my sailor had been out to sea for months
and was returning tonight. It was very erotic."

"And was your sailor dark and dangerous like that guy you
were just talking to?"

She stared at him a long moment. "Jealousy. I'm surprised you
expended the energy."

"Curiosity. What did he say to you?"

"He told me where a party is tonight. Wanna come?"

"Wait until the weekend. All the guys I know should be in from school by then."

"Oh, this is the yacht crowd. Come on, Hunter, it'll be a blast."

"My curiosity remains unsatisfied."

"Okay, okay. I met him last night."

"Where, here?" Hunter grabbed her by the arm, glancing up and down the boardwalk. "Last night?"

"Panic. Whoa, two emotions in one night. One more, and you get a gold star, Hunter."

"Miki, there was a murder here last night."

"Well, duh. Some dope dealer in his bed. So?"

"Who said he was a dope dealer?"

She shrugged.

Hunter took her by the hand and started walking toward home. "Look, there's a bunch of bull going around about this, part of which I propagated myself. But one thing is stone truth: anybody hanging around the docks is under suspicion." He looked over his shoulder as they walked. "Did it occur to you he could be the killer?"

"Just forget it, Hunter."

"What were you doing down here anyway?"

"Forget it, all right?"

They walked in silence until they were within sight of home. "Look, Miki, I know you're gonna do what you want no matter what I say, but don't go to that party. It's really got me spooked."

"Concern. Number three. Here's your gold star." She stopped in the middle of the street and kissed him long, ignoring the impatient honking of car horns. "You could be the sailor in my dream, you know."

He sucked in a sharp breath. "Any sailor would be crazy to turn down an offer like that," he murmured against her neck.

"Then come on," she whispered, and led him to his dock where his uncle's skiff waited in its moorings. "Handy little boat for making love; don't you agree?"

He looked into her eyes, her face in the moonlight more mature than by day, the shadows emphasizing the striking bone structure. "Call me crazy, stupid, anything you like, Miki, but we can't. Not this summer."

Her voice was demanding. "What difference does it make as long as we're not right in your granny's face?"

"I don't know. It just does."

"Hell. So you want me to believe you play at virgin-boy every summer?"

"That pretty much says it. I know it doesn't make sense to you." Hunter shrugged and reached a hand to touch her breast. "It doesn't make much sense to me at this moment, but it's the way it is. Granny Jen may be strict, but she doesn't stay on my ass like my mom does. If she kicks me out, I have nowhere to go but back to Raleigh. I can live a straight life for three months. It beats three months in hell with a mom who barely tolerates your existence."

Miki slapped his hand away. "Everybody's mom barely tolerates their existence. That's life. Get over it." When he did not reach for her again, she turned away and started off at a brisk walk toward the house. "I'm going to bed. Try to grow up by morning, would you?" she threw at him over her shoulder.

He stared after her as she walked away, then called out, "Miki, wait a second." She slowed her stride, and he caught up. "As long as you're mad at me anyway, I need to ask you something."

She grunted in exasperation. "What now?"

"Granny Jen is suspicious of something malodorous coming from your room."

"Incense, Hunter. I'm not smoking pot in your granny's house. God, now you're the weed patrol!"

He grinned and tried to embrace her. "If I put on my patrol uniform, will you think I'm cool again?"

Pushing him away gently, she answered, "Not tonight. Maybe tomorrow. See you, Hunter."

He sighed and watched her slip inside his granny's house, then climbed the stairs alone to his garage apartment.

Later that night, Hunter lay sprawled upon the sofa that had mysteriously appeared in his apartment, one leg propped on the back, eating popcorn and drinking a soda. He hated arguing with Miki. What he wanted to do with Miki, the reason he had brought her to Beaufort, was laugh. Pull pranks on people. Harass the tourists. Miki was entertaining, bright, sassy. She made every day an adventure. And of course, Hunter wanted Miki in his bed; he wasn't dead. But the risk of Granny Jen finding out and sending him back to his mother's home was too great.

Hunter's relationship with his mother was complicated. He didn't doubt she loved him, but he knew she didn't like him much. When Hunter was three years old, his father had skipped town, and he hadn't been seen since. Hunter had grown up feeling responsible, as if he should apologize for his father's disappearance, but he wasn't sure why. It seemed to Hunter that the older he grew, the more he reminded his mom of Rob Kittrell, and the more she couldn't stand to be around Rob's son.

Some days, he hid the hurt by pretending not to care; other days, he struck back by deliberately annoying his mother, step-father, and two half-sisters. His entire life had been a struggle to hide the confused and disillusioned little boy behind an exterior of indifference.

But not at Granny Jen's. At her house, he felt he was genuinely liked, and that meant home to Hunter. Living by her rules, living a clean life even now that he considered himself a man, was a small price to pay for a home.

No particular sound—just the restlessness within him—brought him to his feet to stand by the windows facing the water. Moonlight, caught in the mist rising from the water, softened the midnight darkness. A figure passed within his view, walking quickly, long skirt swaying, hair lifting slightly in the breeze. He moved behind the center window so she was distorted by the ancient stained glass, crackled blue. He did not change this vantage point until long after Miki had become a shadow and disappeared.

Grayson Tucker did choke on his gravy biscuit the next morning while reading the printout of the previous night's activities. Big drug bust on the waterway, too far into the morning hours to make local headlines. All he had in hand were bare details, but evidently the State Bureau of Investigation had received a tip that a particular dealer was working a yacht party within sight of Beaufort's own drawbridge. The whole gang had been requested to move its party to the Brunswick County jail for the night, and no doubt, possession charges were being filed even now. They had come up empty on the dealer himself, however.

Grayson pushed his biscuit aside. He'd had a bellyful of nauseating facts this week anyway. This drug bust was being handled by the SBI and the county sheriff's department, but Grayson had a feeling it was related to the murder in his harbor. He may not have big-city resources, but he had a Southern gut. Sometimes that was enough. This time, it had to be.

❦ ❦ ❦

Hunter sat slumped in his chair on Granny Jen's shaded porch, one foot on the seat, nonchalantly devouring a pimento cheese sandwich. He noticed Granny Jen watching Miki out of the corner of her eye. Miki was picking at her lunch, her face pale; he guessed she had been partying all night. He hoped Granny Jen's sharp eyes would miss something just this once.

"Hunter, for heaven's sake, sit up straight at the table, please," Granny reprimanded in her refined, Southern voice.

"Sure thing."

His grandmother cleared her throat. "Miki, dear, you look a little peaked today."

Hunter tried to catch Miki's eye, but she kept her head down, a stubborn set to her mouth.

"Perhaps a bowl of soup would taste better," said Granny Jen. Miki shook her head, not looking up.

"Tell me something, kids," Jen said carefully, "are you accustomed to these late hours?"

Miki pushed back from the table.

"Sure, Granny Jen. Every weekend at school. It's no big deal," Hunter said quickly.

"That's what I figured. And you two certainly looked healthy when you arrived. Are you sure there's not something else bothering you, dear?"

Miki stood, her napkin tumbling to the floor. "No. I have to get to work." She headed outside, letting the screen door bang behind her.

Jen caught Hunter's eye and nodded toward the girl's departing figure.

"Wait up, Miki!" he called, grabbing another sandwich and following. He caught up with her on the street. She was walking quickly, a defiant set to her shoulders. "What gives, Babe?" he asked.

She walked on, not answering, not looking at him.

"Hey, this is just me, okay?"

After a long pause, she flared, "Where does she get off grilling me like I'm some kind of criminal?"

"Ah, c'mon. She just asked how you felt."

She whispered something fiercely. All he caught were a few curses.

"Listen, Miki. Granny Jen's not like other old people. She's not your mom."

"You got that right."

"I mean, if she asks you something, it's just because she wants to know what's going on with you. It's not her against us." They seemed to be walking less intensely, if not more slowly. He chanced a look at her, but she was staring at something across the water. "When she asks me a question, I give her a straight answer, when I can. When I can't," he shrugged, "well, I try not to be rude."

She stopped suddenly, and he tripped to a halt beside her. "Oh man, I was rude, wasn't I?" she asked.

He closed the distance between them and stood very close, only his breath touching her. She sighed and rested her forehead on his chest. "Now I've gotten on her bad side," she said softly.

"Not necessarily." He tore the sandwich in half behind her back. "If Granny Jen has a bad side, I never found it. Here, eat this," he said, nudging her.

"Is food the Southerner's answer to everything?" she asked, taking her half.

"Pretty much."

They stood in the grass beside the water and watched the wild ponies across Taylor's Creek grazing the scruffy grass on the sand bank. "So, how was the party?" Hunter ventured.

She didn't answer. When he looked at her, she was staring at the ponies, face set. Then her sandwich sailed toward the water and sank without a splash.

"Shoot, I was still hungry," he grumbled.

She looked at him then and laughed shortly. "Ever been around a bunch of middle-aged spoonheads?" she asked.

"Can't say that I have."

"You don't want to be."

When she didn't say anything else, he said, "Come on, we'd better get to work," and he started walking away.

"Hunter."

He stopped and looked at her. She was squinting at him through tear-filled eyes. "I was almost busted," she whispered. When he stared at her without moving, she said, "I'm not kidding."

"Damn."

Suddenly the few feet that separated them seemed very wide. When he moved toward her, she side-stepped him and began walking briskly once again toward town. Another hundred feet and she'd be brushing shoulders with the tourists.

He ran after her and stopped her with both arms. She couldn't get away without causing a scene, and so she looked at him squarely.

"You said 'almost.' What happened?"

"That guy—the one you saw last night. He seemed to know it was about to go down. Got me out of there in a hurry, on a speedboat. Dropped me off at your Granny Jen's dock." There was silence. "Don't look at me like that, Hunter. Nothing happened." More silence. "Trust me, Hunter."

"That's not what I was thinking. I wasn't worrying about you and that guy. Miki, you could be in jail right now. Or you could be offshore with that bunch if somebody had decided to make a run for it."

"Don't think about that. I'm okay." She wrapped her arms around him. "I'm okay."

He drew her into his arms more tightly and rocked her slowly. "You scare me, Miki," he said.

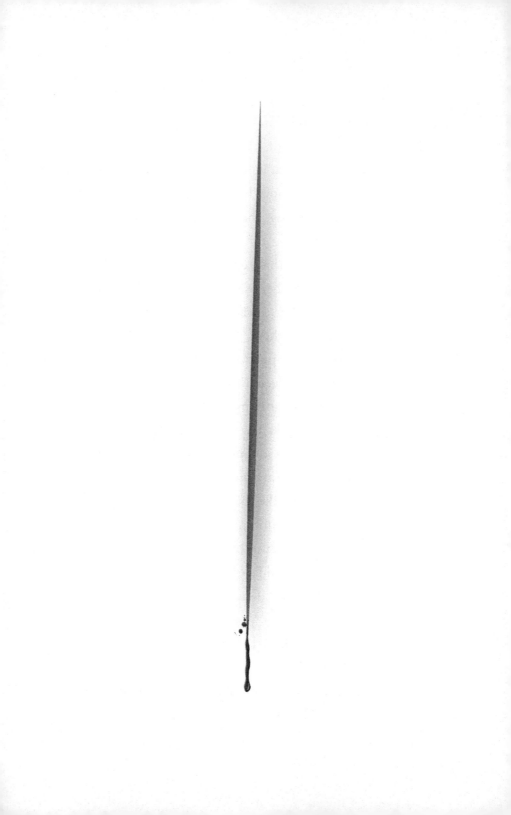

THREE

Grayson Tucker was too sick to his stomach to consider breakfast the next morning. His gut had told him this was coming; still, neither his gut nor his eyes were prepared for what faced him now. He unwrapped a stick of gum as he stared at the body slumped in the yacht's dining alcove. This victim had been murdered in the same manner as the first: quick knife blow to the windpipe, the throat sliced. This man had been awake, evidently, drinking a nightcap and smoking a cigarette. His struggle against his attacker must have been pitifully brief. The cigarette had politely burned itself down in the ashtray.

What was odd about the scene was that there was an implied coziness. Surely the killer had been sitting at the same table, talking comfortably. There was no evidence of this, however: no rings from a second glass on the table, no cigarette of another brand in the ashtray. This guy was thorough. A professional. The

SBI would be combing the boat for evidence, but Grayson had a feeling their search would come up empty.

And the victim, Grayson discovered minutes later, had a fresh drug charge against him, so fresh it was from the day before. This dead guy was just out on bond from the yacht party raid, released late yesterday afternoon.

Grayson chewed his gum mechanically and tried to picture the scene. The dead guy had spent the night partying, and then had sat most of the day in a noisy jail waiting his turn before a magistrate. Surely he had been tired. Was he expecting a visitor? How long did they sit at the table and chat?

Unlike the first victim, this man did not travel alone. His two crew members had found him at breakfast time. Their story was that their skipper had been in a foul mood upon returning late yesterday evening, had cursed the system for detaining him, had eaten a light supper, and had warned them not to disturb him, because he was exhausted. As a result, the two had closed down a bar in Morehead City and had flopped in a nearby hotel until morning.

Now, they dogged Grayson as he moved about the yacht, swearing they knew nothing else, stinking of beer and cigarettes. Frankly, they were getting on his nerves and turning his stomach one more flop. When the short one whined again, "We didn't do it. You believe us, don't you?" Grayson stared him down and drawled, "Then, you won't mind if I search your quarters, will you?' He studiously looked over his notes to hide a grin at their panic. Guys probably had a stash of their own tucked away. But no knife with a medium-length, straight, thin blade, he would bet. They might have hefty working knives and maybe a long-blade fillet knife or two, but not the type of knife the coroner had said was used on the first victim.

When Grayson squatted down to inspect the blood-stained floor for tracks, a movement caught his eye. "Hello," he murmured, "come here. Come on over here." A young cat skittishly approached his extended hand, and he soon had it firmly in his left hand, rubbing it with his right, notebook tucked under his arm.

"And where did you come from, Sissy? Hmm? Do you belong here?"

The two crew members looked at him stupidly.

"Have you boys ever seen this cat?"

They shook their heads in unison.

"You sure? Maybe your boss picked it up on his way in yesterday?"

"Huh! Naw!" came from the boys.

"Uh-huh. Get her some food." Grayson scratched the cat's neck thoughtfully as he watched the two scramble to look in the refrigerator and behind doors, banging about.

They were clumsy and nervous, watching him over their shoulders as they spilled food and left compartment doors open. Whatever these two were hiding, it had nothing to do with the murders. Whoever had sat at the table with their boss and slit his throat in mid-sentence was smooth and efficient. Whoever the killer was, he would not be unsettled by the presence of a simple police officer.

Finally they produced ice cream in a saucer with wheat bread on the side. Now the odd detail from the first murder fell into place. There had been no cat food or dish in that yacht, either. Grayson had not wondered about that for long; for all he knew, the guy fed his cat caviar in a crystal bowl.

Now he clutched his first bit of concrete evidence, and it purred back at him. "So, you're a little calling card, are you, Sissy? Too bad you can't talk. But you know what? They've got all kinds of stuff on the internet nowadays. Maybe your daddy likes cats, hmm? Maybe he hates cats. Maybe his name is Cat. Maybe for once that computer will spit out some useful information. You reckon?" And he left the yacht and walked up the dock, not offering a comment to the forensic guys who were on their way in.

❧ ❧ ❧

Hunter blasted his stereo until midnight and then cut if off. He had needed a complicated bass to untangle all those annoying tourists from his mind. "Get a life," he had almost told one woman who had pestered him for gossip about today's murder and would not be distracted, not when he pointed out ponies belly-deep in water, not even when he tried to show her a happy pod of dolphins.

Now, at midnight, he needed that windy silence peculiar to the coast to let him know he really was at Granny Jen's. He sat on his sofa in the dark and just listened. There were no traffic sounds, no human clamor of any type. For this moment, he could be the only person on the planet. There was only the wind, ripping across the water as it had always done, whistling at him through the open window like an old buddy.

Something seemed skewed this summer. Maybe it was the murders. Maybe it was Miki. Well, definitely, it was Miki. Always, Hunter had calmed down at Granny Jen's, had slipped into the quiet groove of the place. He might party with the local gang a couple of nights a week, but never hard, never like he had learned to do at school. Somehow, he had assumed Miki would get the hang of the place after a few days. This was beginning to seem unlikely.

A clatter of stones against his stained-glass window brought him to his feet. He leaned out of the side window.

"Hey, what's happening?" he asked easily.

"You tell me." Her voice was mischievous, and she swayed girlishly in her jeans, the jacket wrapped about her waist moving with her.

"I'm fond of my blue window, Miki."

"Good for you, Hunter. What else are you fond of?"

"Blue sky. Blue water."

"You're wicked."

"Uh-huh."

"Are you too lazy to take me out on that blue water?"

He looked across at the water, black and sparkling with diamonds of moonlight. "I'm busy."

"Doing what?"

"Contemplating."

"Any other good-looking boys up there who might take a girl out?"

"I dunno. I'll check."

He disappeared from the window and reappeared thirty seconds later on his landing above her, long-sleeve shirt unbuttoned, insect repellent and flashlight in hand.

"Come down, Rapunzel."

"You've got it backward, don't you?" He jogged down the steps and approached her.

"Expecting company?" she asked, eyeing the bug spray.

"Yep."

They boarded his uncle's skiff and eased away from the dock. The tide was low but coming in, he noted. Could be worse. Could be the other way around.

He had no trouble navigating the shoals, sometimes guided by strategic signal lights, sometimes just lucky he had a flat-bottomed boat. Other boats were on the water, many surrounded by pools of light.

"What's everybody doing?" she asked.

He cut the engine and let the boat drift toward a sand bank. "I'll show you." A flip of the switch, and the area off their bow was flooded by a lamp mounted over the water.

"Neat."

He slipped into the water and walked at the edge of the light, tow rope in one hand, a four-pronged spear in the other. The inland water had its own sounds—wind whistling across the water, waves slapping the boat, an occasional low murmuring voice from another boat—and Hunter did not interrupt. A match flared, briefly illuminating Miki's face. The next few minutes were comfortable.

Hunter eased through the shallow water at a steady pace, pulling the boat behind him. The trick to flounder fishing was to move without a splash, keep the light ahead of his spear, and not let the boat bump his backside. To be successful, he had to see the fish before it saw him, and be quick and accurate with the spear before his prey could even move.

Eventually, Miki's voice cut the silence. "Whatcha doing, Hunter?"

"Gigging for flounder."

Another silence.

"You're in a mood aren't you?"

"Why do you say that?"

"I can tell. Tourists getting to you?"

"Yeah, something like that."

"Tell."

"Half the tourists think they're about to be murdered in their beds even though their bed is in a condo on Atlantic Beach and they've never seen the inside of a yacht. The other half . . ." He stabbed at something within the circle of light and came up empty.

"Ever gigged your foot, Hunter?"

"Not yet. The other half is thrilled by it, like they think a movie is being made around them or something."

"You ought to try being stuck in a booth on the waterfront."

"Harassing the tourists not as much fun as you thought?"

"They're harassing me! No one wants to know about harbor tours. 'Honey, tell me which boat that poor man was murdered on.' 'I don't know ma'am.' 'How many times was he stabbed?' 'I don't know, ma'am.' 'Where do you think the killer will strike tonight?' 'I don't give a . . .'"

"Gotcha!" Hunter speared and came up with a healthy, flopping fish. And he hadn't even made a splash. He still had it; he was smooth.

"Shine your flashlight on the cooler, Babe, so I can see what I'm doing. There. Supper in the box."

"Happy now, Hunter?"

"Getting there."

"Here. Take a toke." She leaned forward, offering him her joint. "Make all those bad tourists go away."

"Nuh-uh."

"Stubborn streak. Didn't know you had one, Hunter."

"It's the Southern gentleman in me."

"Huh?"

"Never mind." He continued his slow walk, the boat behind him, staying in the shallows. Outside of their circle of light, the water was black, constantly moving toward them in sparkling crests of waves. The nearest sand bank appeared as a dark, immovable hulk in the water. Hunter knew that it, like the water, was not static. The wind ruffled the grass in timeless patterns of motion, crabs scurried along the sand, the tides changed the shape of the bank day by day. But within their light, all was comfortable and safe. Familiar, at least for this moment.

"Are we going in circles, Hunter?"

"Yeah."

"You mad at me, Hunter?"

"Worried."

"Don't be. Look how safe I am tonight, my big, strong fisherman towing me around, supper in the box."

"And tomorrow night?"

"I'll tell you what." She flicked her joint in the water. "I'll go straight tonight, just for you. How's that?"

"Blue eyes," he said softly. "I'm fond of blue eyes."

"Hi, Granny Jen."

Jen heard the voice and the screen door open, and she looked up to see a pretty face grinning at her, friendly dimples, sweet blue eyes. "Amy! You're home from college. Come give me a hug." The young woman who bent to squeeze her warmly was petite with a mass of red curls pulled back in a single clasp. "How are you feeling, Granny Jen?" she asked, looking into the old eyes with concern.

"Pretty good. I'm happy, which is more than most people can say. You know, you just missed Hunter."

The blue eyes looked away. "I know. I missed him on purpose."

"What happened between you two?" Jen asked tenderly.

"I guess we tried, you know," Amy cocked her head to one side and smiled wistfully, "being more than just buds toward the end of last summer. Big mistake."

"Have you heard from him since?"

"No, but you know how we always went our separate ways every fall and just picked up again the next summer."

Granny Jen nodded. "You've been his best friend since y'all were three years old. I don't think that has to change just because it didn't work being sweethearts."

"It's hard to explain. I feel like we messed up a great friendship, and I doubt Hunter wants to see me."

"Oh, I believe he might. If anybody is his soul mate, dear, it's you."

Amy seemed surprised. "I don't know, Granny Jen. When he's away from here, Hunter is, well, Hunter is into some things that are totally foreign to me. We can't exactly be soul mates."

"But what if Hunter closes himself off from his soul when he's away, Amy? Think about it."

Amy brushed at a wisp of hair that was happily dancing around her face. "Well, anyway, I've seen that drop-dead gorgeous blonde he brought home. Definitely his type. Maybe you'd better be looking to her for a soul mate." Amy shook her head. "I doubt Hunter needs a buddy this year."

"Don't be so sure. He may need one now more than ever."

"We'll see. But you and I can still be friends. Hunter can be an old Pooh if he wants, but he can't stop me from coming to see you. So, tell me what you've been reading lately." And Amy made herself at home on Granny Jen's porch as she had always done, pouring them both tea, telling jokes, talking about books. Granny Jen settled comfortably in her chair and smiled with more content than she had in several days.

➤ ➤ ➤

Grayson studied the computer screen. The small swivel desk chair squatted beneath his weight. He had accessed SBI files, FBI files, and sheriff's department files from dozens of counties. He had studied profiles of killers, drug dealers, and underworld traffickers of all descriptions. Nobody fit his killer. He had tried every combination of cat name he could think of.

Only one name caught his attention, a name with ties to Beaufort: Kittrell—Hunter's family name. Grayson leaned back and thought about that. Hunter's uncle, Donald Kittrell, had died three years before. Hunter's father, Rob Kittrell—now there was a piece of work. Rob had been only twenty-two when he disappeared, slipped right out of a drug agent's hands the day he would have been arrested for dealing.

Even though it made no sense for Rob to turn back up in Beaufort slitting stranger's throats in the harbor, Grayson thought it might be a good idea to see what the computer had on Rob Kittrell. Grayson's thick fingers hit a wrong key, and he lost the screen he was on. Nuts. He smacked the side of the monitor, and the screen went black. Whatever happened to a machine a man could fix with a good whack or a wrench to its insides? With a sigh, he started over, massaging his neck while he waited for the computer to reboot. Sissy, the kitten from the yacht, purred as she brushed her little body against his ankles.

Beyond the closed door, the commotion that had been going on nonstop for two days continued: reporters demanding a statement, the town's residents demanding an arrest. It sounded like a small riot. His bedraggled staff, accustomed to small-town stuff, handled abuse only in small doses. "I'm not saying it again," he heard one of his officers growl, apparently to a reporter. "The SBI is handling it. That is the only statement Chief Tucker is issuing at this time." Grayson rubbed his eyes and stayed in front of the computer.

The Cat knew what he was doing. He was a genius, and pretty soon the world would know it. His vision was coming together, the timing and execution perfect. Execution. He liked that word. He sat alone on a bench on the waterfront. Yes, executioner; that was a challenging title. To be a killer, you only had to hold the knife and stick it where it would do the job. But to be an executioner: Aah! You held the keys to a man's life; you held the knowledge of good and evil; you held justice in your very hands. To be an executioner, you had to know who must live and who must die. And The Cat knew exactly who must die. He knew because he had made it his business to know, had learned the life stories of each tagged name on his list, had gotten in close. Close enough to smell, to touch, to kill. Yes, The Cat knew who must die and he knew which ones would be dying in Beaufort this summer. He must be patient until each was executed. Then he would move on.

FOUR

"You have got to be kidding!" Miki's voice was edged with exasperation as she stood in the doorway of Granny Jen's sunny kitchen.

"What?" Hunter asked innocently.

"Now you're going to church?"

"Already been, Miki." Hunter removed his tie and started clattering about the kitchen, aware that Miki was staring at him.

Miki poured herself a cup of coffee and sat on a stool at the counter. Irritation slipped into her voice. "Why the hell would you want to do that?"

He shrugged. "Why not? It makes Granny Jen happy. She likes to show off her good-looking grandson to the blue-haired bunch," he added with a grin.

"Oh, please."

"What's it to you?"

"Just tell me you don't do this every Sunday," she said.

"Of course not. Just when the notion strikes me."

"That's my Hunter: dependably undependable."

"Whatsa matter? Afraid a little religion might rub off on your bad boy?"

"Something like that. It's been pretty scary just watching you play at good boy this summer." She continued drinking her coffee. The silence between them stretched as he pulled food from the refrigerator, his motions efficient. Finally, she asked, "Where is Granny Jen, by the way?"

"In her room. I don't think she feels well today. The trip to church seemed to wear her out."

"So you're staying with her today?"

"Uh-huh."

"Fixing lunch?"

"Yep."

"You reek of good boy." She set her cup down and pushed it aside.

"No, that's my new aftershave, Babe."

"Will you walk me to work?"

"Sure." He began slicing cold roast beef for sandwiches, wielding the knife with surprising dexterity, not seeming to notice that the long silence was straining her.

Carefully, she said, "I want you to meet someone."

"Who?"

"A guy."

"I don't meet guys, Miki."

"This is the guy you saw the other night."

"Your dark and dangerous yacht-type party guy, huh?"

"Look, he's cool."

"Yeah, right. That was a real cool party he found for you the other night, wasn't it?" He kept his back to her, his knife slicing the roast in quick strokes.

"Hunter, don't be like this. He knows about stuff going down all over the harbor. It's just for kicks. Something new to do."

"What's his name?"

"Jack."

"Jack what?"

"I—I don't know."

"Now, that's intelligent."

"Damn it, Hunter. I don't need you to play father." She stood up.

"Mustard."

"Huh?"

"Hand me the mustard."

"So will you, Hunter?"

"I'll tell you what. If Mr. Jack yacht-boy wants to meet me, he can walk his ass to where I am. And I suppose you've ruled out Jack-boy as the harbor killer?"

"Well, Jack says . . ."

"Please. Don't tell me what Jack says." He looked full into her blue eyes. "How about listening to what your Hunter says? Roast beef and mustard are a good mix. Now, chocolate and codfish— well, that's not so good. You and yacht-boy's crowd are not a good mix. Trust me."

She didn't respond for a moment, and when she did, her voice had an edge. "Is that some sort of weird Southern analogy?"

"I'm cursed with a Southern stomach; what can I say?" His

voice was as careless as ever. "My Southern stomach tells me your yacht-boy stinks like rancid codfish. And isn't he like your dad's age or something?"

"Forget I mentioned it, Hunter. I wasn't trying to start an argument."

"Good. Come eat lunch with us then."

"No, thanks. I'm going to walk on, okay? I'll grab something to eat at break."

He almost let her go without saying anything else. "Miki," he called after she was out the door. "Wait a minute, and I'll walk with you."

"No, that's okay. You take care of Granny Jen."

"Miki?"

"What?"

"Nothing. Bye." He stood in the door and watched her until she was out of sight, the knife still in his hand.

Unsettled, he began assembling the sandwiches. Something about the conversation with Miki snagged on the edges of his memory. It reminded him—oh, crap, it reminded him of the day his mother had introduced him to Patrick Barton. He had just turned seven years old; once more, his father had not even sent a birthday card. "I want you to meet someone," she had said, her voice careful. He could still taste the acrid fear in his throat when she said that. She was going to leave him. She was going to leave him just like his dad had done. "You're going to like him," she had said. Hunter had made up his mind that day to never like Patrick Barton, no matter what he did, no matter that he became his step-father three months later, no matter how hard the man tried. It was Hunter's way of keeping his mom. It was his way of keeping his self-respect.

Hunter arranged the sandwiches on Granny Jen's Sunday dishes, poured tea in her best stemmed glasses, and put two white linen napkins on the tray. He was particular about the way he did this, wanting it to look nice. And then he walked down the hall to her room, carrying the tray aloft as if he had done it for years.

"Shouldn't you be leaving for work soon?" asked Granny Jen from her bed as Hunter cleared away the lunch dishes.

"I traded days with Bill. He didn't mind." Hunter's voice was pleasant.

"Oh. Are you kids going to the beach today?"

"No."

"Well, Hunter." Granny Jen adjusted the pillows behind her back and searched through the sections of newspaper.

"What?"

"Surely you don't intend to spend a beautiful summer day cooped up in here with me, do you?"

"Hey, I've got to catch up on the funny paper. Something important might have happened. Charlie Brown didn't grow up and marry that little red-haired girl since last summer, did he?" He set the tray of dishes on the floor and reached for the newspaper.

"Hunter, get out of here."

"Want me to read to you? I do a killer Mr. Wilson and Dennis."

"Sometimes your stubborn streak serves you well. Sometimes

you're just plain stubborn. Go fishing. I'm not going to die today."

"Fish aren't biting. And nobody said you were dying."

"Go out in the sunshine. I'll be fine."

"If you don't let me stay, do you know what I'm going to do?" He grinned at her wickedly. "I'm going to tell that prissy daughter of yours that you're bad sick, and you know what will happen then?"

"Don't call your aunt 'prissy.'"

"My non-prissy aunt will priss down here from New Bern and fuss and call the doctor and dust everything twice and insult your maid and then . . ."

"Hush, Hunter." She was starting to chuckle.

"And then she will force-feed you asparagus soufflé."

"Okay, okay, you win," she said with a laugh, shaking her head.

"That's better. Now, listen closely. There may be a pop quiz at the end." He unfolded the comic section with drama and settled down to read. After a few minutes, he could no longer ignore the appraising look she was giving him.

"What?"

"Tell me how you see Miki."

"Miki?"

"Yes. I don't want to form an opinion just on what I've seen. What do you see when you look at her?" Her voice was matter-of-fact, not demanding an answer. He knew she was genuinely interested.

He chose not to answer. "Can we talk about something else?"

"Okay. How are your grades?"

"Good enough." This was not a great improvement in subject, but he let her get by with it.

"Good enough for what?"

"Good enough that my scholarship has miraculously survived intact. I just don't know how I managed to choose a major that takes five years to complete."

"In other words, you've worked just hard enough not to lose it, no more."

"Sure. That's good enough." He said, unoffended by the observation.

"Well, that's one way to do it, I guess. Would you like to hear another way?"

"Maybe we'd better go to another subject," he suggested.

"So, tell me your impression of Miki."

"Besides that."

"Tell me what courses you'll be taking next year."

Hunter smiled. One thing about talking with Granny Jen: she was persistent.

"With pleasure," he said. And he launched into a litany of various architecture and design courses he would be taking, speaking with uncharacteristic intensity. On this one subject, at least with Granny Jen, he had a hard time feigning disinterest. The truth was, he was quite capable in his field, and he knew it. Still, he refused to give even architecture his total commitment, refused to give his mom and step-father the satisfaction of knowing he cared. "I'll be so buried under projects, I won't be able to breathe until Thanksgiving," he finished a little proudly.

"Sounds to me as if you're looking forward to it."

"Don't bet on it."

"And have you applied for an internship?"

"Nope."

"Won't you need one to be licensed as an architect?" she asked.

"I guess."

"Don't count on Uncle Donald."

"Huh?"

"Don't play innocent. You're betting your uncle left you all his money."

"Well, he didn't leave it to anyone else," he said. "And I'm pretty sure he didn't take it with him."

"Just because the dispensation of his estate must wait for your graduation doesn't mean any of it actually goes to you."

"I know that." His voice took on the sarcastic edge he used with his mother.

Granny Jen was not put off. "He took a great interest in you that last summer. He knew he was dying, and he saw such potential in you, Hunter."

"He saw my dad in me, you mean." Anger shook his voice. He looked down at the paper, disgusted with himself for showing how much he cared.

"Yes, he saw your dad," she answered quietly.

"And you think he tricked me into finishing school so I wouldn't turn into a full-fledged asshole like my dad."

"Hunter."

"I can't apologize for what he is."

"You should have seen yourself as you talked about school a minute ago. You love it, whether you admit it or not. And that's what your Uncle Donald wanted for you, son. He wanted you to grab that chance and claim it for your own."

"So you think that's all he meant when he said he was leaving me something to get me through life?"

"I honestly don't know. I'm sure that possibility has occurred to you."

"Of course. He was so screwy I wouldn't put it past him." Hunter picked up the paper, ready to end the conversation.

"He was a fine, wise man who loved you, and you know it. And you're about to get that degree in spite of yourself, and I hope I live to see it," she said with passion.

"Granny Jen, I hate when you talk like that."

"My old heart's wearing out, Hunter. That's the truth."

"Never."

She didn't miss a beat. "So, do you love her?"

"Who?"

"The girl you refuse to tell me about."

"Miki?" He gave a short laugh.

"You care about her."

"Maybe."

"Would you marry her?"

"I don't think Miki's quite the marrying kind," he said. He passed a hand over his face, hoping Granny Jen wasn't scrutinizing his expression too closely.

"Do you think she's good for you?"

"Hey, we're great together at school. This just isn't her scene, you know?"

"So, define her."

"You do it for me."

"No. I don't know her well enough. But I'll tell you one

thing." She pointed a finger at him for emphasis. "I think *this* is your scene and the life you live at school with Miki is not, and that bothers you more than you want it to." Her voice remained conversational, not demanding an answer.

"You think too much, Granny Jen. Now, if my name was Charlie Brown and she had red hair, I'd marry her in a heartbeat. And speaking of Charlie Brown . . ." He rattled the newspaper emphatically and went back to reading the comics aloud to her.

Hunter spent the night on the sofa in the living room so he could hear Granny Jen if she called. She had gotten in and out of bed with difficulty, and he almost wished he had called his prissy aunt. He awoke the next morning to find Granny Jen feeling stronger. And Miki had not come home from work at all.

🐜 🐜 🐜

Onions and peppers sizzled in butter, filling the small galley with aroma. Through the raised hatch, Miki could hear the morning sounds of the waterfront: boats creaking in their moorings, sneakers stepping by on the boardwalk, dinghies motoring in for supplies, people laughing over coffee or Bloody Marys. She stood barefoot with a terry robe wrapped loosely around her, coffee cup in hands. She did not touch the chef, yet she didn't appear out-of-place.

"You're a master with that knife, Jack," she observed as two plum tomatoes became neatly diced bits in seconds.

"Never thought about it. Just something you pick up when

you bach it as long as I have, I guess." With one swipe of the blade, he cleaned all the tomato bits off the chopping board into the pan. "This used to be a fillet knife, I think," he said, indicating with one finger that the knife had once been two inches or so longer than it now was.

"How big was the fish you broke it on?" she asked sarcastically.

"You're quick. I bought it at a second-hand shop just as you see it. My guess is it was used commercially and sharpened so many times it lost its length and curve. See how much wider the handle is than the blade?"

"Huh. Why don't you buy a new one?"

"I had to furnish this yacht on a budget. Now I'm attached to the stuff; know what I mean?"

She didn't respond. She watched him with fascination, taking in the way his nicely-kept hands maneuvered the kitchen utensils, the movement of well-toned muscles across his broad shoulders, the curl of thick dark chest hair, just touched with gray.

"You don't talk much the morning after," he observed.

"This isn't exactly the morning after," she said lightly. "It's just too early for me, and besides, your couch sleeps like hell."

"Too bad. My bed is big enough for two." He cracked eggs into the pan with one hand. Jack Franklin had the look of a self-satisfied man, and Miki knew she was probably not the first young woman who had stood in his robe in his galley.

Noticing her wrinkled nose, he explained, "Sort of a scrambled omelet. I'm too lazy to make a real one."

"It's not that. I'm just not used to smelling eggs this early."

He smiled, the lines of his face strong, the tan just right.

"Well, I don't want to send you home to face your boyfriend on an empty stomach."

"Oh, Hunter's easy. I'll just tell him I didn't want to disturb his sick grandma, which is partly the truth. Besides, he's not exactly my boyfriend."

"So he won't care you got blasted last night and had to crash on an old guy's lounge sofa?"

"Well, he—I don't know. It's hard to predict what Hunter will care about."

"So, what is he, if not exactly your boyfriend?" He dished the egg concoction onto plates and motioned for her to sit.

"Hunter is Hunter. He's easy, like I said. Besides, he's cute, and he may even be rich."

His laughter was perfectly-timed, carefully friendly. "Well, you'd better not let that one slip away. Those qualities would be hard to duplicate."

She laughed politely and began toying with her food.

"Eat hearty, there, my young friend. It's hard to lie on an empty stomach."

"I thought you said you were from Jersey. You have a Southerner's preoccupation with food. And I can't lie to Hunter. He has this uncanny way of getting at the truth eventually." With that, she began to eat without offering more conversation. She quickly changed into the clothes she had worn the previous night, leaving his robe in a heap on his stateroom floor. When she left, it was with a distracted "thank you" and an impatient swing to her walk, not even glancing back at her host.

Jack Franklin watched her go intently, nothing distracting his dark gaze. She was young, and she thought she had the world by the tail. He remembered what it had been like to feel that way, to think you knew it all, to think there was nothing you couldn't conquer. Well, she knew nothing of life; she had no concept of the things of the world, of the tools life used to slice a soul, to destroy a heart. Perhaps she would learn this summer. Perhaps Jack would teach her.

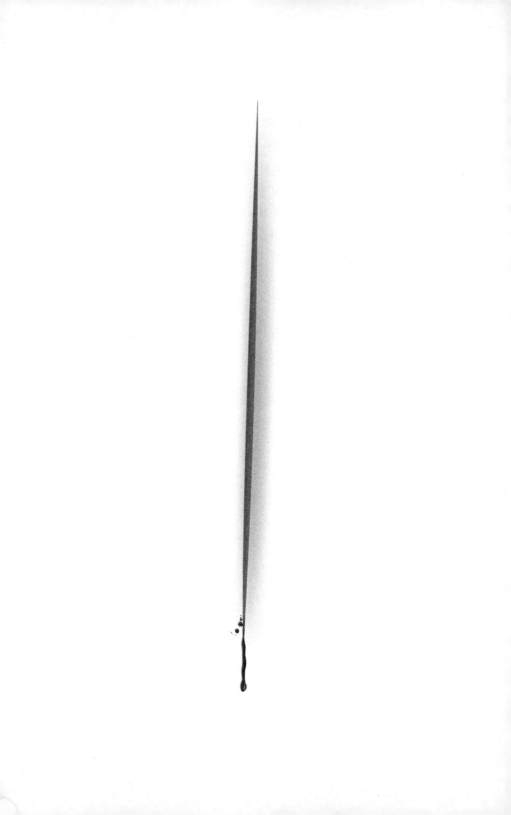

FIVE

The Cat waited on the shore for the signal. To his right, the beam from the old Cape Lookout lighthouse sliced the night sky at prescribed intervals. Lights from nearby pleasure boats glowed and rippled on the black water. Low voices could be heard conversing on a nearby boat: a friendly gathering. Farther away on another boat, music blared and figures moved in silhouette against yellow light. A comfortable night for most, The Cat mused. A fatal night for one.

Thirty minutes before, he had watched from a sand dune as a cruiser approached from the open sea, passed the last day beam, and rounded the tip of land to slip into the sheltered bight. Its running lights were extinguished as soon as it anchored. As The Cat waited, he focused on the silhouette of the man behind the curtains in the dimly lit interior of the boat. He knew the man's name. He knew where the man bought, where he sold, and what samples he was carrying tonight. He knew the color of the man's eyes. In a few minutes, he would know how fear looked in those eyes.

The cabin door on the boat opened and closed, and a shadow moved toward the boat's stern. The Cat ticked off the seconds with the fingers of his left hand, enjoying the anticipation. An executioner had to enjoy sending souls to hell, or what was the point? The knife was sharpened, openly visible in a holster outside his shirt. He was ready.

There. A match flared, a face was illuminated as a cigarette was lit, and the match remained lit eight seconds before dropping to the water. That was the final signal. The Cat gave the man credit for perfect timing.

He shoved off from shore in his launch and idled in the water for a moment, preparing himself. Luring this particular mark had required delicate negotiation. The man had his own profitable run from Venezuela to Miami, and he had come to North Carolina only under the promise that this market would be sweet and this contact could move his goods into the right hands. Cash up front, no snags, no trail left behind. The man had been assured that the contact was professional, a native who knew the water and the lay of the land. Yes, The Cat was a professional, all right. And the first ten seconds with the man would be critical. The man would either believe that he could do the job or blow The Cat's head off.

He motored slowly, leaving no wake, cutting through the still reflections of the pleasure boats snugly harbored for the night. He was a man at the top of his game. There was no rush. The bite of salt air against his face, the sparkling dance of black water and diamond light fed his anticipation. Excitement grew within his body, demanding as passion, cold as steel.

When he neared the boat, The Cat cut his motor and glided in. He had not yet seen the man's face, and he did not look now. He let the man scrutinize him as he caught the boat's ladder and tossed a mooring rope up to the deck. He let the man wonder about the cat. As the man secured the rope, The Cat reached inside the cage at his feet for the kitten. She sat hunched and still, her eyes narrow slits. Perhaps she was seasick. Perhaps she sensed what was about to happen and did not want to watch.

Without a word, the man stepped to the cabin door and opened it. The Cat boarded the boat with the kitten in one hand. He stepped down into the cabin and turned, letting the man see his face in the light, letting him see the knife. The man shut the door and sat at a table. The Cat sat close to him, taking the knife out and laying it on the table. The man drew a gun from a holster beneath his jacket and kept it in his hand. There were no pleasantries exchanged.

The Cat set his face carefully as he looked the man in the eye. The man's brown eyes were guarded, calculating. The clean-shaven face was tanned to leather by the sea; one tense jaw was scarred just where it angled into a prominent chin. His full lips appeared incapable of a smile, and yet, a short laugh sounded in his throat.

"Nice touch," he said, nodding toward the kitten. "What's it for?"

"Luck." The Cat stroked the kitten, his hands steady, deliberately sensual in movement. He was courting the man now, poised for conquest. He knew every nerve in his body by name, so heightened were his senses.

"A price was quoted to me. Cash. When will it be available?"

"The cash is always available," said The Cat. "And the goods?"

"The goods are still three days away. I haven't moved them."

"The samples?"

The man reached beneath the table with his left hand, his right hand still holding the gun. He laid two small square packets on the table, powder in one, crystals in the other. Raw cocaine and crack. A regular pharmacy.

"Hold the cat."

For the first time, the man flinched. "Can it swim?" he asked.

"You don't really want to find out." The Cat extended the trembling kitten across the table, mid-air.

A dollar amount equaling the fiscal budget of a small country rode on the man's response. The man cursed and took the cat. When the kitten strained to get away, he laid the gun on the table and held the cat with both hands, making it hunch down on the tabletop. He did not rub it.

From his shirt pocket, The Cat produced a magnifying scope. He picked up the knife and deftly slit the packet of powder, drawing out a small amount on the tip of the blade. Unhurried, he examined it under the glass, his hands steady. He did not sample the powder.

The cat was not purring. Shouts and laughter carried across the water from one of the boats. The man cleared his throat. A hum formed inside The Cat's head. The knife fit his hand perfectly, the handle smooth. Struggling now, the kitten began to claw, twisting in the man's hands.

"Two seconds more," The Cat said in a soothing, Southern voice. He set the magnifying glass on the table and returned the powder to the packet with the knife blade, his hands sure. His eyes were on the kitten, and his arm kept moving. The knife flashed one precise stroke as the arm behind it plunged it with power into the man's throat. The Cat watched the blood spurt red and red again as he sliced, carrying through the motion with his whole body, standing, his weight behind the knife, his left fist knocking the gun to the floor. The man's eyes were screaming fear, but his mouth was gurgling, blood drowning him.

In wild hate, the kitten clawed the man's hands until he let it go, and then the man clawed for the knife, but The Cat had both hands on the knife, one knee on the table, forcing the man down by his throat. And he held him down, blood turning the chair arm red, until the gurgling ceased.

The Cat donned rubber gloves to wipe the blade clean before folding the packets inside a handkerchief. Garbage. His blood-soaked shirt was garbage. He had touched nothing inside the yacht. No one on the water cared about the lone launch that motored off into the night. The boats would disperse the next morning. The body would bloat in the heat for three days. By then, the cat would be crazy with thirst.

>• >• >•

Grayson Tucker coaxed the cat to cease its mad skittering about the cruiser and warily approach the dish of water. She finally lapped the water, trembling, eyes closed against the men who stared at her. It was now time for Grayson to reveal the cat secret to the state authorities who had called him to this death scene. This third murder fit the two in his own harbor with the added detail of claw marks on the victim's hands. Grayson did not look at the body and did not search for clues. He left that to the state guys. Let them figure out for themselves that there were none.

In his boat, Grayson opened a small tin of tuna for the cat. He would check again with animal rescue folks, check the waterfront, but he knew the killer was too smart to have picked up the cat where he could be seen. The killer was too smart, period. And he was not through with Beaufort. Grayson felt certain of that.

SIX

"Flowers? You brought me flowers?" Miki hooted.

"Look what you've done. You made one of them droop," Hunter said with mock petulance.

"Which one? I don't see any droopers." She inspected the huge bouquet Hunter held, hands behind her back.

"That purple one there. And it was my favorite, too," Hunter replied quite seriously.

"If I'm not mistaken, that rare iris is one of Mrs. Spencer's favorites, also," put in Granny Jen from her chair.

"You *stole* flowers?" she laughed again. "You'll have the garden club hot on your trail now, Hunter."

"I was very careful to swipe only one from each yard, thank you. Aren't you going to take them?"

"Well, of course. A hot bouquet has always been my idea of romance." She eyed him slyly from behind the flowers. "What's up, Hunter? Have you been bad or are you wanting to be bad?"

"I'm wooing you, for your information."

This sent Miki into peals of laughter.

Granny Jen looked up from her book. "You kids take this conversation outside before I have to give you wooing lessons."

"I am an expert at wooing," said Hunter with exaggerated offense as he opened the screen door and bowed for Miki to pass.

"Wooing?" she whispered, taking his hand as they walked toward his Jeep.

"Yes, wooing." He opened her door for her. "This officially begins a real date. Just you and me and the moon, a little food, a little music. Whadaya say?"

"You're hard to resist, Hunter," she said as she settled into the seat.

There were times when Miki looked like any other college kid, blonde hair down, youthful figure, pretty face. When she chose to, however, Miki could turn heads, and she chose to today. She walked into the restaurant with the grace and purpose of a woman who had experienced the world and liked what she found, her chin lifted to just the angle that said she had the room under control. To a man watching, she looked like a woman who had never been surprised but whose lips held many surprises, just a hint of a smile. Her eyes were less bright than usual, mysterious, hiding secrets a man desired to know. And a woman might watch her with envy, for Miki embodied the mystique of womanhood.

The restaurant owner greeted Hunter as an old friend, touched Miki's hand as he took the flowers from her, and led the couple to a back table, carrying the flowers aloft in a glass. Miki walked her purposeful walk, and Hunter sauntered behind, swiping a couple of candles from tables as he went.

"Are you working the waterfront this year, Hunter?" the owner asked as Hunter plunked the candles down on their table.

"Yes, sir. On board the *Pirate's Lady* again."

"I've stayed completely away. It's a bizarre place these days."

"Yeah, it's a trip. Every tourist is an expert on the murder of the day."

"Is your business still good?"

"Oh, yeah. Better than ever. 'Forget the ponies,'" he mimicked. "'Show us where those three guys croaked.'"

"And now every stray cat is a suspect."

"Yeah, really. I'd hate to be a kitty these days." Hunter settled in to study his menu. After a bit, he peered at Miki through the flowers and asked pleasantly, "Are you feeling romantic over there in the bushes?"

"If I can manage not to set fire to my menu with all these candles, I'll try to work on the romantic part."

"Let me order for you," he said, taking her menu with drama.

"And what do you recommend?" she asked formally.

"We will have . . ." And then he froze.

"Hunter Kittrell," a Down East voice said. "It's good to have you back in town, son."

"Good to be back, Mr. Tucker," Hunter said, shaking the big hand of the Beaufort police chief. He looked past Grayson and stared into the eyes of Jack Franklin.

"So they sent the cops after you, did they, Hunter?" said Miki, and then she, too, locked eyes with Franklin.

"Ah, Miki, this isn't just a cop. This is *the* Grayson Tucker who will soon crack Beaufort's most famous murder case." Jack Franklin's voice was not Southern, and it carried distinctly across the room as he stepped into their space. "And this must be your not-exactly boyfriend?"

"Exactly," said Hunter, subtly refusing the extended right hand.

"Ha! You're quick. Almost as quick as my Miki here." Jack put his hand on the back of Miki's neck, a possessive gesture.

Hunter kept his gaze on Jack, not a flicker of interest, not a glance at Miki's face.

Jack leaned forward, deliberately too close to Hunter's face, his voice lowered. "And what have you done, boy, to warrant having the cops sent after you?"

"Not a damn thing. It's just a kid's joke," And with that, Grayson Tucker took over and steered Franklin away with a quick look of apology into Hunter's eyes.

Hunter closed his menu and set it on the table. His eyes held Miki's for a moment.

"What is the matter with you?" Miki's whisper was sharp with fury. "Why couldn't you at least shake his hand?"

Hunter stood slowly from the table, six feet of lanky young man, and extended his right hand to Miki, palm up. "Let's go," he said. She took his hand and stood also, lifted her chin, and they walked hand-in-hand out the door, leaving the flowers and candles for the next patrons.

As soon as the restaurant door closed behind them, Miki punched Hunter on the arm and started up the sidewalk at a quick walk. He caught up with her and took her by the arm. She shrugged him away and kept walking. This time, he stepped in front of her and stopped her, both hands on her arms, and kissed her fiercely.

"Are you insane?" she demanded, punching him again. "Let me go."

"We're still on our date, Miki," he answered, drawing her more closely into his arms. He kissed her again, this time long and warm.

She broke away from the kiss. "I don't understand you, Hunter. I told you Jack is my friend."

He let her go and stepped back, studying her face intently. "Miki," he finally said, and his voice was matter-of-fact, "one of us is your friend. One of us is your worst nightmare. You choose."

She looked away. "I don't believe you, Hunter." When he didn't respond, she said, "Say, is our date still on?"

"It's just beginning. Wanna go for a burger?"

"Yes, thank you," she answered politely, and she took his arm and walked with him to the Jeep.

The summer crowd was in full party mode by the time they drove down the little spit of land the locals called "the beach."

"This is not a beach," Miki pointed out.

"There's water. There's sand. A beach," Hunter stated.

"There are no waves."

"We give the waves to the tourists in the summer."

"The beach" was a wind-swept bank of dunes jutting into the

sound with little to recommend itself except that it did not appeal to the tourists. Parking was at a premium, and Hunter maneuvered his battered Jeep, rag-top down, between parked cars. People waved and thumped the side of the vehicle in recognition as he passed. He did not stop until he was in the center of the action.

"Hey, there's Hunter!" someone shouted, and he stood up in his seat to applause.

A guy handed him up a beer, which he passed on to Miki. "Where've you been, boy?" asked the guy. "We could've used you shooting hoops the other night."

"Working my ass off, as usual."

"Your granny don't cut you much slack, does she?"

"Naw, sir," agreed Hunter. Miki nudged him with the beer, and he took a swig and handed it back to her.

"Is this your lady?" the guy asked.

"Yeah." Hunter blasted the Jeep's horn twice. "Everybody, this is my lady, Miki."

"Hell, Hunter, you mean you know this one's name?" someone called.

Hunter laughed easily and coaxed Miki onto the hood of the car. Music was blasting from someone's car stereo, the noise banged about by the wind. Kids stopped by to talk, leaning on the Jeep.

Suddenly, Hunter pounded on the hood, calling, "Hey, you! Amy! Come over here!"

Somebody dragged the petite redhead from another group and shoved her over to the Jeep. There was expectant laughter all around.

"Where have you been?" demanded Hunter. "I've been looking for you all summer."

Amy's blue eyes searched his before giving him her dimpled smile. "Oh, around. Working. You know how it is," she said.

Hunter encircled Miki with his arm. "Amy, meet Miki Stone. Miki, this is Amy Goodwin. She used to be hell on a tricycle."

"Now they've turned me loose with a Camaro." Amy brushed impatiently at the jaunty curls dancing away from an attempted ponytail. "Good to meet you, Miki." She gave Hunter's sneaker a squeeze and started away.

"Wait a minute. I'm trying to make a date with you, here." Hunter pulled her back by the ponytail, grinning wickedly.

Her eyes were hidden as the wind tossed the curls around her face. "I thought you two were, like, tight," she said.

"Technically, this is our first date," said Miki.

"Technically, you sleep until noon," responded Hunter. "So," he turned back to Amy, "will you?"

"Will I what?"

"You know, come over in the mornings like you used to. Go fishing and stuff?" When she hesitated, he added, "It's only half a summer without you, Amy."

Amy glanced at Miki before answering, "I know what you mean." Before she could say anything else, some guy had her by the hand, pulling her toward the music. "See ya," she called over her shoulder.

Hunter looked at Miki. "Technically, you're a liar," he said.

"Nuh-uh. You never actually asked me out on a date. We just sorta happened."

He smiled his easy smile. "Yeah, we did. And we happened to be great."

"And are we great now, Hunter?"

"You tell me."

"Hey, you're the one who's changed, Hunter."

"Me? Nah. I'm still my same bad self, Babe."

"You left your bad self at school—the one who was always ready to make love and who would have been getting high with me about now instead of barely tasting his beer. Remember him?"

"This is my summer self, I guess," he answered with a shrug. "And your summer Hunter is as crazy about you as ever." He touched her hair. "Crazy enough to woo you. And I'm having a great time on our date."

She laughed. "Well, I should say so. You made a date with a red-head right in front of my eyes." She gave him an affectionate hug. "I'm having a good time, too, Summer Hunter."

He grinned and jumped down from the hood, reaching up to help her down. They walked through the crowd, stopping to talk with the groups they passed, until they were closer to the music. Finding a spot where the sand was packed hard, they danced, the breeze catching Miki's skirt and tossing it seductively around her legs. Hunter had an easy way of moving, unhurried and smooth; together, they appeared to be the perfect couple. If he noticed the appraising stares his buddies gave him and his girl as they danced, Hunter did not acknowledge them. If he cared that Amy left early with another guy, he didn't show it. The party broke up just after midnight when flashes of lightning warned of an approaching storm, and Hunter and Miki said their good-byes and drove straight home.

On Granny Jen's back stoop, Hunter kissed Miki sweetly, tasting her. "I had a nice time," he said politely. "Can I see you again?"

"Depends on how many flowers you swipe," she said, not letting him go. Her kiss was long and inviting, her young body pressed insistently against his.

He whistled low and shook his head. "You're too tempting, Miki. I've gotta go, like, right now."

"I don't understand you, Hunter," she said, stepping back reluctantly.

He released her quickly and bounded up the steps to his apartment, turned at the landing, and waved gallantly. She waved back from the stoop just as great splatters of rain hit him in the face. With a whoop and a slam of the door, he was inside.

No, he couldn't explain himself to her. He didn't have the words to say that it had nothing to do with wanting to be good but everything to do with home. Home meant that when he came to this place, the sickening feeling that he wasn't worth a damn to anyone left him. And only here did he feel a hope—maybe an expectancy—that the gnawing hole in his chest could be filled. He could not have put that into words, but he knew one thing: Home was worth any sacrifice.

⁕ ⁕ ⁕

Granny Jen sipped her coffee and studied Hunter's back as he poured juice and clattered cereal bowls. Rain still pattered outside, promising a gray, lazy day.

"You're too quiet, Granny Jen," he said, slicing a peach. "I told you to stop thinking so much. It'll stunt your growth."

She chuckled. "Okay, so tell me how your wooing went."

"It went." He set the bowls on the table, peach slices over granola. "Do you love her?"

"I don't know, Granny Jen." He sounded impatient. Perhaps he was impatient with himself; perhaps he did not yet know how to define love. "Why is it so important to you?"

She looked away. The silence felt awkward.

"Look, I'm sorry. Things are just weird right now, okay?" When she didn't speak, he said, "Granny Jen, aren't you talking to me?"

"I have some things to tell you, and I don't quite know where to begin." When she sipped her coffee, her hand shook.

"Well, start with the good stuff. Make it easier on both of us." A quick frown of concern, then his face was impassive as he waited for her to speak.

After another silence, she said quietly, "I'm giving you the apartment, Hunter."

"What?"

"You heard me."

"Don't do that."

"It's done."

"But why? I mean . . ." He looked away, unable to face her or the truth.

"This is my last summer in this house, Hunter. You know it, and I know it."

"No, Granny Jen." His voice strangled over his anguish.

"Yes, it's time," she said. "We're each coming into a new season in life. When you're young, you think you have life and love and time in your grasp, and you can do with it as you please. You get a little older, and you think life's got you, pulling you along too fast. But that's okay, too, for the ride can be sweet, even if the scenery is a little blurred by the speed." She paused. "And the sorrows . . . well. Maybe you're too young to want to hear about those." She looked him in the eye. "There comes a time when the ride slows down and you have to turn it all loose, if you ever held it in the first place."

"Not yet."

She patted his arm. "Hey, I'm going to live as long as I can. But probably not much longer in this house. It's too big. And I'm afraid I'll soon need help just getting around. You love it here nearly as much as I do. I want you to have a home here, and I want it settled now. So just say 'thank you' and enjoy it."

He didn't say thank you or anything else. Jaw clenched, he stirred his cereal into mush.

"You know, Hunter, now that the apartment is yours, you can make your own rules."

He looked up from his stirring.

"It's not my property, and I can't ask you to live by my rules."

He appeared bewildered, almost afraid.

"I have a word for you from the Bible," she said.

He grunted, exasperated.

"Paul told another young man named Timothy to guard carefully the things he had been taught."

"That doesn't have a damn thing to do with me."

"Hunter."

"Excuse me. A darn thing. Granny Jen, you see way too much in me. You seem to think I'm going to turn into this . . . this amazing person, when all I'm trying to do is just hang loose. You know, see where the wind blows. See if life turns out to be worth the trouble."

"You *are* amazing. And you will never know what life is worth until you have given it your heart and soul to the end. *Then* you can look back and say what it was worth." Her voice had risen with unaccustomed passion, and he waited to speak until she was no longer shaking.

"Thank you for the apartment, Granny Jen. In my mind, it will always be yours, and that's enough said on that subject." He pushed away from the table. "Was there anything else you wanted to tell me?"

"Yes. My reason for wanting to know whether you love Miki. She didn't come home again last night."

"She—well, of course, she did. I brought her home myself." He stood and strode quickly to her door. "Miki!" He yanked open the door without knocking. She was not there.

When he walked back into the kitchen, Granny Jen asked, "Are you all right?"

"Sure. So I'm lousy at wooing. It's no big deal."

But it was a big deal. She knew it, and he knew it.

SEVEN

"Hey, let me in!" Someone pounding on the hull of his yacht brought Jack Franklin from reverie. When he looked out, there stood Miki with her skirt clinging about her legs, her face illuminated by light from within the boat.

"I can't believe I did this," she exclaimed as he motioned for her to come aboard. She seemed chagrined, almost laughing, almost angry. She shook her skirt. "Oh, man, I'm dripping everywhere. Do you have anything dry?"

Wordlessly, he stepped into the stateroom and returned with the terry robe she had worn before. She took it with a laughing, "Thanks," and moved out of view, not quite sliding the compartment door closed. Jack had not spoken, and he settled back and lit a cigarette, staring at her moving shadow.

"What a storm!" she was saying through the opening. "Hunter's friends' party broke up early, but I wanted to find something to do besides sleep, you know? I didn't realize it was raining so hard until it was too late to turn back. I was going to get soaked either way."

She slid the door open, and her shadow merged with her figure, casually wrapped in the robe. "Thanks for letting me in." He said nothing as she stepped closer. "Hey, I'm sorry about Hunter tonight. He's, well, he's . . ."

"He's a boy." Jack dismissed the subject with one word.

Neither spoke again as she settled opposite him, running her fingers through her hair, sending droplets of water flying. "Am I interrupting something?" she finally asked.

"There's a murderer loose, Miki. The harbor is no place for you at this hour."

Shrugging off the implication, she said, "How about you? Aren't you afraid to be here?"

Without changing expression, he slid open a drawer beneath the table, flashed a .38 revolver, and returned it to the drawer. The gun was only in view for a breath of time, but its presence sharpened the room. "I'm ready for him," he stated, and his voice was as clear a threat as the gun.

"I thought he was only after drug dealers." Whatever casualness she might have been trying to achieve was swallowed by the hardness of his stare.

"Why are you here, Miki Stone?" he finally asked.

There was a defiant tilt to her head, a narrowing of her eyes.

"You're bored with your boy. You're bored with this town. You want something. What is it?"

She started to stand. The hand he put out did not touch her, but stopped her nevertheless.

"I can be many things for you, Miki." Rain was slapping the boat. He kept his voice low, distinct, hard as steel. "What do you want? And why do you think I can provide it?" When she didn't respond, he continued, "I can be your innkeeper. I can be your friend." His words came slower, like a man talking to his lover. "I can be your teacher."

She did stand, then, and so did he. "My point is, whatever it will take to fill that dissatisfied void in you, I will not be your dealer." She seemed to relax, but he did not. "If you want to get wasted somewhere else and come here to sleep it off, I can do that. There is much I am willing to do for you." She looked into his eyes, her face tilted up. "But I will not be your dealer." With that, he moved past her. "I'm going to bed. You do as you like."

And he left her standing alone in the robe, wind and rain and lightning outside.

Hunter was alone on his sofa, rain still falling. Something about the gray day caused him to think of his uncle, and he zapped his stereo louder, filling his head with noise enough to squeeze out Uncle Donald. One leg draped over the back of the sofa, keeping time with the music, one forearm covering his eyes, he did not realize someone else was in the room until she plopped on the floor beside him. Out of the corner of his eye, he saw a flash of red curls, and he started to laugh.

"You're a brave woman, Amy, you know that?"

"Why?"

"Between Granny Jen, Miki, and my current mood, you are treading dangerous territory."

"Actually, Granny Jen told me to come on up."

"Huh. Who would have ever thought?"

"And your moods never mean anything, Hunter. So explain to me about you and Miki."

"I wish somebody would explain it to me." He zapped the music off and sat up abruptly. "Now, what if you had caught me naked?" he teased.

"Wouldn't be the first time, would it?" Her eyes were mischievous, and he grinned, anticipating. "Remember the time we got in a water hose fight, and your granny hollered for you not to get your new shorts muddy?"

"So I stripped off everything I was wearing. My shorts stayed clean, and I beat you, too, didn't I? Admit it; you were terrified of my little naked self."

"Ha! I couldn't aim for laughing. And explain why you've refused my demands for a rematch for fifteen years."

"Probably has something to do with having to pull weeds every day for the rest of that summer."

Her laugh was hearty for such a little body. She looked around. "You know, I haven't been up here since we were kids. This place could use a coat of paint."

He stood and pretended to haul her up by her curls. "Maybe you're what I've been missing all summer. What's your favorite color?"

"Green."

"Might clash with my blue window."

"You mean you're actually going to paint?"

"Sure. Why not? You did just say you would help, didn't you?"

"Not exactly."

"Sure you did."

"Lord, Hunter, you never change."

"That's up for debate. So what color are we painting?" asked Hunter.

"If it were mine, I'd paint these three walls white and that one wall with no windows something bright, like coral. But Granny Jen may not go for that."

"She won't care." He stood in the center of the room and surveyed his domain, hands on his hips. "Man, this is going to be a job. Why are you making me do this?"

"Me? I . . ." Amy sputtered.

"How much does paint cost, anyway? I'm on a budget."

"Just charge it to your granny."

"No. Let's charge it to your dad," said Hunter. "He won't know the difference. He'll just think your mom went on another decorating spree."

"Tell you what. You pay for the paint, and I'll supply the rollers and stuff from Mom's stash."

"Deal." Hunter stuck out his hand to shake on it.

"I wish I knew precisely at what point I managed to volunteer for this."

They were both laughing when they stepped out on the landing. Crossing the yard below them, Miki stopped short and looked up at them.

"Hey, Babe, where've you been?" Hunter's voice was casual.

She looked at him with a rare desperation in her eyes.

"Come with us. We're boldly going where this man has never gone before."

"To the paint store," put in Amy.

"How domestic." Miki turned toward the house.

They started down the steps.

"Really, come on. It'll take two interior decorators to keep me colorfully coordinated."

She smiled briefly. "No, thanks. I'm really wiped. I'll catch you later." And Miki walked to the house without a backward glance.

"Go talk to her. I think something's wrong," said Amy when the screen door banged behind Miki.

"Nah. I have a mission to complete." He jumped in his Jeep and motioned for her to follow. With one more look at the door, she climbed in. "To seek out new life and new paint colors," he quipped as he cranked up.

🐜 🐜 🐜

Inside, Miki sank to the floor, head on her knees, shoulders shaking. Her hands were clutching her hair, and she did not seem to hear Granny Jen approach.

"I wish with all my heart I could get down on the floor with you," said Granny Jen.

Miki jumped and tossed her hair back, quickly wiping her cheeks. Shoulders back and chin up, her body posture changed from pitiful to defiant; her eyes dared Granny Jen to speak again.

But she did speak. Slowly, she lowered herself into a nearby chair and said, "What's wrong, child? You can't be spending all those tears on Hunter."

Miki stared at her blankly. "You don't like me, do you?" she finally asked.

Granny Jen sighed. "You perplex and confuse me, and I don't understand you. But I do care about you a great deal."

"Why?"

"Perhaps I have been blessed with a caring heart."

A long time passed as Miki looked at the floor. Her features softened. "If you had any idea of the crap I've gotten myself into, you would be more than perplexed. The easy part, I'll try to explain. I just wanted to talk to Hunter so bad, you know? And there he was laughing, and I knew it wasn't a good time. And somehow—" she leaned her head back against the wall and spoke to the ceiling—"somehow I don't think there will be a good time again."

"Why not?" Jen prodded.

"He and I were so . . . together . . . back at school. This place has pulled us apart."

"No it hasn't."

There came that defiant angle of the chin again; the blue eyes narrowed.

"Shh. Just let me say this." Granny Jen blew out a breath and proceeded carefully. "I think there is a great emptiness inside you and Hunter, and you reach for each other and maybe some narcotics to try and fill it."

Miki eyed her suspiciously.

"As long as you keep reaching, you think, 'Maybe this is happiness. Maybe I'll be satisfied.' But here in this place, you see Hunter realizing that somewhere close by is something that will truly satisfy him, and that makes your emptiness even more acute."

Miki stood abruptly. "I have no idea what you're talking about, but if it has something to do with Amy, you are so far wrong you're not even on this planet."

"It has nothing to do with Amy. But your heart knows, as Hunter's does, that the things of this world dissolve quickly and leave a bad taste on your heart. You crave truth, and you both must search somewhere besides where you've been searching to find it."

"Bull. I'm going to take a nap." She started out of the room.

"Are Hunter and Amy coming back here?"

Miki stopped but did not turn around. "I guess. They said something about going to the paint store."

Granny Jen laughed a truly tickled laugh. "Well, I'm going to wake you up after a bit. It will do you good to be with those two when they get to going."

Miki shook her head and started off again.

"Now you don't want Hunter to think you're hiding away jealous, do you?"

"You are cagey, Granny Jen. All right, you win. I'll get up eventually and join them. Or will you allow me into the sanctuary of Hunter's room?"

"Only Hunter can answer that, dear." And Granny Jen closed her eyes before Miki's stare could hit her.

Beatrice Jenny Kittrell kept her eyes closed and sat very still for a long time. She was completely drained. Always a plain-spoken woman, she was not accustomed to speaking with such passion. It almost felt as if she had been in a fight with Hunter this morning, and now with Miki. Maybe it *was* a fight. The line between good and evil certainly seemed to have pierced her home this summer. She thought back to a time many years before when the battle lines had been clear, the battleground her own son's heart. And now, the heart of her son's son was at stake.

But there was a difference. Her son's battle had been fought on pure granite. Oh, how hard his heart had become! Kiln-fired stone. Hunter's heart was still clay. For all his emptiness and indifference, his heart was still malleable. And she would fight for it to her dying breath.

Granny Jen did not move for a very long time after Hunter and Amy returned. It was not that she had not heard them—half the neighborhood heard them. There was a great clattering of buckets and ladder, shouts and laughter. She could hear them even after they finally hauled all their equipment up to the apartment: windows opening, furniture moving, more laughter. She imagined the scene as it progressed: the ladder set up, the fight over who would paint the trim, splatters of paint on hair and drop-cloths. Eventually they would actually get some on the walls. The only thing beyond her imagination was the hot Caribbean coral being smeared on one wall.

It was Miki who found her there, eyes still closed. "Granny

Jen," she asked softly, "are you all right?"

Opening her eyes, Jen glimpsed an expression bordering on concern peering at her. "Yes. I'm just tired."

"Have you eaten lunch?"

It was the first time the girl had ever expressed interest in her welfare. Jen realized simultaneously how pale she must appear and how late it was getting. Why, it was past two o'clock.

"Oh, goodness, time slipped completely away from me." She struggled to get up, pulling on her cane.

"You stay there. I'll fix you something," Miki said, not unkindly. She appeared a bit frightened. Soon she brought fruit and chicken salad on a plate, along with a tall glass of iced tea. Jen accepted it gratefully. "Can I do anything else for you?" Miki asked.

"No, child; thank you, though. I'm just going to sit right here and eat this. I'll feel better soon."

"You sure?" Miki appeared uncertain about what to do.

Jen solved the dilemma for her. "Take the tea and some paper cups up to the painters for me, would you?"

Miki smiled in acknowledgment that she had been conned and went off. Carrying tea did make it easier to enter the room where Hunter and Amy chattered away.

"Hey, Babe. Finally, a fresh recruit."

"Not hardly." Miki surveyed the job in progress.

"What do you think?"

"Quite impressive." She opened the freezer compartment of the ancient Kelvinator. There was ice, three inches of frost, some popsicles, and not much else. Soon she had cups of tea in their paint-sticky hands.

"So, if you're not going to be our assistant, what will you be?"

"Supervisor."

"Supervisor?"

"Yes. You missed a spot just to your left." Miki perched on the back of the sofa. There was silence for a while.

"Good choice of colors, Amy," Miki finally said.

"What makes you think I didn't choose the colors?" Hunter broke in.

"Get real, Hunter. Are you an art major, Amy?"

"Accounting, actually." Amy continued painting, her back to Miki.

"See? I told you she was boring," teased Hunter.

"That's not what he said about you," Miki countered.

"Exactly what did he say about me?" Amy did look at Miki then.

"Uh, well . . ."

"He's never even mentioned me, has he?"

"He doesn't talk about Beaufort much," Miki said carefully.

Amy looked at Hunter in surprise and went back to her painting. "And what are you studying?" she asked Miki.

"I'm not sure. I can't seem to decide." Miki crossed her legs, letting her shoe dangle. "I like drama, but I'd hate like hell to have to sleep with someone to get a job, you know?"

"Um, my roommate's a drama major. She plans to teach, but there's always community theater," said Amy.

Hunter tried to catch Amy's eye, but she was working with intense concentration and would not look at him.

"Hey, assistant, you're too slow," he said, tapping Amy on the back.

"So fire me."

"I can't. You're too cheap."

"Give me a raise."

"Then I'd have to fire you."

"Please give me a raise," Amy laughed.

"Bet you can't do that trim before I finish this wall."

"Just watch me," she said. They painted quickly for the next few minutes. "Look what a mess you're making, Hunter. You're splattering my trim."

"Whose trim?" he asked.

"Hunter."

"What?"

When Amy didn't answer, he looked at her. She gestured toward the sofa. It was empty.

He hopped off the ladder and went to the window. Miki was just pulling away from the dock in his uncle's boat.

"Does she know where she's going?" asked Amy.

"No."

"Go after her. Take my dad's skiff."

"Miki is very self-sufficient."

"She'd better be. The tide's going out."

He sighed. The rain had stopped, but the chop was nasty on the backwater. This was the reason he had not gone in to work: the *Pirate's Lady* wasn't sailing.

"Good. Maybe she'll beach herself somewhere until this blows over instead of drowning," he said.

"You are evil."

"I just know Miki's moods. C'mon. Let's paint. I don't want to miss any of this great fun, do you?"

"You can't fool me, Hunter," said Amy as she returned to her painting. "You can act like you don't care what Miki does, but something's eating you. What is it?"

He was quiet for a long time as he rolled paint like an expert. "She's not happy here, and she's not happy with me. And I don't know what to do about it."

"Maybe she should go home."

"It's not that simple. Her mom's a country club-alcoholic back in Pennsylvania. She spends her alimony all day and entertains her friends' husbands all night. She doesn't want Miki in her way. And her dad—well, her dad will give her anything she wants, so long as she stays out of his face."

"I'm sorry. You never know what some people have to live with, do you?"

"Hey, don't go feeling sorry for her. Miki's a big girl. She can take care of herself. She's just having a hard time adjusting to the slow pace here, you know?"

"Have you two been together long?"

"All semester," he said a little proudly.

"Must be some kind of record for you, Hunter."

"Hey, don't start."

"Just kidding. How did you manage to hang on to her so long?"

"Oh, gosh, she's just such a blast, you know? And we fit together so well, I just thought, I guess, that we would fit the same here. And don't come out with one of your lectures. I'm doing my part. I even swiped her some flowers yesterday."

Amy was concentrating on trimming Hunter's blue window. "Well, are you serious?"

Hunter gave her a quick look before answering, "I hate that

word. I don't even know what it means." When she didn't respond, he added, "I can't define how I feel about her. Tangled, maybe. We're tangled together, and I don't want to let go of her."

"Hey, I'm impressed. You said all that and you didn't even mention her boobs once." She let out a shriek as Hunter came after her, waving his paint brush. "Stop, Hunter. You'll get paint on your window."

Lights were winking on along Taylor's Creek when Miki returned. The fading light glowed with rosy haze; the squall had blown over. Waves tapped the dock gently where Hunter sat, feet in the water.

"Did you bring back supper?" he called.

She held up a seashell. He guessed it had a hermit crab inside and smiled.

"Check the tide table before you go out next time," he said as he grabbed the rope she tossed him.

"You're too smart for your own good, Hunter," she said wryly. "How come you never get stuck?"

"I know where I'm going." With a strong grip, he pulled her from the boat. "You okay?" he asked.

"No." They sat on the end of the dock and held each other. "Why does everything feel so screwed up this summer?" she asked.

"You tell me."

She was silent.

"Where did you go last night?" he asked.

"Halfway to hell."

"What did he do?"

"Nothing."

"Miki."

"Nothing. He ignored me."

"But you'll go again," he said.

Silence.

"Why, Miki? Why can't you just stay here and enjoy the view?"

"There is no view from my window."

"I didn't mean literally."

"I don't know, Hunter. Let's just drop it." She looked him in the eye. "Let me see the view from your window tonight. Please."

"Can't do it."

"You can. It will make things right between us again."

"I *won't* do it. And that's not what's wrong between us and you know it."

She was silent when faced with his subtle accusation.

He reached for a rope tied to the end of the dock and hauled up a crab trap, nice bluefins dancing on the wires. "Tell you what. You are cordially invited to my apartment, which will be on all the magazine covers next month, for a fine seafood supper. These guys are buying." He indicated the crabs.

"Shh. Don't tell them."

Supper was very late, but great in the Down East tradition. Hunter did not have many utensils, or for that matter, ingredients, but he sure could steam crabs, spiced just right, butter on the side. He could make a horseradish sauce for his steamed oysters that would have made old Blackbeard breathe fire for real. And his hush puppies were the melt-in-your-mouth kind, not too big, just a hint of onion.

"That was a respectable dinner, if I say so myself," he bragged as he scrubbed the dishes.

"Does your mom cook like this?" Miki asked, leaning on the counter to watch him.

"Sometimes," he said with a frown. He preferred not to think about his mom. Keeping his eyes on the pot he was rinsing, he asked softly, "Where are you going tonight, Miki?"

"I don't know, Hunter," she answered wearily. "Why won't you let me stay here?"

He shook his head and did not look at her. It was a matter of principle now. He had made his choice as to how he would live this summer. It may seem artificial to her since it was only for the sum-mer, but it meant something to him. It meant there was good in him after all. It meant he was worthy of this apartment. She would have to choose. Hunter or Jack. He would not ask her to stay.

Without a word, Miki left, her footsteps soft as a kitten's on the hardwood floor. She did not kiss him good-bye, and he did not watch to see where she went. He still had his self-respect, for what it was worth.

EIGHT

Grayson Tucker should have been smiling. Another night had passed with nothing on the report besides a couple of traffic violations, a domestic incident, and a rustling in somebody's bushes. No murders, no drug busts. Small-town stuff. And on top of that, his scales were tipping five pounds lighter, thanks to his recent aversion to fatty breakfasts.

But Grayson felt uneasy. His gut may have been thinner, but it still told him the killer was close by and poised to kill again. And no matter how many times the forensic guys turned over the evidence and said "Aha!" it still amounted to zilch. The only connections were drugs and cats. Grayson himself was sure the killer was a man, and he was sure he was only with the victims briefly. So what?

While the state guys pursued the cat theory down the same avenues Grayson had followed to dead ends, Grayson's mind snagged on the implied coziness of the scenes. Who was this guy? How did he get so close? Where did he learn to kill so effectively?

Picking up his hat, Grayson headed for the door. As always happened toward the end of June, the days became hot and the sun was murder on anyone out in it all day. These days, Grayson parked his car in favor of walking the harbor and downtown area. He wanted his presence known, and he wanted to look every person in the eye, friend and stranger alike. For certain, there were no clues to be found anywhere else.

Besides, Grayson was searching for someone in particular, a man he had not seen in many years, a man he wasn't sure he would recognize if he did. This man would have Jen Kittrell's gray eyes, for sure. The feds had alerted Grayson that Rob Kittrell might be in Beaufort, maybe on the water. It seemed federal agents had been about to bust Rob last fall in some drug sting when he had given them the slip and vanished from California. His yacht had recently been found beached on a tiny cay in the Caribbean. Presumably, he was traveling in a new yacht under a new name. According to a "source," Rob could be in Beaufort. Maybe. Grayson never knew what to make of those federal guys and their sources. For all he knew, Rob was in China.

Adjusting his hat against the persistent harbor breeze, Grayson tried to remember Rob Kittrell. Bigger guy than Hunter, darker hair, maybe even better-looking, and he would be, what, forty-ish by now? Pretty wild in high school, but so were some of the town's model citizens. The difference was, about the time most in his crowd were marrying nice girls and settling down, Rob got a nice girl in trouble and married her because his older brother threatened to kill him. And then, when one guy in his crowd had gone off to prison, Rob was just gone. Period. Briefly, Grayson wondered how much of this Hunter knew, if he realized why Jen was so strict on him, whether he even remembered his dad.

Well, it was a shame, but not really any of Grayson's business. His job was to find Rob for the resident narcotics agent. If he could recognize him. If Rob Kittrell was even in the country.

Jack Franklin was sitting on his deck enjoying a cocktail and the evening breeze when she appeared, striding briskly down the ramp as if she belonged there. With a brief questioning glance but no hesitancy, she stepped on board his boat and sat beside him. She snatched his drink boldly, as if she deserved it.

"So, you're back, Miki."

"For now."

"Why?"

"I can't answer all those questions you asked the other night, and I can't deal with everything you threw in my face. But I could use a friend."

"Go on," he said.

"And at this precise moment, I'm a little scared."

"You?"

"There's this guy who keeps hanging around my booth," said Miki with a glance toward the boardwalk.

"For how long?"

"Nearly two weeks. Well, since before that last murder."

"Yes, I know. I have been watching him," he said, his hand touching hers as he reached for his drink.

She seemed startled by this revelation but did not comment. "Anyway, just now, as I was waiting for Hunter to get off work, he came toward me as if he wanted something. Old guy. It scared me, and I had to get myself somewhere, fast."

"Old guy? He looks about my age."

She laughed.

"You did the right thing. Old guy Jack will take you in any time. And the other old guy won't bother you again." He reached beside his chair for the bottle and poured generously.

Silent, Miki stared long at the darkening shoreline opposite. Whether she noticed the stately silhouettes of sailing yachts moored in the channel or the shadowed forms of ponies moving on the bank, it was hard to tell. Her expression was determined, yet distant. If she felt his eyes studying her profile, she did not acknowledge it.

"Were you afraid of the dark when you were a little girl?" Jack asked, lighting a cigarette.

"No. What makes you ask that?"

"Just wondering. Why would you be afraid of an old guy hanging around the docks?"

"Because he gives me the creeps." She seemed irked that she had to explain.

"Does he remind you of your dad?" His voice was smooth and low.

"Of course not. Why do you keep asking these questions?"

"I want to know everything about you, Miki Stone." He leaned closer to her, the glow of the cigarette between them.

"I want to walk around inside that brain of yours. Now tell me what your dad is like."

"He's like, well . . ." She looked away, her expression annoyed.

"He's like me, isn't he?"

"No! I mean, not in any way I could put my finger on."

He laughed a pleased laugh. "He is a powerful man, yes?"

"I don't know. Okay. Maybe I could give you that one."

"Not like your boyfriend."

She stood abruptly. "Oh, Hunter's boat came in, and I didn't even notice. Hunter must be waiting for me."

"Yes, Hunter. Tell me again his last name."

"Kittrell."

"Kittrell. Interesting." He stood also, and his open hand touched the small of her back, his heat passing through the thin cotton blouse to her skin. "And how long do you think your boy will wait?"

"Probably not long. He . . ."

"I would wait all night. And do you think he cares for you?"

"Well yes, he . . ."

"No, he must not. Has he ever come after you when you were down here after midnight, alone? Has he stopped you from coming to me, alone?"

"I never wanted him to. I . . ."

"A man would have."

She stared into his face, her features sharp in the dim light. And then, without a word, she left, her stride brisk and certain.

Miki stopped when she reached the dock. Hunter was not there. By the glow of streetlights, she finally spotted him, hands in his pockets, walking home. He must have waited a while. But not long enough. She looked back at Jack's dark form, cigarette glowing. "Hunter! Wait!" she yelled and walked quickly to catch up. His smile was easy when she put her arm around him, his hand light and careless on her back.

➤ ➤ ➤

Mornings on the water are forgiving. Mist clings to the sea grass, shore birds scoot and stalk for breakfast, gulls fuss overhead. Morning water is still, the skies a fresh canvas. No wind to stir up trouble, no clouds to mar the pale blue. Morning is always the same, and it erases the stains of the night before, makes a person believe life could start fresh one more time.

Such a morning found Amy and Hunter on the water, easing around the shoals, the wake behind them a precise V that dissipated quickly and disturbed nothing. Theirs was the silence of companionship; they had been here before. Now and again, Amy pointed out a pair of dolphins, a cormorant diving. It all felt pleasantly familiar.

They set shrimp nets along the creeks early and went back to gather them in while it was still early. Their haul was light but sufficient: leave the rest for the real fishermen.

Amy did her share of the work, her body the small, sturdy type that dives in heart-first, shoulders square, legs stocky. Having Amy along completed something for Hunter: the scenery?

The peace? The summer?

As they started in, Amy sat on the live-well facing Hunter, her feet propped on the cooler. Arms folded across her chest, she asked, "Hunter, don't you miss Beaufort when you're not here?"

He was silent for a long while as if he had not heard her above the growl of the motor. His eyes were on the water ahead when he finally said, "I try not to."

"I feel like I've fallen off the planet whenever I leave here," she said. When he didn't respond, she continued, "I don't understand why you haven't told Miki all about this place. Every single detail. It's part of who you are, Hunter."

He adjusted his ball cap lower over his eyes. Maybe he was looking at her now. Maybe not.

"And I find it odd that you haven't told her about us."

"What 'us'?" The hat cast an angled shadow just above his lips. She looked away.

"Us. You know, doing this." She made a gesture that spanned the boat, the water. "Every single summer of our lives. I didn't especially mean last summer," she added in a small voice.

He shrugged. He could have been saying that he tried not to think about his summers or he could have meant he had forgotten last summer.

They came alongside and passed a cruiser proceeding slowly in the narrow channel. Although the skipper could barely be seen behind the tinted glass in the pilot house, Amy waved at him. He did not appear to wave back.

* * *

"Hey, Granny Jen," exclaimed Amy as she and Hunter stomped in carrying the cooler. "Look at you sitting there all pretty and cheery."

Jen chuckled as they passed through the porch on their way to the kitchen.

"I predict y'all are going to be pigging out on shrimp tonight," continued Amy.

"Forget supper. What's for breakfast?" came from Hunter.

"There are homemade muffins and some fruit in there," called Jen.

"Muffins? I want a man's breakfast." There was a banging of doors, a general clatter, then, "Oh, wow, look at those muffins!"

It seemed a happily disorganized gale had blown in when they hauled their breakfast to the porch to join Granny Jen.

"How are your folks?" Jen asked Amy.

"Great. Which juice is mine?"

"The one I'm not drinking," said Hunter, grabbing a glass.

"And what are you doing this summer, dear?" Jen asked as if there had been no interruption.

"Helping my dad, as usual. Hands off my muffin, Hunter. He's got these delusions of me taking over his business when I'm out of school." Amy grabbed Hunter's hand as it sneaked toward her plate. "I told you once, Hunter, that's my muffin."

"Your muffin? No, this little one is yours," said Hunter, grabbing the muffin from her plate with his other hand.

"Oh, Hunter! They're all the same size." She helped herself to two from the basket. "Granny Jen, I miss how you used to take us on those history walks. Remember?"

"Oh, yes. In fact, I still have pictures of you two taken on those walks. Would you like to look at them over breakfast?"

"Sure. Hunter, go get them."

"I'm eating my breakfast," he complained, his mouth full.

"Well, how are we going to see them over breakfast unless you go get them? Keep up, Hunter. And give me back my fork. What are you doing, starting a fork collection over there?" She took the fork from his hand, cantaloupe slice and all, and bit into the fruit before he could grab it back. With a sigh, he stood up and went inside the house to look for the pictures.

Amy looked toward the garage. "Do you have a picture of the time we climbed on top of the apartment?" she asked Granny Jen.

"Heavens, no! You two nearly gave me a heart attack. What possessed you to do that anyway?"

"That was the year Hunter took it over as his bedroom, and you wouldn't let us play up there anymore. So we decided to play on top of it. Good, Hunter, drop the pictures in the cantaloupe," she said when Hunter plunked the neatly labeled box of photographs on the table.

And so on. Jen never was sure if their banter was a continuation of the previous summer or a rerun. When they were through looking through the pictures, she asked, "Are you doing anything else until time for work?"

"No."

"Yes. Hunter is not through decorating," declared Amy.

"I'm not?"

"Come on; I'll show you."

"Take the camera," said Granny Jen. "I can't wait to see pictures of what you've done."

"Good idea, Granny Jen. Pick up a little speed, there, Hunter. You act like decorating is work."

For a while, Jen could hear sounds of furniture moving, which amused her, since there were only three pieces to move. There was a brief altercation, laughter, and a tremendous amount of hammering. Someone evidently fell off a ladder, which was followed by more laughter. Then there was relative quiet.

"Well, I must admit," Hunter said, surveying their work, "for a guy who can't afford pictures, it's not bad."

Amy stood back to admire. "I say it's great."

They had artfully hung the old badminton racquets, croquet mallets, and fishing gear on the walls. There was even a croquet ball balanced on two nails. It was not quite ready for *Southern Living*, but it was okay.

"What you need is a screen to hide that pitiful kitchen area," said Amy.

"I'll have you know I cooked a gourmet meal for Miki in that kitchen the other night."

She clapped him on the back. "I'm proud of you, Hunter. Now let's move this dining chest."

"Again?"

"Yes. This time, let's turn it face out so that it blocks the view of the kitchen."

"Then I'll have to look at the back of it every time I get a soda."

"You'll get used to it. Hey, put some muscle into it. This thing's heavy."

The chest scraped the wooden floor with an agonizing screech; the teacups rattled ominously.

"Well, would you look at that?"

"How did we miss this when we moved it out to paint?" asked Amy.

"I guess we just pulled it straight out and dropped a cloth over it. And every time you've made me move it, we've pushed it straight up and down the wall."

They stared in silence at the back of the chest. There, tacked to the wood, was a handwritten note:

Hands off!
This cabinet belongs to Hunter.
Donald Kittrell

"I guess that explains why this piece wasn't carried off when the rest of the stuff walked out of here. Come on, let's push it back."

"Stop, Hunter. Don't you want to keep the note?"

"No way. I don't want anybody walking out with my chest."

"Well, wait; don't move it. It looked good there."

Hunter pushed in a frenzy. It seemed important that he put it back where it was, fast. There was a furious scraping and rattling, then a clunk when it stopped.

"Well now you've messed up your flow of rooms."

"What rooms? It's all one room. Fix the teacups nice there while I look at my chest."

"You mean you actually like this old thing?"

"It's mine. And Granny Jen says it's, like, ancient and worth a bundle."

"So, are you gonna sell it?"

"Sell it? No, I told you; it's mine."

"I don't get it. Why would your uncle want you to have this?" Amy rattled the teacups as she arranged them, and then stepped back with Hunter to admire the effect.

"Don't know."

"Surely it's not all he left you."

"Could be."

"Aren't you disappointed?" she asked, looking up at him.

He shrugged.

"Well, good grief, I would be. There must be more to it than just an old cabinet. Let's see what's in this drawer." The only drawer was a shallow one above the cabinet doors, and she pulled it out and stood on tiptoe trying to see inside. "What's in there, Hunter?"

After glancing inside, he closed the drawer. "Nothing. Just some old papers."

"Let's look at them."

"Nah. It's nothing important."

"Hunter!"

"Come on. I want to see Miki before we go to work." He turned his back on the cabinet and started toward the door.

"Shoot. You are so weird." She followed him, shaking her head.

* * *

Hunter walked Miki to work. Neither said much. At the dock, he kissed her. When she tried to break away, he kissed her again.

"Um, I've got to get to work," she said. "Wait for me tonight, okay?"

"Miki, you get off before I do, remember?"

"Oh, yeah." She looked confused. "Scc ya."

"Wait for me, Babe, okay? Miki?" His eyes searched her face for an answer.

All she said before turning away from him was, "I've gotta go."

So did he, actually, and he ran ahead before the ship sailed without him. As he ran, he brushed past a man who glanced at him and stared at Miki as she went toward her booth.

The man did not bother Miki today, just as Jack had promised. Miki no longer had a job.

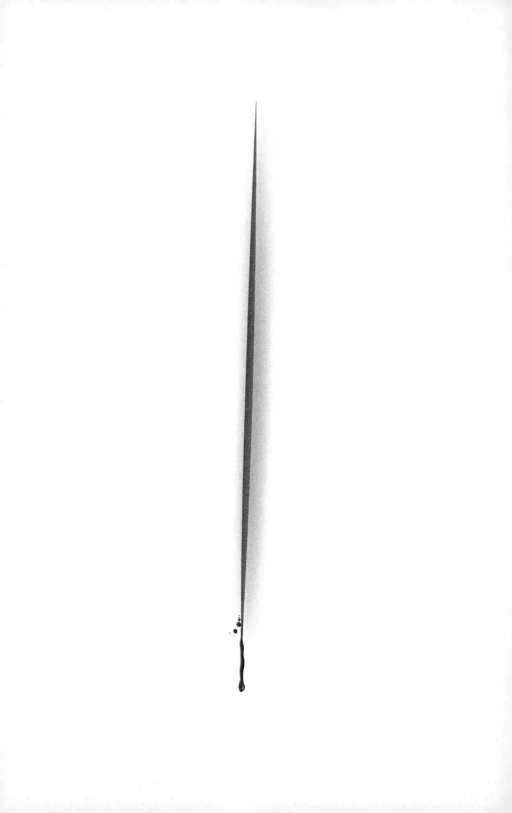

NINE

Miki sat with her head leaning on one hand and stared at her uneaten lunch. *Nice going, Girl,* she thought. *Lose a job a twelve-year-old could do.* She looked down the boardwalk toward her old booth beside the water where a pretty brunette was handing a brochure to a white-haired couple. She couldn't understand it, really. Her boss had called just before she was to leave for work and told her she was fired. Something about her work not being satisfactory. What work? All she had to do was hand out brochures to tourists and be polite. And she had been polite, in her brisk way.

It wasn't that she cared about the job or the money. The job was just someplace to be, something less boring than doing nothing. Barely. And Miki Stone did not need money. Dear old Wall Street Dad, living fast and high with his girlfriend in Manhattan, saw to that.

It was just so damned embarrassing, losing a ridiculous job like that. What had she done? No way was she going to tell Hunter or his granny until she figured out a suitable lie. She had a feeling Granny Jen would find the truth out pretty fast. But would she tell Hunter?

At the thought of Hunter, an unsettled feeling came over Miki. She despised that feeling. The good thing about being with Hunter had always been that she didn't have to think or feel anything. Just have fun, get high, push all of life's buttons at once or push none of them. What did it matter? She had decided life was pointless, and Hunter didn't care whether it had a point or not. That had made a pretty good match, in Miki's view.

The problem was that Hunter was acting as if he believed there might be a point. My God, he had been *decorating*.

A dark shadow crossed her table, and Jack Franklin sat beside her. She ignored him and pretended interest in a ninety-foot yacht which was docking at the end of the boat slips. More confusing thoughts pushed around in her head. Had Jack been right? Did Hunter not even care about her? And which Hunter did she want: the one who didn't give a crap what she did or the one with the uncharacteristic concern?

Thinking about Hunter was hard, and it hurt, so she turned to Jack and smiled instead.

"Finally! There's my Miki. What brought on such a fit of heavy thought?"

"Oh, man, you wouldn't believe it. I lost my job."

"Well, I can see where that would portend the end of the world."

"It's not funny. Hunter's granny got me that job. I'll feel like a total fool telling her I lost it."

"Then let's think of something else." He made a pretense of thinking. For the first time, Miki became aware that people passing the dining porch looked twice at the two of them together.

"I know," he said with a dramatic snap of fingers. "Tell her you got a better job."

"Oh, yeah, right. Like that's going to work in a town this size."

"Then we'll make it true. I have a sudden need for a secretary." He pushed a napkin toward her. "Fill out this application and you're all set." Maybe it was because he was looking at the harbor, his gray eyes in shadow; maybe it was because she didn't know him well. She thought she saw triumph surface in his eyes just before they narrowed, but she couldn't be sure.

"Secretary? Nobody is going to believe that."

"Oh, but they will. I will tell the old granny her name was on your application as a personal reference. And perhaps if I mention to Grayson Tucker that there could be a dilemma over my hiring you, he will put in a good word for me with Mrs. Kittrell."

"What?"

"What part did you miss, Miki?"

"You said, 'Mrs. Kittrell.' How did you know her last name?"

"Well, she is Hunter's grandmother." His voice was smooth.

"So? Hunter has two grandmothers. And people remarry."

"It was an assumption."

"And why do you hang out with Grayson Tucker? Isn't he the police chief or something?"

"You're sharp, and you ask questions. I'm not sure that is an asset for a secretary. I may have to promote you to executive assistant."

Again, Miki noticed passersby staring. "Bull. So what could you possibly need a secretary for?"

"The usual. Correspondence. Messages. Appointments."

"Appointments?" she sputtered.

"Yes. You'll see."

"What kind of business are you in?"

"Oh, it's all very confidential. But legitimate," he added in response to her raised eyebrows. "I'll explain it bit by bit as we go along. You accept, I hope?"

"I guess. People are going to talk, though. They're about to break their necks staring at us now."

"You love it. Admit it, Miki Stone. You thrive on being the center of attention, and you get double the attention when you're with me. Admit it."

She turned her head and ignored him. But he was right. He looked like he ought to be somebody—somebody with absolute power—and she could make heads turn herself when she wanted to. Let the whole town talk. Here was her first new kick in weeks.

"You'll begin tomorrow morning. Eight a.m. sharp."

"Are you crazy?"

"This is the real world, Miki. My office hours are in the morning. Of course, I'll take responsibility for getting you up on time if you happen to be under my roof."

He was not looking at her as he said this, and her eyes took in the cut of his face, the way his masculine hand gripped his thigh. "Sleeping with you will not be part of my job," she said flatly.

"Your mind is playing games with you," he responded. "There will be one more requirement, though."

"What?"

"You will eat a decent meal daily while you're in my employ."
He indicated her rejected lunch.

"Somewhere you have Southern genes, Jack."

His laughter carried across the water.

Hunter met Miki's revelation of who her new employer was
with stony indifference. All he asked was, "So what do you actually do in this phantom secretary job?"

She laughed easily. "Believe it or not, he does need a secretary
for a few minutes a day. If he wants to pay me to sit in the sun and
shoot the breeze the rest of the time, why not? And don't even ask
what he does because I can't tell you."

"I wasn't going to."

Her third morning on the job, Miki left quite late without
even a good-bye. Hunter happened to step out of his apartment
in time to see her walking down the street. He called after her,
"Miki! Don't forget our date this afternoon."

She stopped and looked up at him on the landing. "Oh, I can't,
Hunter," she called back. "Jack needs me to work this afternoon."

"But this is important. I told you I can't deal with going to
Grandma Baker's by myself."

She looked away from him toward town. Then she gave a
small wave, giving in, and started off again in a hurry, calling over
her shoulder, "I'll ask Jack if I can get off. I can't promise. 'Bye."

He watched her go, tucking in his t-shirt. Today was his

Grandma Baker's birthday, and Granny Jen always insisted that he visit her at least this one day. He had never gone alone; Amy had gone with him every single year. This year, he had really counted on having Miki along.

Walking to work by himself, Hunter tried not to brood over his impending visit to his maternal grandparents. This morning would be hectic. He had traded his afternoon cruise for a morning harbor tour which would include lunch for the passengers on deserted Shackleford Banks. The *Pirate's Lady* was booked to capacity today, July first, carrying fourteen passengers and a crew of three.

The ship's skipper was a friend of the family's, a stern old salt named John who had retired from commercial fishing to haul tourists around in the summer. He steered the ship with the wheel from the menhaden fishing boat his daddy had sailed in the 1920s, watched the sails and the tides, and kept his mouth shut. Hunter and the other mate shoved off, got the ship underway, manned the lines, talked with the passengers, wrestled with the little kids to keep them in life jackets, and occasionally chased a kid down before he pitched off the rolling deck into the water. At least once a week, one mate would have to keep a supply of paper bags going to a seasick passenger. They took turns with this chore.

Although the skipper knew every single tale that had ever been told about the town or the water, he never repeated a single one to his passengers, leaving it up to his crew to entertain the tourists with whatever stories they chose, true or invented. The only question Hunter had ever heard him answer was the often asked, "Do you know where Blackbeard's treasure is buried?" No matter where on the water they happened to be, the old man always answered, "Yep. Right off to starboard there," pointing toward a spot on the water which some open-mouthed guy would inevitably try to mark with his eyes.

This morning, after only an hour on the water, Hunter was ready for a break. After anchoring off Shackleford Banks, he and the other mate, Bill, had dinghied two loads of tourists over to the island. While Bill stayed on shore with the passengers, Hunter went back to the ship for the coolers of food and stopped a minute to rest. He sat on the polished wood of the deck, one foot propped on the gunwale, and popped the tab on a soda. It was hot now that the ship was not moving, the breeze no match for the sun.

"How old are you now, Hunter?" asked John from his seat at the wheel.

Hunter glanced at the skipper as he swallowed his drink, suspicious of the sudden interest. "Uh, twenty-one next month."

The old man nodded. "Yep. That would be about right." He didn't volunteer another word.

Hunter almost let it go. After a few gulps of soda, he finally asked, "About right for what?"

"Your dad's age the last time I saw him. He could have been a year or two older. You reminded me of him sitting there just now."

Hunter turned and sat up straighter, not looking at the man. He reached inside the cooler for an ice cube and rubbed it on the back of his neck.

"I guess you get tired of hearing that as much as I get tired of people asking about Blackbeard," said John.

Hunter stood up. "Actually, no one ever mentions him to me," he said, finishing the soda and crushing the can in his hand.

"We passed a man on the water a while ago who made me think of Rob. That's what put it in my mind to bring him up, I reckon," John said and looked out at the water, ending the conversation.

Hunter looked across the wide expanse of the sound, squinting, halfway expecting his father to materialize right beside Blackbeard's treasure. He blinked and reached for the cooler. That was a joke. He figured he had about as much chance of seeing his father again as he did of finding that treasure.

"I'd better get this over to the passengers," he said. "They ought to be pretty well baked and ready to eat by now."

John grunted. If he noticed the joke, he didn't laugh.

After work that afternoon, Hunter deliberately took his time walking down the boardwalk. He was in no hurry to get on the road to his grandma's and in even less of a hurry to approach Jack Franklin's yacht. At the boat owners' ramp, he stopped. Yes, there was Miki on Jack's deck, a notebook in her lap. She was wearing a white hat and a bright blue sun dress, impossible not to notice. What had she been wearing when she left home?

Easing down the ramp, he saw Jack in the flybridge, talking on a cellular phone. Hunter put both hands on the dock rail and leaned forward. "Hello, gorgeous," he said.

"Oh, Hunter, you startled me. What are you—shoot; I forgot to ask off."

"Kittrell," came in Jack's loud voice as he appeared on deck, putting the phone in his pocket. "Has no one taught you water etiquette? Don't touch my boat."

Hunter, who hadn't touched the man's boat and who did not intend to, didn't flinch. He didn't even glance at Jack. Keeping his eyes on Miki, his voice low, he said, "It's time to go, Babe."

"Hunter, I promise, it slipped my mind. Jack, can I take off?"

"Take off? Your third day on the job?"

"It's something important Hunter has to—"

"I need you to finish this."

"What are you doing?" Hunter asked.

"Keeping a tally of arrivals and departures, each boat's registration numbers, make and model, city of origin. It's really interesting."

"I'm sure it is. Most of it you can get from the dockmaster, though."

Miki looked into his eyes, confused.

"I know what I'm doing, Kittrell, and you are trespassing."

Hunter did not move, his expression indifferent, his eyes on Miki.

"Jack, chill," said Miki. "It's my fault for not ask—"

"Nothing is your fault. The boy has to take responsibility for his own trespassing. Isn't that right, Kittrell?"

Hunter looked at Jack for the first time, and it was a long, hard stare. It was met by an arrogant, equally hard stare. Then Hunter looked back at Miki.

"Come on, Babe. You don't need this. Quit, and let's get out of here." His voice was still quiet, but his eyes searched hers for an answer. She looked away, but Hunter could read her, and it was plain what she wanted: for him to leave.

Without a word or gesture, he walked away a few steps, then turned and walked backward up the ramp, his eyes locked on Jack Franklin's. It was Jack whose eyes narrowed first, and Hunter turned again and walked away for good.

* * *

"Cocky little devil," Jack said harshly.

"Shut up, Jack." Miki leaned her chin in her hands, eyes shut. That damned unsettled feeling came back. She did not need this; Hunter was right about that. She breathed deeply and tried to force the feeling away.

"So what was so important that Hunter had to have you with him?"

"Nothing. Just something he doesn't like to do alone."

"So will he do it alone?"

"He'll probably take Amy."

"Amy? And she's his sister? Cousin?"

"Just an old friend."

"Sweetheart?"

"I don't know. Maybe one time."

"Interesting."

"Leave it alone, Jack. It's not interesting."

"One-time sweethearts are always interesting."

"Look, just leave it. Let's get back to work."

Miki hated this. Despised it. She didn't want to hurt Hunter, didn't want to care if he was hurt. That unsettled mood jammed its way back in. She couldn't stop her mind from going over the incident, over a summer of incidents. Why couldn't things just be cool with Hunter again? Easy and uncomplicated. He seemed to want too much from her lately, to care too much.

Granny Jen had said something about an emptiness inside

Miki that demanded to be satisfied. And Miki had thought at the time, *That would be nice. Just to be empty.* Not perpetually bored. Not filled with these incessant cravings. Just empty. Drugs, kicks, Hunter—nothing had satisfied the great need inside her. She had never known what she needed. Now she knew. She wanted emptiness. Sedation. A cessation of her longings. Wouldn't that be peace?

Something inside her began to shut down at this revelation. She had never pretended that the raw craving within was for love. Maybe as a child she had craved love, but she had been disappointed so many times that her heart no longer bothered. She didn't know what she craved now, but she knew her desires would swallow her whole if they were not satisfied. Or if not satisfied, sedated.

It was late afternoon when Jack returned from an errand. As he looked over Miki's notes, his hand—demanding attention— touched her back. Fearlessly, she looked into his eyes, her tormented soul wide open to him.

When he kissed her, it was deep and possessive, and she felt doors in her heart slamming shut, closing avenues to love, purpose, fulfillment. These were not things she desired anyway.

Sedation. That was all she wanted. Desperately, she yielded to the heat of his hands, the insistence of his seeking tongue, the driving demands of his experienced body. "Jack," her lips whispered, but her soul was crying, "Burn me, empty me, satisfy me, sedate me." Sedation. An end to all cravings.

✹ ✹ ✹

"Now this is novel." Amy was speaking into the wind as Hunter sped down the narrow road, top down. "You usually whine all the way down here. Today you're just not speaking."

He nodded to show that he had heard her.

"Did you do your shopping?"

"Oh, crap." He slammed on the brakes and checked his mirrors, preparing to make a U-turn.

"Just harassing you. I took care of it for you."

"Amy." Just speaking her name was a laugh, a grin.

"You owe me big time now, boy," she said.

"I do, I do."

"I always like to go Down East, myself."

"Me too, I guess," Hunter admitted. "Tell me—I forget every year—how old is my Grandma Baker today?"

"She was sixty-seven last year. You do the math."

"All I can ever remember is she's old and not old-old like Granny Jen."

They drove on in silence, bumping along the road that hadn't seen a paving crew in too long, until they reached the fishing town where his mother had grown up.

Down East, the world feels bigger, timeless, with the broad expanse of the Pamlico Sound stretching flat and brilliant in the sun. Life slows down; the noises of the world subside, and the water speaks with its own voice. It takes a certain heart to hear just what the water has to say. Hunter's Grandpa and Grandma Baker had such hearts. The water had taught them an uncommon kindness, an unhurried acceptance of life's storms. Still, they had not taken too kindly to their daughter's sudden and necessary marriage to Hunter's father and had taken even less kindly to his abrupt abandonment of their daughter and grandson. Unbidden, this particular storm of life was called to memory whenever Hunter was around.

Not that they in any way showed any disapproval of Hunter; it was just the opposite. They bent over backwards to be good to him, and that was the problem.

The Bakers were a prolific bunch, and there were cousins and more cousins in and out of Grandma's house, on and off of Grandpa's boat, up and down the road on bikes. As a kid, all Hunter desired was to troop along with the rest of them. What he got instead was special attention, extra hugs, the biggest cookie, an unwanted spotlight. And worse, there was a general expectation of excellence. Horrors! The last thing Hunter wanted was to catch the biggest fish or ride the fastest bike or even have the most mosquito bites. He did not in any way want the responsibility of making up for whatever it was his father had done.

Still, the visit never killed him, and they were his grandparents. Good people. And so it was that Hunter reluctantly visited on the required birthday, with Amy along to share the spotlight, and a nice present that was as much a surprise to him as to Grandma Baker.

After this visit, just like always, when it was time to leave, he walked toward his Jeep, feeling vaguely guilty for not coming more often.

Grandma Baker followed him out, one arm around Amy. "I declare, you sweet little thing, you get prettier every year. You come on back—don't wait for Hunter—you're just like family. You know, I had an aunt with red hair. Hunter, give me a kiss. Look how tall you've gotten. My gracious, do you knock all the girls dead at that college or are you waiting for Amy? Look at that blush, girl . . ."

When Hunter saw his grandpa motion for him to step aside, he left his grandma still chattering and joined him beside a stack of crab traps. Grandpa Baker was stocky; years of working the water had hardened his body and given him thick, calloused hands. Now, as dusk settled the day down to a whisper, the gentle eyes in the weathered face were dark with concern.

"Hunter, I have something to ask, and it is mighty hard to say, so I'll just come out with it. Have you seen your father?"

Hunter felt a chunk of ice land in his chest with his next breath. He looked away, struggling to keep his face composed.

"Son, I am so sorry to bring this up; you know I wouldn't hurt you for the world. There was some investigator fellow around here yesterday. He seemed to think Rob Kittrell might be in this area. I figured if he had come here for anything, it would be to see you."

"His ass is dead if he comes near me."

Grandpa Baker sized Hunter up, seeing him in a new light. "Do you think you would recognize him?"

"Yeah. Just look for the big sign on his back that says 'gone to hell with no forwarding address.'" Hunter heard his own voice shake with the rage he usually hid. There was a silence. Far off to sea, heat lightning bounced from cloud to cloud. Hunter drew a breath, and in a voice that was now almost too calm, he asked, "Grandpa Baker, what exactly did my father do?"

After a hesitation, his grandpa asked, "Do you mean when he left?"

"Whatever."

"Drugs, so I was told." Grandpa's voice was thick with Down

East accent, and when he lowered his voice, Hunter had a hard time catching all the words. He heard, ". . . Rob Kittrell never came around me, anyway," and ". . . Jen did the right thing," and a couple more sentences he could not catch. Hunter felt more confused than enlightened.

"You said an investigator wanted him," Hunter persisted. "Does that mean they're still after him for selling?"

"Could be."

"Good. Maybe he'll get his throat slit in the harbor." Hunter's voice was flat and smooth, all emotion controlled.

"Hunter! What's gotten into you?"

"I'd just like to see him get what he deserves."

"I'm really sorry I told you about this." Grandpa Baker put a hard, worn hand on his grandson's shoulder. "Don't you do anything rash, son. Don't do anything at all. He's not worth going to prison for."

Hunter felt some of the tension leave his body.

"And he could be dangerous by now. You don't know. Do you hear me? You just lay low."

"Sure." Hunter smiled an easy smile. He could do that; he could lay low. He had done it all his life.

"Just watch out for Jen. I already told that investigator fellow to stay away from her. This would upset her with her bad heart and all."

It would kill her, Hunter thought.

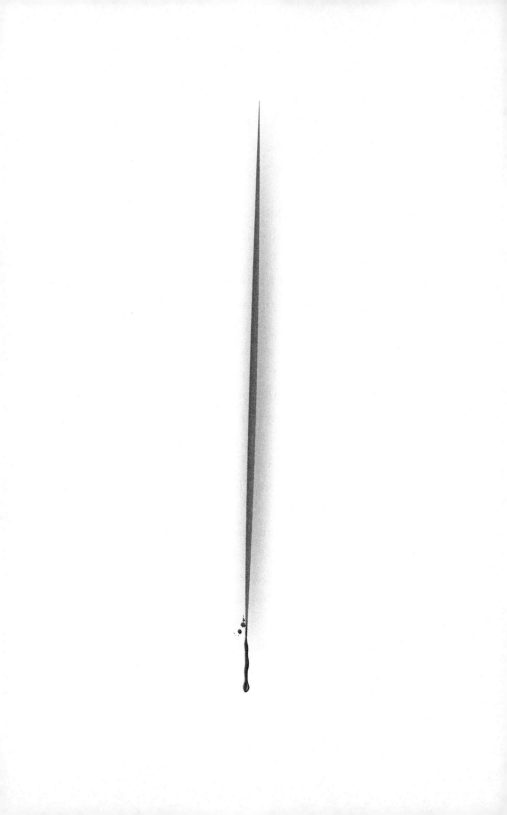

TEN

Hunter tiptoed around his apartment, much the same way he had done during the days after his uncle died. His mood was not restless, not peaceful; it was resigned. Rock and roll had not invented enough noise to hold back his thoughts on this night. Giving up on the usual cross-breeze off the water, he finally switched on the air conditioner and lay sprawled before its unnatural hum, sucking a Popsicle.

Moonlight glowed blue through his stained-glass window. He stared at the old-fashioned design—an ivy-entwined door which framed a scene of blue mountains and a peaceful sea in the distance. Perhaps the window had once been in a church; in fancy script at the bottom were the words, "*The Lord shall preserve thy going out and thy coming in from this time forth.*" He used to believe that. When he was a little kid, he would come up here and stare at the words and think they meant that somebody who went out would come back. God would put things right again. Well, that was bull. If his father really had returned, it was too damn late and things sure weren't going to be right. Maybe his uncle hadn't been man enough to kill Rob Kittrell, but Hunter was.

His uncle had come home to die the summer after Hunter graduated from high school. No children. Married once but never remarried. Powerful in Atlanta's business community. Everyone said he was rich. Donald Kittrell had been handsome, robust, charismatic, the man all eyes followed in a crowded room, the person whose conversation everyone sought at a dinner party. Hunter had grown up in awe of him.

That last summer, as they spent quiet early mornings on the water, doing nothing of more importance than setting a few crab traps, fishing for a few panfish, Hunter found, beneath the facade, just a man. This man puzzled him, sometimes frightened him, even disgusted him, and finally, almost tore his heart open.

"Hunter," Donald had asked once without preliminary, as the dawn reflected still and mellow on the water, "what will you do with your life?"

"Don't know."

"What do you want to do?"

Careless shrug.

"You do. You have a dream, Hunter. God puts a dream in every heart. You have to have the will to pursue it."

No response, and the subject was dropped.

It was not on the water but in this apartment, however, rain pattering outside and running in droplets down the blue window, that Hunter learned more than he wanted to about himself and his Uncle Donald.

"Hunter," Donald said, prowling around the collected antiques that were just beginning their departure from the apartment, "I ought to leave everything I own to you."

"Huh?"

"Would you accept?"

"Daggone right!"

"What do you think I'm worth?"

"Enough."

"What do you think is most valuable to me?"

This was met with a shrug.

"If you've been listening to me this summer, then you should know. And someday, when your heart embraces the answer, you may just find that I've left you with all you need to get through life."

Donald was opening and closing drawers, poking around. Finally, Hunter asked, "What are you looking for?"

"I thought you'd never ask." He closed a drawer and stood before Hunter an uncomfortable while. "This is what I want you to ask yourself: What am I looking for?"

Hunter had not been able to keep the impatience out of his voice. "Go ahead and get it over with. Tell me what the hell I'm supposed to be looking for."

"Truth."

"In a drawer?"

Donald smiled and looked toward the blue window. "Maybe. It's usually closer than you think." There was a brief silence. "You haven't even asked why I would consider leaving you everything— or anything, for that matter."

"So I'm not inquisitive. Shoot me."

"Do you think you deserve it?"

This question was met with a cocky lift of Hunter's head.

Donald sighed. "We rarely deserve the good gifts we get. But in your case, in a way, you do."

Hunter had not been able to disguise a flicker of surprise.

"You should have been my son." The blunt statement hung in the air. Had Hunter been inclined to speak, he could not have for the rush of questions that tangled his tongue.

"I loved your mother. I planned to marry her. I will never know why your father went after her when he knew how I felt. Maybe just to prove he could get her. Whatever Rob wanted, Rob usually got."

A scream began to form inside Hunter's head: *Shut up. Shut the hell up!*

"When I found out . . ." Donald began. There was another long pause, and Hunter started to feel sick. "When I found out he had fathered you, I went berserk. After I bloodied his nose, I beat him all the way up those steps into this very room." Hunter glanced around the room and stared hard at his uncle. "I told him I would kill him if he didn't marry her, give you a name, allow her the respect she deserved. I refused to see past my own anger and humiliation to the inevitable disaster Rob would bring upon you both."

Donald began prowling again, avoiding Hunter's eyes. "What a fool I was. People look at me and they see success and money. No one, not even my wife, ever knew that I would trade it all in a minute to have the chance to do it right. It is a bitter regret that has nearly destroyed me. I'm the one who hurt your mother, hurt you. Not Rob, not really." He came and stood before Hunter, who sat at the table, circling the rim of a glass round and round with his finger. Hunter met his eyes.

"I should have married her. You should have been my son. Never would I have told you that I wasn't your father."

And as Hunter stared into his uncle's eyes, in that moment, he both loved and hated him with a matchless intensity that ripped his heart. He turned his back on his uncle and quenched the flare of emotion with one careless, obscene gesture. Then Hunter walked out.

Remembering this now, on a hot and still night three years later, Hunter again left the apartment. He wished Donald had killed his father. It would save him the trouble of doing it himself.

Quietly, Hunter let himself in Granny Jen's back door. By memory, he eased through the dark rooms, avoiding furniture, and opened Miki's door. She was not there. The old house was still, as if waiting for his next move. Walking with a quiet assurance, he went to his grandfather's old desk, located the key Granny Jen thought was well-hidden, and opened a certain drawer. Inside was an old .32 Owlhead pistol. It was loaded. Taking it out, he slipped it beneath his belt.

Then, still moving quietly but quickly, he opened his grandmother's door. The air was warm, stuffy. He crossed the room and closed the windows.

"Hunter? What are you doing?" Her voice was calm, not startled.

"Turning on the air conditioner. You'll smother in here."

"Thanks. Good night."

Hunter did not climb the steps to his apartment. Reaching up, he placed the gun on the landing and took off at a steady pace toward town. The muggy air was unsettling, electric. When his steps reached the spot on the dock nearest Jack Franklin's yacht, he stopped and stared at it, hands in his pockets. There appeared to be only one light on; soon it was extinguished. He thought he heard Miki laugh. How long he might have stood silent and unmoving, staring at the boat, he would never know; Grayson Tucker joined him. Grayson did not touch him, but his voice was kind.

"Go home, Hunter. You don't need to be down here at this hour."

Hunter's steps were less purposeful as he walked the silent streets. It was nearly dawn when he returned to his apartment and placed the gun inside the drawer of his dining chest without a glance at the drawer's other contents.

The sharp outline of Miki's face was somewhat softened by the shadows of the magnolia tree in Granny Jen's yard. "Well, come in, Miki. What are you doing standing out there knocking?" Granny Jen asked.

The girl stepped inside. Her pretty face seemed honed by tension today; she appeared older, maybe more sophisticated. "Is Hunter here?" she asked, still standing near the door.

"You know, I haven't seen Hunter today," Granny Jen said.

"Oh." Miki hesitated, seemed about to ask a question, then gestured loosely toward her room and stepped past Jen.

"I haven't seen your hair up like that," Jen commented. "It's very classy."

"Thanks. I needed a new look for my job." Miki's laugh was brief. She disappeared down the hall for a few short minutes and returned carrying a small bag.

"Stay and talk a bit," urged Granny Jen.

"Uh, no. I need to get back to work."

"Do you like it?"

"I guess." There was a brief pause. "Okay. Well. It's been good to see you."

Granny Jen frowned slightly. Was it just yesterday morning that Miki had bounced out of here a college kid, a guest? Who was this formal young woman?

"Oh, and tell Hunter I stopped by."

Jen's frown grew deeper, and she glanced at the bag. "No, Miki, I don't think I'll do that. This is between you and Hunter."

Miki met her eyes briefly, then turned and walked away.

The doctor's voice on the telephone was careful, patient. "This has been coming on for some time, Hunter. I'm surprised she hasn't told you."

"She's got me freaked me out with all her talk about dying and moving and stuff. If you knew about it, why haven't you fixed her?"

The doctor's laugh was comfortable. "Sometimes, it's not that easy."

"What's wrong with her?"

"Your grandmother's heart is failing, Hunter. It's just wearing out."

"Okay. Get her a new one."

"At her age, that's not an option."

Hunter was silent a moment. "And that's why she gets tired so fast?"

"Yes. Just everyday efforts put a great deal of strain on her heart."

"Can't you do anything?"

"Bring her in and let me see for myself how she's doing. It could be that adjusting her medicine could make her feel better. For a while."

Hunter drew in a breath but did not speak.

"Your grandmother is spunky, Hunter. She'll do as much as she can for as long as she can. That much I can promise. And one more thing. Try not to upset her."

That's what I was afraid of, thought Hunter as he hung up. With a killer loose and his father possibly lurking about, that was not going to be easy.

ELEVEN

The Cat had a lot on his mind. There was still scum on his list in need of execution. But not today. Someone else would die today. A pest, not on his list, but in need of extermination anyway. Extermination had not been part of his original plan; but why not? It all boiled down to pest control in the end.

A kitty need not be involved this time, but a Kittrell would be.

* * *

July Fourth was hot, and the tourists were out in droves. Together, the heat and the full passenger load made a demanding day for Hunter. Still, when he got off work and a couple of the guys asked, "Hey, are you coming to the beach?" he answered, "Sure, why not?"

"Are you bringing that babe you had with you last time?"

"Don't know."

"Come easy, go easy, huh, Hunter?"

"Yeah, well. Look, I'll catch up with you later."

Hunter walked the dock alone. On a dining porch, a lone guitarist sang mellow James Taylor tunes. Moonlight cast a radiant path on the black water. As a child, Hunter had thought if he could just set his feet on that path, he could walk straight to the horizon. Somehow, the path always seemed to dissolve beneath his feet, and he would end up with his knees in water. Remembering that now, Hunter wished the path had been real.

Without hesitancy, he walked down the ramp and straight to Jack Franklin's yacht. "Miki," he called. "Miki!"

She appeared on deck wearing an elegant sweater and long silk skirt. "Whatcha want, Hunter?" She looked a little puzzled, maybe a little pleased, to see him. Then, Jack Franklin stepped on deck, and something distant, formal, came over her features.

Hunter held his eyes on hers, would not let her look at Jack. "Hey, Babe, you look great. There's a party down at the beach. Wanna come?"

"Well, I . . ." Her voice trailed off.

"You're not working. Come with me. Might be some fireworks later on."

"Get lost, Kittrell." Jack's voice was patronizing. "Can't you see she doesn't want to go with you?"

Miki didn't look at him, and neither did Hunter. "It's not that I don't want to go, Hunter. But Jack and I have a party to go to; you know, sort of an obligation thing, so . . ."

"So get out of here, Kittrell." This time, Jack's voice was

threatening, and he took a step.

"Jack, stop." Miki put a hand on his arm. Hunter narrowed his eyes slightly; otherwise, he kept his face impassive as he looked up at her.

Miki looked from Jack to Hunter. One man was virile, handsome, all raw, boiling motion. The other stood his ground, hands in his pockets, an unnatural calm beneath his boyish good looks.

"You said this yacht party thing wouldn't get underway until after midnight. I'm going with Hunter for a little while, then I'll be back. Good-bye, Jack." And with that, she left the boat and joined Hunter. His arm was firmer around her waist than usual as they walked away.

"Wait, why are we going this way?" she asked, trying to pull back.

"My Jeep's still parked at home because of the tourists, remember?"

"Oh, yeah." There was something tense about her, and then he felt her body draw up more.

"What's wrong?" he asked.

"Nothing."

"Miki."

"Nothing. It's just this guy. I think I saw him on the dining porch there. He seems to be watching me or following me or something." She leaned into him as she looked toward the porch. "He's tried to talk to me before."

"The one sitting by himself?"

"Maybe. I don't know. It's dark."

"Stay here, and I'll go see what he wants," Hunter said.

"No, Hunter. Are you crazy?" She pulled at his arm.

"It's no big deal. I'll just ask him what his problem is."

"No, don't leave me," she said.

He did not miss the way she glanced back at the yacht. "You're afraid of Franklin, aren't you?"

"No, of course not."

"What's he done to you?" demanded Hunter.

"Nothing. Honest. I just don't want him to see you abandon me out here. He doesn't like for me to be on the dock alone."

"Because of this guy?"

"Him, the killer, I don't know. Let's get out of here." She pulled on his arm until he gave in and continued walking.

They walked a block in silence. "Vanessa Singer," Hunter said.

"What?"

"That guy may just think you're Vanessa Singer and want an autograph. She was reported seen in Beaufort a few weeks ago, you know."

Miki smiled at the recollection and seemed to relax.

"And you look even more like her the way you've worn your hair this week," he added with a glance at the elegant twist.

"Could be. Thanks, Hunter."

"No problem. Now let me go talk to him."

"No, let's just go have fun. I'll ask Jack to speak with the guy later."

The party was louder, more boisterous than before. Maybe the tourists were getting under everybody's skin. Shorts and sneakers seemed to be the preferred dress, and Miki brought more than a few appraising stares. Hunter caught a couple of sly thumbs-up from his buddies and a friendly wave from Amy who seemed to be presiding over the shrimp boil. Miki didn't appear inclined to join any conversation, so they passed through the crowd and eventually drifted away from the noise to the seclusion of a sand dune.

She seemed hesitant to sit down. "Oh, here." Hunter peeled off his T-shirt and spread it on the sand.

"Won't you get cold?" Her sweater had long sleeves.

"It's hot, Miki."

For some reason, she brushed off her skirt before sitting down. Hunter sprawled beside her, leaning back on his elbows, staring out at the water. The music and voices of the party seemed distant, part of another scene, another story. After a bit, he became aware she was staring at his chest; when he looked up, she looked away.

He sat up. "What's going on, Miki?"

She shrugged. From somewhere—an inside pocket of the sweater?—she produced a joint and lit it.

"Jack supplying you?"

"No, he's not, as a matter of fact." Her voice was weary, and she took a deep drag.

"Then what is it with him?"

"I don't know."

"Miki," he spoke softly against her neck. When she didn't move away, he slipped his hand beneath the soft folds of her sweater and touched her skin, warm and smooth. "Miki," he whispered again.

He touched her face and kissed her, and it was just as he remembered. With a sigh, she laid the joint on the sand and drew him down to her. He let his weight settle over her carefully, lifting her head away from the sand, feeling her hands move with deliberate pressure down the sweaty muscles of his back.

It was a long, jubilant kiss. For Hunter, as his hands found familiar warmth, all his promises to his grandmother momentarily retreated in a youthful rush of passion and glory.

And then, he felt her hot tears against his cheek.

"Oh, God, Miki. What is it? What has he done to you?" he whispered.

She sat up with a long, shuddering gasp. Sitting beside her, he tried to hold her, but she pushed him away and reached for the joint. After deep, practiced drags, she wiped the tears with the back of one hand and was again composed, formal, distant.

"I've gotta go," she said, standing abruptly.

"Don't. Wait. At least let me drive you."

"No. Just loan me your Jeep." She was several feet away already. "You left the keys under the floor mat, didn't you?"

"Miki."

"Don't follow me, Hunter. And stay away. It's better for both of us. I mean it." She stared at him in the moonlight. Regret passed briefly over her features, and she turned to go.

"Miki." She stopped, but did not turn. "Don't drive with that." She tossed the joint to the dune behind him and was gone.

Hunter had not moved when Amy joined him. "I've been sent to see how bad you're bleeding," she announced.

He looked up at her.

"Pretty bad, I'd say," she said and plopped down unceremoniously on his shirt. "Stabbed in the heart again?"

Falling back flat against the sand, he cradled his head on one arm. "Actually, I think I've been gut-shot."

"Hmm."

Several moments passed. When she looked over at him, he had the joint in his free hand, contemplating it.

"Good Lord, Hunter." She took it from him and dug a hole with her heel, burying it.

There was another long silence. "Can you still name all the constellations?" he asked.

"Maybe." She lay back beside him. The night was too bright for star-gazing, but she studied the sky and pointed. "There. Hercules."

"You always pick the easy ones," he fussed. He pointed. "Leo."

"No, it's not. You still get Leo and Gemini confused." She took his arm in her strong grip and moved it.

"Leo used to be over there," he insisted, pushing his arm against her hand. She laughed a low, familiar chuckle, and for a moment, he felt her hand more warm than strong against his arm, and then she moved it. "You're the only person in the world who would know that was supposed to be funny," he said.

Abruptly, she sat up and put a hand to his forehead. "In my professional opinion, you're gonna make it," she declared.

"I don't know. It hurts pretty bad."

She rested her arms on her knees and looked him over. "Seems like you wind up stabbed or shot every summer. What's the problem?"

"Beats the hell out of me." He was not looking at her when he said softly, "I bled almost this much the time you stabbed me. You tell me what the problem is."

"You, Hunter. The problem is you. I told you last summer you would have to make some major, big-time changes before we could ever make it."

"Me? Why not you?"

"Because I'm perfect." She stood up and grinned at him. "I'm going back to the party. Are you coming?"

"Yeah. Help me up. I can barely move what with these wounds and all." He held out a hand for her to pull him up. Amazingly, she did, putting all of her stout, little body into the effort. She brushed the sand off his back briskly, her hands not lingering over the contours of his muscles.

"Tell me something, Amy," he said, shaking out his shirt. "Has any other guy gotten lost in those dimples of yours?"

"Not lately." She started off toward the party.

"Wait. Let me put this on. Gotta hide my wounds, you know." She looked away while he pulled the shirt on and started walking again.

"Amy, wait. I've got to say something. I don't think it's me this time."

"I think it is." She looked at him levelly.

"What? What do you think I did?"

"You chose a girl and a lifestyle that you wanted to be right for you, but they're not. You didn't have to do anything. Disaster was inevitable."

"You sound like Granny Jen."

"Thanks. I'll take that as a compliment."

"I think I meant that you and Granny Jen just don't understand about Miki."

"For sure, I don't. I feel sorry for her because I think she's very unhappy, and I believe she's heading down a road she may never know how to get off." She pushed on his chest with her finger. "You are not the cause of her problems. But you brought this mess on yourself the minute you became involved with her. You've got to be honest with yourself about who you really are and who is going to be right for you."

"And do you have anyone in particular in mind?" he asked with mock sarcasm.

She ran a hand through her curls. "Yeah. Let me go warn her to sharpen her knife."

He chased her into the crowd, both of them laughing.

Grayson Tucker stood a distance down the beach. Music and laughter had been drifting on the wind toward him for about ten minutes. Now there were moments of silence broken by exaggerated *oohs* and *aahs* as the fireworks began. The kids knew he was there. A few had waved at him.

The days of impromptu beach parties were over. These kids had parents who clamored in his ear from the time he got up in the morning until he closed his eyes very late at night. The entire town was looking to Grayson to do something about the killer in its harbor. Never mind that state and federal investigators were turning the town upside down looking for the guy. It was Grayson's town; it was his fault no arrest had been made.

Grayson had begun an eleven o'clock curfew last week. The residents seemed pleased and locked themselves and their children in with time to spare. The tourists pushed it to the limit, sometimes lingering around the waterfront as if expecting to see the killer rush aboard a yacht, knife in hand, poised for a snapshot. The retailers and restaurant owners along the waterfront complained to the press but complied. It was the residents of the harbor who ignored the curfew, and they were in the most danger. There was little Grayson could do about it. If he told them not to party, they would just motor away from the harbor toward open water, and Grayson preferred they stay where he could watch them. Actually, he preferred they all pack up and move to somebody else's harbor, but so far, his harbor remained full.

As for the kids, Grayson had given them permission to party until after the fireworks tonight. They knew he was there to break up the party. What they didn't yet know was that home was the only place they would be going. He had officers posted at the highway ready to direct them across the drawbridge toward Beaufort, and he planned to raise the bridge until he had seen as many home as he could. Some of them would elude him, he knew, and drive forty miles out of their way to get back to Morehead just to prove they could. And some would get in a boat and spend the night on the water. But most would be locked in safe for the night. That was all he could do.

TWELVE

It was time to exterminate the pest. The Cat took the old pistol out and oiled it. No doubt, it had been years since the gun was shot. The only bullets he had were the ones in the cylinder. One bullet, well-placed, was all it would take.

The Cat had studied the man closely. Doug Sanders. Forty-two years old. Lived with his mama in Raleigh. Laid off from his job as a dishwasher. Taking a vacation in Beaufort and didn't seem inclined to leave.

Evidently, Doug fancied himself a detective. The Cat had seen Doug snooping around the waterfront waiting for a Kodak moment. Doug took pictures, read the newspaper, and mumbled to himself. He appeared to be looking for clues to The Case of the Harbor Killer.

Doug was not as harmless as he appeared. He was getting too close; he was a pest; he needed exterminating. So far, the national news media had only sent scouts to Beaufort. One more execution, The Cat predicted, and every network news outlet would set up camp on the waterfront. Doug Sanders could be dangerous then, mumbling in the reporters' ears, pointing his finger around the harbor. The Cat was going to cut Doug off before he pointed in the right direction by accident.

The Cat knew just the bait to use on this pest. He could read Doug Sanders' mind. He knew every one of Doug's fantasies.

Just this morning, The Cat had extended an invitation for Doug to join him on board a real yacht. He had approached Doug as a concerned philanthropist whose pleasure it would be to take dear Doug under his wing. He could see that Doug had class; he had potential. All Doug needed were a few introductions. He could be somebody.

The Cat walked the two blocks from the waterfront to Doug's boarding house purposefully. He had already prepared himself for this execution. As he strode past the practical old seaport homes, their historic markers proudly displayed, he concentrated on the task before him. It was past the town's curfew, and he walked briskly as if he were a resident in a hurry to get home. A patrol car cruised by but did not stop him.

Doug greeted The Cat on the front porch of the boarding house, anxiety in his eyes. The Cat was gracious. Doug was eager to please. He showed The Cat a shortcut through backyards and down an alley. They kept in the shadows.

Oh, by the way, whispered The Cat, *the party has been moved off-shore due to the curfew. Such a nuisance. I have access to a boat at one of the private docks on Taylor's Creek. Stick with me. I'll get you there.*

They eased away from the dock, the boat's motor purring, the midnight air still and sultry. The houses along Taylor's Creek were darkened with their residents smugly locked in for the night. Marsh frogs hollered in chorus just as they did every night. All was well. No boogey-men out tonight.

Once they passed the flashing channel marker, they picked up speed, open water before them. The boat bumped and shimmied as it met the waves.

"Will this take long?" asked Doug, both hands gripping the side of the boat.

"No, not long at all," said The Cat, his hand on the gun in his pocket. "I promise I'll be quick."

"Hunter, you're not pulling your weight," complained Amy, leaning over the bow of the skiff, both hands on the shrimp net.

"I can't," he said in a pitiful voice. "I've lost too much blood."

"Get over it." Her voice carried exaggerated testiness. "Here, swap places with me. You've got longer arms." She shrieked as he caught her off guard and nearly tumbled her into the water. "Keep trying, Hunter. Just remember, I always take you with me when I go under."

"Not this time, kid. It's gonna be Amy and the shrimp swimming in the sea." As they maneuvered around each other in the tiny boat, swapping ends of the net, she nearly managed to flip him into the water. His yell sent a heron flapping toward the sky. "Shoot, we lost most of the shrimp. It's your fault for trying to dunk me."

"My fault? You're the one who let go of the net."

The day had begun with Amy and Hunter on the water, talking about nothing in particular. They had been together most of the night, in fact, just talking, no more lectures. And now, in the golden light of early morning, they were attempting to haul in the shrimp nets they had set at dawn.

"Take me around this point," Hunter said to Amy, who was now in the stern, steering.

"Like clockwork," said Amy.

"Huh?"

"You've been peeing on the same clump of sea oats at the same time for the past ten summers."

"And you have a problem with that? Would you rather I just cut loose off the bow here? I can do it."

"Yeah, yeah, you don't scare me. I have two brothers, Hunter." She eased toward the bank and let the boat scrape to a halt on the sand, catapulting Hunter from his stance in the bow. Without missing a beat, he strode up the bank, grinning perversely at her over his shoulder, and disappeared from view.

In two seconds, he was back, yelling at the top of his lungs, sand flying before him.

"There's a dead guy up there!" he shouted. He hit the bow at a run, shoving the boat off the sand.

"What? What are you doing?" Amy looked stunned.

"Go get somebody. Call somebody as soon as you can get a cell signal."

Amy started the motor. "And leave you here?"

Hunter lifted both arms, a no-choice gesture. "Hurry! No, wait." He splashed after her. "Leave me a paddle."

Shaking, Amy pointed the boat toward open water. Until she rounded the point, she kept looking back at him. He stayed in one spot, knee-deep in water, the paddle in both hands in front of him. Then, just as she passed from view, he swung the paddle to his shoulder and gave a long, high wave.

Hunter stood still in the water until he could no longer hear the motor. Glancing around, he finally climbed the bank with slow, determined steps. He was on one of the many flat, sandy banks that dot the sound, scruffy pines and seagrass the main vegetation. There could be no one hiding close by. Looking toward open water, he could spot one cruiser lying at anchor.

Reluctantly, he approached the body. The man was lying on his back, eyes open, mouth open, thick blood from his nose and mouth, a small round hole in his throat, less blood there. He was fully clothed. The sharp odor of human waste permeated the area.

Once more, Hunter glanced around. He had the distinct feeling that he was being watched. With a resigned sigh, he walked closer to the body. Using the paddle, he flicked away the sand crabs that were investigating the bloody face. Careful not to let go of the paddle, he peeled off his shirt and laid it over the man's face and neck. He was particular about this, as if it mattered that it was straight.

Then he stood by, leaning on the paddle. He would not sit. Occasionally, he would send a crab or sand beetle flying with the paddle.

As the morning heated up, he crooked his arm to his nose and breathed his own sweat rather than the corpse's acrid stench. It was then that it occurred to him: this was not an odor of decomposition. The swollen blue hands were grotesque; the face had been frightening. But this man had not been dead very long. For the first time, he noticed that one shoe was missing. He did not notice that the cruiser was no longer at anchor.

He thought about that missing shoe. Did it mean the man had died someplace else and was dumped here? Why here? Surely it was coincidence that he was left here, in a spot familiar to Hunter. The thought that it might not be coincidence was too creepy. Hunter glanced around again. Where was Amy?

The air became very still. Black gnats began to swarm. With the paddle, Hunter waved them away from the body. Nothing would keep them out of his own face. He had trouble swallowing. *It's just a dead guy*, he told himself. *Nobody you know. Don't let it get to you.* Fantasies of chewing gum rolled across his tongue. Cinnamon. Sweat broke out on his temples. He closed his eyes. No, spearmint. Yes, that was working. He opened his eyes. A dark stain was beginning to outline the contours of the man's face beneath the shirt. Hunter barely made it to the nearest scrub pine before he threw up, a blackbird scolding above his head.

The sound of a boat approaching fast was sweet indeed. Amy plowed a solid wake before her as she rounded the point, barely letting off the throttle before crunching onto the bank.

"Are you all right?" she asked after one look at his face.

He left the paddle on top of the bank and slid down.

She looked him over and opened the small cooler. "How about some pop? You look a little sick."

"Maybe just some ice. Stick a piece in my mouth."

She raised her eyebrows, but did so.

"I haven't touched the guy, but I still feel like my hands are dirty," he explained through the ice. "It's been creepy by myself.

What took you so long?"

"You wouldn't believe it. The first boat I waved down—their radio was on the blink. The next one I saw—I waved and waved, but the driver turned at the channel marker and kept going. I had to go halfway to Beaufort before I could get a signal."

"What about that cruiser—well, there was one anchored just across the water there."

"Sorry, I didn't see it. I did pass one speeding toward Beaufort on my way back. Anyway, the two fishermen I first stopped will probably be here in a minute. I came back across the flats."

"I wish they wouldn't."

"What?"

"Be here. Stomp around and look at him. You know, before the coroner or whoever gets here. It doesn't seem decent."

She studied him seriously a moment, then offered him another piece of ice. "Do you want to talk about it?"

He shrugged. "He—I guess he was stabbed like the other guys. Here." He pointed to his throat. "Not long ago."

"Do you think it happened here?"

He shook his head. "Maybe not. I don't know."

"Where's your shirt?" she asked suddenly.

His face twisted involuntarily, and he turned and went back up the bank and disappeared. She didn't know, but he checked on the body, battled a couple of crabs. When he returned, he sat down on the bank.

In a minute, the two fishermen approached. Without consulting Hunter, Amy pulled away from shore and met them, conversed briefly, then returned. They idled in the channel awhile, then left.

"What did you tell them?" asked Hunter.

"That this is a crime scene and footprints are evidence. I bet they'll be back, though."

Hunter glanced at his own feet but didn't comment.

When help arrived, it was in the form of two men, both big, both familiar. Grayson Tucker pulled up first in a skiff wearing khaki slacks, a button-up shirt, and a Panama hat. His eyes crinkled with humor briefly when Amy pulled the skiff onto the beach by herself, but he stepped onto the sand all business, striding up the bank in an unhurried, Southern manner.

"I wanted to see this for myself before the state guys get here," he explained as he walked. There was something reassuring about Grayson, and Hunter joined him beside the body. Grayson squatted. "I hate you had to get mixed up in this, Hunter," Grayson said sincerely. "It's something you'll never forget, for sure." He snapped rubber gloves over his hands. "Okay, let's see what we've got here." Carefully, he folded back the T-shirt to reveal the neck wound and then the face. "May not be my boy after all," he said after a pause. "May not be."

He looked up into Hunter's face, pulled off a glove and reached into his shirt pocket for a stick of gum. When Hunter took it with a sheepish Thanks, Grayson continued, "You've heard about the other three murders, how the victims were stabbed once in the throat, and I'll bet you assumed this man was stabbed."

Hunter nodded slightly.

"He was shot." It was a flat statement. "See, this small, dark stain in the sand is blood from a larger hole we'll find in the back of his neck when we move him. I'd say he was dumped here after being killed somewhere else."

"Yeah, I noticed he was missing a shoe."

A speedboat pulled up behind them, and Grayson stood up beside Hunter, but neither turned around.

"Yes, that's a definite sign a body has been moved," Grayson agreed. "I'm going more by the amount of blood. I know it looks like a lot to you, but it's not, really. He bled more than this some-place else." He seemed finished talking.

"So you don't think it's the same killer?" Hunter prodded.

"Maybe not. Hard to say. It has the same professional look to it."

"Professional look, my ass," interrupted a loud, familiar voice. Grayson did not flinch or even look up, but Hunter did, shocked and repulsed to see Jack Franklin joining them. For some odd rea-son, Jack had not climbed the bank but had gone fifty feet down the sand to where the bank began at water's edge and followed the rise to where they stood. "It is professional." His voice was emphatic. He wore a gun in a black holster strapped under his arm. "And what damn fool threw a shirt over his face?" He looked straight at Hunter. "Boy, don't you know not to disturb a crime scene?"

"The shirt will just become part of the evidence," Grayson said levelly. He seemed irritated by Jack's presence, but not at all surprised. "It was a decent thing to do, Hunter. Don't worry about it."

Jack cursed. "No wonder you haven't solved this thing, Tucker. Like it or not, I'm openly getting involved in this investigation, starting now."

Grayson was the one whose face was impassive. The shock that had been building on Hunter's face found his tongue.

"Will somebody tell me what's going on?" he demanded.

"Federal narcotics agent," Jack said, his eyes narrow. "Interesting situation. Very interesting."

"Shut up, Franklin," Grayson said.

"Maybe Kittrell here would like to explain his whereabouts last night."

"Leave Hunter out of this."

"No, let him talk. I'd like to hear what he has to say."

"He doesn't have to say a damn thing to you, Jack. And I know exactly where he was until midnight."

"Oh, this took place after midnight," Jack said, indicating the body. "Go ahead, Kittrell."

"He was with me the rest of the night." Amy was beside Hunter in a half-breath.

"Yes, I thought so." Jack's voice held a suggestive leer. "Didn't waste any time, did you, boy? Like father, like son."

Hunter felt sick.

"Franklin." Grayson's voice was sharp.

"So tell me, *Kittrell* . . ." Jack spat the name, "what were you doing on this particular spot of the planet, right where the Kitty Killer dumped his last victim?"

"Seemed like the thing to do at the time."

"Seems like a strange thing to do to me. Answer the question."

Hunter glared.

Grayson cleared his throat. "We don't all get to travel the water with indoor plumbing like you do, Jack."

"Oh, good save. So is this a regular whiz stop for you?" quizzed Jack.

"Yeah."

"So you didn't stop where the body happened to be dumped. The body happened to be dumped where you stop. Is that correct?"

"You said it," said Hunter.

"Don't you find that odd?" There was a triumphant gleam in Jack's eyes.

Hunter stood his ground.

"I do," sneered Jack. "I find the entire situation very odd."

"Nobody else does," said Grayson with authority. "And nobody wants to hear it. Hunter, you and Amy can go now. I'll call you if we need any more information."

"Not so fast." Jack's voice was loud, and the two fishermen who had just returned certainly heard him in the channel. "I've got a couple more questions. And it all begins with my very odd, very interesting situation."

"Go on, Hunter," Grayson said quietly. "Don't listen to this."

Hunter could not have moved if he had wanted to.

"Here I sit in Beaufort harbor, doing my undercover thing, just waiting for this one particular guy. Heavy drug connections. And as I sit there, behold, people start dying all around me. Obvious drug connection. And so, I start thinking, Could there be another connection? And what do you know?"

"Can it, Franklin," Grayson said.

"I'm looking for a Kittrell. And the killer's signature is a kitty. What am I to make of that?"

Grayson was prepared, and when Hunter sprang toward Jack, fists swinging, he caught the young man and held him back.

"Franklin, I swear, I'll beat you myself if you don't shut up," Grayson growled.

Jack paused, but it was not because of Grayson's warning. It was to let the two fishermen, who had anchored their boat in the channel and who were moving fast through the water, get halfway up the bank. Then, his voice lowered, he spat out distinctly, "And every damn time I turn around, I'm tripping over Rob Kittrell's bastard son."

"Franklin!" Grayson yelled.

Jack stepped back and watched as the fishermen, soaking wet, scrambled the rest of the way up the bank and grabbed Hunter and Grayson. Sand flew and punches were swung, but neither man touched Jack. Jack knew what he was doing. Men had tried to kill him before.

"Hunter, please get out of here. Amy, get him away from here." Grayson's voice was as much a plea as an order. He did not look at Hunter as he backed away, but bent and picked up his hat. His hand was shaking as he put it on his head. Neither of the fishermen moved, nor did Grayson.

Jack finally spoke. "If there ever were any clues in the sand, you idiots have kicked them halfway to hell."

Amy sped around the point and across the flats. Once she had the boat well away, she killed the motor. Hunter had been sitting on the live well, elbows on his knees, his head in his hands. Now his shoulders began to shake, and the sobs he had been holding back broke free.

Amy did what any good friend would do. She put her arms around him and cried with him.

THIRTEEN

"Miki!" The waterfront reverberated with his yell. "Miki!" Tourists stared. The young man who was yelling was sunburned and sweating, shirt off, hair tousled. His appearance was neither as clean and casual as a tourist's nor as crisp and suave as the deckhands' who were now frowning at him. He pounded on the hull of a yacht with one fist, and when this brought no result, he swung himself up by the gunwale and landed on deck. Then he pounded on the cabin door. "Miki, I know you're in there."

"Hunter Kittrell, what is wrong with you? I don't want to see you," Miki shouted from within.

"Get out here and talk to me!" he yelled. "Miki!"

She appeared in a tight robe.

"Miss Stone? Is there a problem? Would you like me to take care of this for you?" called a man from a neighboring yacht.

"No, thank you, Mr. Bennington. I apologize for the intrusion."

She stayed in the passageway, neither offering to come out nor inviting Hunter in. "What is it, Hunter?" Her voice was icy. "You know Jack will kill you for coming on his boat."

"Jack has already done to me the worst a man can do." Hunter spoke in a low voice. "And now, I want to know what he's done to you."

She gave him an irritated stare.

"I think you're in danger, Miki." The statement hung between them a second.

"Oh, bull. Don't turn weird on me, Hunter."

"The man is mean. Just plain mean."

She started to speak, but he kept talking.

"Haven't you wondered why a *narcotics* agent would move a small-time user like you under his roof? Think about it, Miki."

"What? Where have you been, Hunter?"

"Don't change the subject. Why do you think he would do that?"

"He's just after the big guys. He looks after me."

"Yeah, I bet he does," Hunter scoffed.

"I don't have to take this from you." She turned to go inside.

"Miki, he's up to something. I don't know what it is yet. But he's mean, and he's going to hurt you."

"Oh, Hunter. Don't be so paranoid. Please go home before Jack gets here."

"Listen to yourself. You're the one who's paranoid. Deep down, you know I'm telling the truth. You know you should be afraid of him."

"Not me. He's not going to hurt me." She turned and faced him again. "I am afraid for you."

"He's using you, Miki. And when it all falls down, you're

going to be squashed."

"What? You aren't making any sense. Please. Just get out of here."

"All right. I'm gone. But I'll be back." He leaped off the deck onto the ramp and started off.

"No. Stay away. I mean it, Hunter." She backed inside the cabin and slammed the door."

"I'll be back any damn time I like!" he yelled toward the closed door. "You need to know just what a real friend is!"

Grayson Tucker hit the button on his answering machine once again.

I want to report a missing person, I think. My Dougie got gone from the boarding house where he was staying at. Well, he said he was going to a yacht party, which don't make sense seeing as how he don't know no yacht people. But he was all excited he was going to meet Vanessa Singer. But he hasn't called me and I'm real worried.

Grayson wrote down the woman's name and phone number, feeling very weary as he did. Dougie was on his way to the morgue now, along with Hunter's tee-shirt and paddle. And Grayson, having verified the identity of the body this morning, had recognized the fellow from the waterfront. In fact, Grayson had investigated Doug Sanders three weeks ago, after noticing him daily hanging around the docks. Unless further investigation now turned up something new, Doug was just a tourist with no history of drug use. One dead tourist put the entire summer in a new perspective and made it personal.

Grayson headed home for a shower, wondering what on earth Vanessa Singer had to do with anything.

✸ ✸ ✸

"Hunter?"

"Yes, Granny Jen, it's me." Hunter was walking across the lawn holding a drink can in his hand.

"I've been worried."

"I know you have. I'm sorry. Let me get a shower and I'll tell you about it."

Granny Jen had watched for Hunter to return all morning, worried because he had not come in last night. Even seeing her grandson in person, all in one piece, did not make Jen feel much better. She busied herself carrying a few things for sandwiches to the porch, and then sat at the table to make lunch. That seemed to be all she had strength for today.

When he joined her, freshly bathed and shaven, she asked him to bring out the tea pitcher. He did so, and then he sprawled in the chaise lounge and popped the tab on a can of beer. She eyed him, unperturbed, and went back to her sandwich-making. Neither spoke for a couple of minutes until she shoved a paper plate in his direction and poured herself a glass of tea.

"What's up with the paper plates?" he asked.

"That was all I could deal with today."

He nodded in understanding.

"So tell me, where does a person your age get beer these days?"

"People," he said, nodding again.

After a pause, she said, "Hunter, if you're trying to shock me, you missed. If you want to irritate me, now, you might just manage that."

"I'm not trying to do either, Granny Jen. I've just had a really rough couple of days."

"I'll tell you what you're doing. You're reminding me a whole lot of your daddy."

He stopped in mid-swallow, eyed her, and set the can down. "Now that was a low blow."

"I just tell it like it is. How about you join me for lunch and tell me about your rough two days?"

He sighed but didn't move. "For starters, I guess Miki has dumped me for good."

"Are you sure it's not just for the summer?"

"Now there's a thought. Maybe I could just sit on my can all summer and see if she decides she wants me back."

"I apologize. I was trying to be helpful."

"Well, you're not too far off the mark. She may have dumped me, but we're not through in some obscure way I can't quite explain."

"IImm." Granny Jen looked thoughtful as she chewed.

There was a comfortable pause, and then Hunter blurted, "Do you hate my father?"

Her face lost some of its composure before she answered, "No, of course not. Because it hurts so much to love him, I probably love him more acutely than I do anyone else. What made you ask that?"

He shook his head slightly. "Do you ever want him to come back?"

She seemed to have a hard time finding an answer. Finally, she said, "I have to admit, I have been known to fantasize about him walking through the door, healthy and grinning and ready to start over and live life the way I want him to live it. But that's not going to happen. The truth is, he was rebellious at a very early age. And if he's into as much as they say he is, then it's probably just as well he stayed away."

"Yeah. Probably is." He didn't ask where she might have heard any news of him. "And were you, like, really pissed when you heard he'd gotten my mom pregnant?"

She stared hard at him before answering. "Hunter, I can't even imagine what has precipitated this conversation. But I'm going to tell you one thing. You are not a mistake, and don't let anyone tell you otherwise. No matter what mistakes may have brought you here, you are here for a purpose because God doesn't make mistakes. And you have the same chance as anybody to make something good of your life."

"Worthwhile, I presume." There was a touch of sarcasm.

"Absolutely."

"Well, thanks for the lecture, but that's not really where I was going. What I want to know is, would it kill you if he did show up?"

For one heart-stopping moment, he thought he had killed her, so pale did she become. "What have you heard, Hunter? Where have you been all night?" she asked.

"Grandpa Baker told me not to tell you this, but there's a rumor that my father could be around here. And now it seems the cops are looking for him. And it has really scared me to think that you would hear it from them or that he might actually show up."

"You thought I would fall over dead."

"Well . . ."

She chuckled a bit. "So, now I won't. Thank you. Now tell me what's going on."

"Well, I can't do that, Granny Jen." He stood up finally and joined her at the table. "Because I don't understand it myself. Something is going on, but I doubt it's what it appears to be."

"And that's it? That's all you can tell me?"

"Not quite. When you read your paper tomorrow, you'll probably see that I have the distinction of being the person who found dead guy number four."

"What? Hunter, how awful. Are you okay?"

"I might have been if you had let me finish my beer."

"I mean it. That's a terrible thing to happen. Were you alone?"

"Amy was with me. She went for help, so I got to have a nice, long visit with him by myself. It was a blast."

"Let's don't be irreverent. Is Amy okay?"

"Yeah, Amy's okay." His voice was quiet.

"I am so sorry, Hunter. A thing like this will stay with you forever."

"Yeah."

There was more in his voice than that single word could hold. She studied him carefully before pressing further. "What does this have to do with your father?"

"That's the part I don't understand. Just give me some time to figure it out. And in the meantime, don't believe a word you hear from anybody else, okay?" He raised his voice. "And especially not that devil you see walking across the yard."

Hunter jumped up from the table, dishes clattering, and slammed off the porch. "You've got no business here, Franklin!"

"This search warrant says I do." Jack Franklin was smooth in voice and movement, well-oiled, well-practiced.

Hunter faced him, not budging. "Don't you even think about

setting foot inside my grandmother's house." He spoke in a clipped, low voice. "My father has not been here, and she doesn't know where he is."

"Oh, I wouldn't dream of disturbing your granny." Jack appeared amused. "She hasn't left her house in three weeks, and her son definitely hasn't been here." There was a glint of victory in his eyes. "You, however, disappear on the water at all hours and could have made contact with him." He started up the steps to Hunter's apartment two at a time. "And you know what? Even if I don't find anything in here that tells me where Rob Kittrell is, I can damn well bet I'll find something to put your cocky ass in jail."

The door to Hunter's apartment slammed just as a car screeched to a halt on the street. Grayson Tucker ran across the yard muttering something about a body not being able to get a bath around here anymore.

From behind Hunter came Granny Jen's Southern voice with more snap in it than usual. "Grayson, you watch him. He all but said he was going to plant something. You watch him, you hear?"

Grayson nodded even as he pounded up the steps. An excessive—considering Hunter's few possessions— slamming and banging came from the apartment.

When he felt Granny Jen's arm around his waist, he put his arm solidly around her. "Sure hope they don't go breaking my teacups," he said lightly.

She patted him. "It will be all right. You'll see. It will be all right." She called in a loud, clear voice, "Are you watching him, Grayson?"

"Yes, Jen. That's what I'm here for."

There was a curse from Jack Franklin. Granny Jen flinched but continued to pat Hunter reassuringly even as both men reappeared on the landing.

Jack, it seems, was a sore loser. "Next time, Kittrell," he spat as he came down the steps. "Next time, I'll find your stash."

Grayson sat on the top step and waited for Jack's car to pull away. He looked tired, maybe a little sick. "Hunter," he said, looking down at them both, "I have to ask you a question, and you can answer it now or you can answer it in private."

"I'm not afraid of anything my grandson has to say," said Granny Jen. She had begun trembling with fatigue, and Hunter's arm stayed strong around her.

"Is it about what was in the drawer of my dining chest?" asked Hunter.

"No," Grayson said carefully, watching him.

"Then ask anything you like, but I've got to get my granny back on the porch."

"I'll wait."

Slowly, Hunter and Jen made their way back to the house. July fifth in Beaufort was always hot, and this particular one was hard. Jen was leaning as much on her grandson as her cane. He left her in her chair with her tea and a reassuring wink and walked back outside. Grayson remained seated on the top step, still looking tired.

"So ask me."

"Tell me the truth. Why was Franklin so sure he would find drugs in here?"

Hunter made no attempt to lower his voice so that Granny Jen couldn't hear. "I've been known to party. But never here. Never at Granny Jen's."

"How would he have known that about you?"

"Ask him." Hunter's gaze was steady.

Grayson nodded in acceptance, slapped his thighs, and stood up. "He won't be back. You don't have to worry about that."

Hunter trotted up the steps and started inside with a quick nod for Grayson to join him. Immediately, he walked to his dining chest and opened the drawer, aware that Grayson was watching.

"Did you see Jack Franklin take anything out of this drawer?" he asked deliberately.

"No. There was nothing in here besides"—Grayson peered inside— "what's in there now." He looked at Hunter appraisingly. "Why? What's supposed to be in there?"

"Doesn't matter." Hunter shook his head and closed the drawer. "It wasn't anything about my father, and it wasn't drugs."

"Okay." Grayson turned to go, and then stopped. "Hunter, you're a good kid. Don't mess yourself up when you go back to school."

Hunter let him get to the bottom of the steps before he spoke. "Mr. Tucker."

Grayson turned and looked up. "When will they know what caliber gun killed that guy?"

Understanding flickered in Grayson's eyes. "Soon," he answered. "What do you think it might be?"

"A .32. Like maybe an old Owlhead." Hunter spoke in a low voice.

Grayson considered his words carefully before speaking. "Why might a person be hiding a gun of that type?"

"Stupidity."

Again, Grayson considered thoughtfully. "You know, Hunter, your dad may never have been in this area." He spoke in a low voice that would not carry to the porch. "Lord knows there are enough people looking for him, including myself."

Hunter came down the steps and stood face-to-face with Grayson. "Who's been watching this house?"

"Could be some of Franklin's people. Those federal guys only tell me what they want me to know. What have you heard about that?"

"Only that Franklin was mighty proud of himself for knowing my granny hasn't been out lately. It would be interesting to find out who they have seen go in my apartment, say, in the last three or four days."

"Yes, it might." Grayson paused awkwardly before speaking again. "Look, I'm awfully sorry about that scene this morning and this search and all. I think you've handled yourself well, considering the circumstances."

"Yeah, well, you know what? When a guy gets as wound up as Franklin is, there's usually more to what he's not saying than what he is saying, you know? I mean, this whole scene is mega-weird if you take it at face value."

Grayson put a strong hand on Hunter's shoulder. "You didn't get that wise from partying, kid. Now, listen to me. You're going to feel a little shell-shocked from all this for a few days. Stay away from Jack Franklin, and don't do anything rash. When you feel ready to sort through this mess, you know I'm here."

Hunter made no comment as he watched Grayson get in his car. Actually, it struck him hard just then that he had his own way of sorting through things, and for the first time in his life, a reason to do it: Miki.

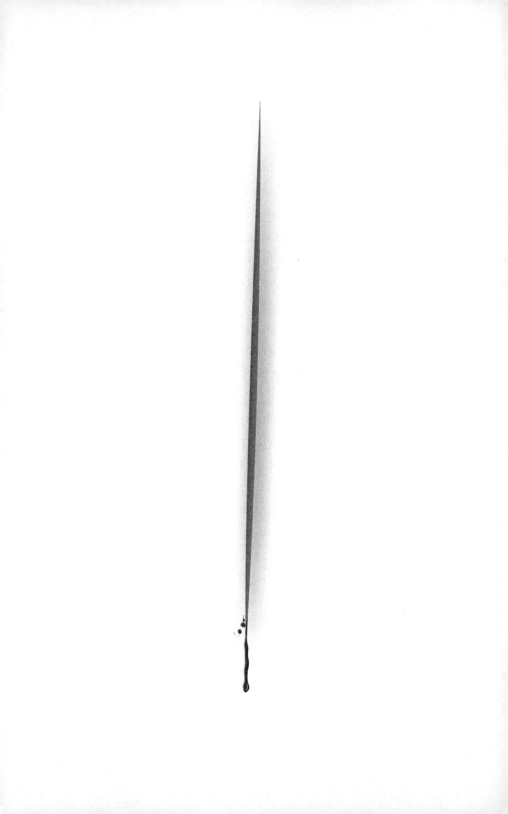

FOURTEEN

ot here. Pretty day. Food's okay.

Beneath this cryptic entry in Doug Sanders' spiral notebook was taped a clipping from the local newspaper:

Vanessa Singer was sighted on the waterfront, lunching with a companion.

There was no comment about the clipping. There were a few remarks on the weather with no dates. Stuck between pages were brochures advertising local points of interest, meal receipts from waterfront restaurants, and a ticket stub from a dinner cruise aboard the *Pirate's Lady*. Every news item involving the murders that the local paper had printed was taped to a page of the notebook, the clippings folded, if necessary, to fit the size of the notebook.

Occasionally, among the clippings would appear an intriguing remark:

Spotted her today.

Almost talked to her today.

It's either that man or that boy. I've been watching them.

Could be that boy.

Why does she like that boy? I saw him pick up a cat today. Every time she leaves with him, I'm afraid he will kill her.

Alone, these messages were meaningless, but guess what? Inside Doug Sanders' billfold was a receipt from a drug store photo processor.

Grayson Tucker picked up the pictures from the pharmacy and carried them down the street to a diner. Once seated, he opened the packet and went through the photos quickly. Doug Sanders had not wasted any effort on historical sites or wild ponies. If he had driven over to Atlantic Beach, he had not taken any pictures. If he had made any friends, their smiling faces were not among the snapshots.

Spreading the photos out on the table, one by one, Grayson frowned. There were pictures of yachts, one after another. Interspersed among these photos were snapshots of specific people: Hunter talking to the blonde girl Grayson had seen him with, Hunter kissing the girl, Jack Franklin talking to the girl, Jack alone on the deck of his government yacht. The only staged photo was one of Hunter aboard the ketch, looking politely bored for the camera. In Hunter's own words, the scene was "mega-weird." That both men in the photos had been standing over Doug Sanders' body just this morning was too much coincidence for Grayson.

The scenario was sick. Doug Sanders had a crush on the girl. Jealous of the two men he had seen her with, he imagined each as the harbor killer. Jack Franklin would carry the scenario to the next level, Grayson knew. Somebody in the photos had killed Doug, and Jack, the investigator, would surely eliminate himself in a hurry. Grayson had never wanted to destroy evidence so badly in his life.

Well, he couldn't do that, but there was one thing he could do. He could blow these photos up and see for himself who might turn up aboard one of these yachts before handing them over to Jack Franklin. Carefully, Grayson picked up the snapshots in order and examined them closely before returning them to the folder. Yes, there was one in particular, a gentleman behind tinted-glass in the pilot house of his yacht, who seemed to be looking toward the camera.

Grayson left his uneaten meal on the seat beside him and hurried out into the sunshine, still wondering what in the world Vanessa Singer had to do with anything.

★ ★ ★

"Hunter, are you up there?"

"Yeah."

"Are you dressed?"

"Come see for yourself."

"You are so perverted." Footsteps clattered up the stairs, walked lightly across the hardwood floor, and stopped. Hunter looked up to see Amy standing in front of him. "I thought you might be zonked out up here," she said. "Mama made me take a nap with a teddy bear when I told her what happened. Haven't you slept at all?"

"Nope."

"You look ragged," she declared.

"Well, thank you, Amy," said Hunter. "I've been waiting all afternoon for you to come tell me that."

"No you haven't. Look at you. I can't believe I actually caught you working."

"I have been known to on occasion," he said dryly.

There was silence as she watched him work, then, "So that's why Granny Jen's car was parked in the driveway."

"Yep. Been measuring. Checking the foundation." With the magic of pencil, paper, and architectural skill, Hunter was transforming his one-room apartment into a cozy home.

"Who would have thought you could do all that with this little place? Is Granny Jen planning on renting this out or something?"

"Nope. This is just for me."

"Ha! You and what millionaire? This place will be fabulous." Amy rattled the completed sheets as she studied them. "Look at this! You've changed the entire roofline to fit your blue window. Check out all these windows. And a real front porch, just like all the old houses in town. It gives me goose bumps just thinking about how pretty this could be."

"Will be. I absolutely will build this with every detail you see plus some I haven't drawn yet." He erased a mark and leaned back to look at his work. "Someday. When I get over being broke."

She glanced at his face and pointed to a sheet. "I'm going to expect a meal from this gourmet kitchen one day."

He took the sheet from her. "This is just a preliminary sketch. Let me work out the details before you start planning my meals for me."

"Oh, Hunter. This is just so cool to see you in action. Let me look some more." She leaned over his shoulder. "Explain to me why you expanded in two directions."

"To make use of my limited lot."

"Your lot?"

"Yes, my lot. You know, you're annoying me right now, Amy."

She didn't speak, and he looked up to see her staring at him with her mouth open. "What?" he asked.

"That's the first time I've ever heard you say how you really felt about anything. There might be hope for you yet, Hunter Kittrell."

"Huh? If that's a compliment, it's a lame one."

"Well, how about this? I'm really impressed with your work. All this time I thought you were just playing your way through school."

"I tried." He studied his work intently, frowning in concentration. His hands, tan and calloused from a summer of working the ship, handled his drawing tools with precision, long fingers spread carefully on the paper.

"What brought on this fit of working anyway?" she asked.

"Stuff."

"Like what?"

"Stuff that needs thinking through," he said, as if talking to a child.

After a pause, she ventured, "I thought architects used computers these days."

"We do." Hunter tapped his pencil on the drawing board. "I happen to like drawing by hand. This is how I get my brain in gear." Without looking up, he added, "You're standing in my light."

"Oh, sorry. I guess I'll take myself outside then. I see you're okay, and that's all I came for." Light footsteps moved toward the door.

"Amy?"

"Yes?"

"Maybe I'm just missing Miki. She always stood behind me and rubbed my back and didn't talk while I worked."

"I can't be Miki for you, Hunter."

"I didn't say I wanted you to be. I was just explaining why I'm sorta testy."

"You have a right to be. It's been a rough day. Do you want me to put Granny Jen's car back in the garage?"

"Uh, no. I was going to wash it after a while." He didn't look up from his drawing.

Her footsteps retreated down the stairs; next the sound of water spraying could be heard through the open window. He smiled and continued working. In fact, he was so lost in his work that he was startled to hear her voice at his side an hour later.

"Hunter? Do you want me to do anything else for you before I leave?" Amy asked.

"Yeah, if you don't mind." He leaned back and stretched. "Check on Granny Jen for me. That crap this morning nearly wiped her out. Tell her I'll be down in about an hour and that I'll fix shrimp Creole for supper unless she needs me now."

"Did something else happen this morning?"

"You wouldn't believe it," he said, looking up at her. "I got raided by the law."

"Wow. What were they looking for, your father?"

"Yeah, him, drugs, anything Franklin could hang me with."

"I am not believing this, Hunter. That's too much for anybody to take in one day."

"Oh, there's more," he said.

"No way." She looked at him with concern, her head cocked to one side.

"Somebody's been in my apartment in the last three days or so."

"You're kidding."

"Nope. And I need a favor. House-sit for me in the morning while I take Granny Jen to the doctor. I'll get a deadbolt while I'm out."

"You don't have much to steal, Hunter."

"Right now I'm more worried about what somebody might put in here than what they might take out, you know?"

"You think that Franklin guy will be back?" Her eyes were wide with alarm.

"Probably," answered Hunter. "Mr. Tucker said he wouldn't, but I'm not sure he can stop a Fed. Especially not one with a personal vendetta like Franklin seems to have. If I don't get this thing figured out in a hurry, he's going to find some way to put me in jail."

"But why? What's his problem?"

"Miki."

"Mik . . ." And then, reality sank in. "Oh, Hunter, I'm sorry. I had no idea."

"See what a mess I'm in? Franklin knows I'm going to try to find out what he wants with Miki, plus what my father has to do with that murder today. In other words, he's going to be tripping over me, as he said, every way he turns."

"Man. Your life just got weird. Aren't you scared?"

"Terrified. Have you got an extra teddy bear I can borrow?"

"You may need two bears tonight, Hunter," came Grayson Tucker's deep voice from the doorway.

Hunter and Amy both turned.

"I'll get right to the point. May I come in?"

"Sure."

Grayson opened the screen door and entered, his presence making the room seem small. "The victim this morning was Doug Sanders. Does that name ring a bell?"

"No."

"Did you recognize his face?"

"No!" Hunter was repulsed.

"It seems he had noticed you." Grayson laid the two photos of Hunter and Miki on the drafting board.

There was stone silence.

"Do you mean the dead guy took these pictures?"

"Yes. And this one." Grayson laid the picture of Hunter aboard the ketch down.

Hunter cursed softly.

"Now, do you remember Doug Sanders?"

"Sort of."

"Well, either you do or you don't, Hunter."

"Mr. Tucker," Hunter began, looking the man in the eye, "I have a lot of people in my face every day. And I have to keep the ship sailing and stop the little kids from falling overboard and be polite and answer the same stupid questions a million times. After a while I don't really see their faces."

"But they don't all take your picture," Grayson persisted.

"Actually, quite a few do. They seem to be under the delusion that, instead of a tip, I want to be immortalized in their scrapbook or something. Usually it's with some old ladies, though. That's why I sort of remember this, since he wanted a picture of me alone. It was a dinner cruise about two weeks ago. But I didn't pay that much attention to the guy, and I don't remember really talking to him at all. Man, this is creepy."

"Okay, good. That's pretty much what I expected. Now, when Jack Franklin questions you, you give him your story just like you did then."

"What? Should I have had a lawyer just now?"

"No. This was off the record. I just wanted to verify what I already figured to be true."

"Why am I in trouble, exactly?"

"Because the guy is dead, and you're the one who found him. And he seems to have had a crush on your friend here. And he seems to have pegged you as the harbor killer. And dead guys don't talk, Hunter. If they could, my job would be a whole lot easier."

"Wait a minute. Turn this boat around and sail that channel again. You got all that from these pictures?"

"Mr. Sanders kept a notebook."

"And so now I'm a killer because some dead guy says so? I should have let the bastard rot in the sun!"

"Shh. Calm down, Hunter. Granny Jen will hear you," said Amy.

"I don't care who hears me." He stormed to a window, unlatched the screen, and leaned out. "I didn't do it," he yelled. "Hey, you! Yes, you. Are you a Fed? Well, put this in your gun and screw it. I haven't done a damn thing all summer."

The confused fellow, who was probably a tourist, folded his

map and drove away. On the water, however, close by, somebody chuckled and lit a cigarette.

"Hunter, shut up and get over here," drawled Grayson with the patience only years of experience can muster. "There's another picture I want you to see."

"Hold on," said Hunter, latching the screen. "You say this guy had a crush on Miki?"

"The blonde?"

"Yeah."

"These photos, combined with the few notes he kept, point to that possibility."

"You know, Miki was about to jump out of her skin last night. She said some guy had been following her, and she thought she saw him on the dock. It was dark, and I didn't get a good look at him." He stabbed the air with his finger. "I'll tell you what. You need to be talking to Jack Franklin. He probably smoked the guy just to get him off Miki's back."

"You're coming unglued, Hunter. Now listen to me. The Feds may question you, but nobody is going to accuse you of killing anybody just based on this. So take a deep breath and calm down. Okay. I want you to look at this blow-up." Grayson pulled an enlarged photo out of a manila envelope.

"What am I looking at, the boat or the guy?"

"Either. Is either familiar to you?"

"No. Should they be?"

"Look at the man closely. We'll have a lab zoom in on his face, but this is the best I could do locally."

Hunter shrugged.

"Have you seen any pictures of your father taken recently?"

Hunter shut down, like turning off a switch. Finally, he asked in a voice that betrayed no emotion, "Are you saying this is my father?"

"No, I'm not saying that at all. I'm asking your opinion."

"I don't have an opinion."

"Hunter, cooperate. You're in this thing neck-deep, whether you want to be or not. What's your gut reaction?"

"Amy," Hunter said slowly, "remember that favor I asked a few minutes ago?"

"Check on Granny Jen?"

"Please."

"Sure," she said. "I'll be by in the morning about nine, okay?"

"Thanks."

Not until he heard Granny's screen door bang did Hunter speak. He kept his eyes on the picture, not looking at Grayson. "Yesterday, my gut reaction would have been to track this man down, and if he were my father, shoot him for what he's done to my mom, Granny Jen, and me. Now, after all that's happened . . . ," he shook his head, "I don't know. I just want him to disappear again and not be in trouble. But to answer your question as to who this guy is, I can see why you'd look twice at this picture."

"Whoever he is, he seems to be looking straight at the camera."

"Yes, he does." Hunter tapped a pencil on the drafting board. "He sure does." Hunter was silent as he stared at the picture, frowning, not sure whether to tell Grayson that the skipper of the *Pirate's Lady* had seen a man on the water who reminded him of Rob Kittrell. Finally, he asked, "Mr. Tucker, why is Jack Franklin looking for my father?" When Grayson hesitated, he added, "Be straight with me."

Grayson cleared his throat. "Possible drug connections. He's never actually been charged with anything that I know of."

"Do you think he's the harbor killer?" After a pause, Grayson said, "Let's just say that I would like to find him before Franklin does and ask a few questions of my own."

"Yeah, I've got a few questions I'd like to ask him too," Hunter muttered.

Grayson began putting the pictures away. "One more thing. Like I told you before, stay away from Jack Franklin. I mean stay far away."

"I can't promise that."

Grayson studied him before asking, "The blonde?"

"Yeah."

Grayson's face twisted, and, with a sigh, he left.

FIFTEEN

Miki lay awake at two a.m., listening to Jack's steady snore, longing for sleep. Sometimes sleep was the only escape she had.

Jack's heat made its claim on her skin; his body, his hands, his tongue knew many ways to burn her flesh with pleasure. But he hadn't brought her the sedation she craved. Maybe no one could.

Still, she wasn't ready to leave Jack. There was a dark, possessive side to him that thrilled her with its carnal masculinity. It excited her to be seen with him, to catch heads turning. She guessed he could be brutal, maybe dangerous, as Hunter said. But she didn't fear him.

At this moment, she only feared not sleeping. As a girl of fourteen, she had lain awake too many nights while her parents screamed at each other: Accusations, lies, obscenities. Afterward, when the huge house was finally quiet, she would pursue sleep through the night's long hours. Dawn would often find her still awake, the deafening screams of her own soul still reverberating in her heart.

Tonight, she blamed Hunter for her lack of sleep. Why couldn't he just leave her alone? He made her feel guilty for leaving, even though there had been no promises between them. She wanted desperately to forget Hunter, but somehow the memory of his hands warm on her skin, his lips moving in sweet, lazy circles on her mouth, wouldn't leave her.

Damn.

Careful not to wake Jack, she slipped from the bed. In the darkness, she found a bottle of liquor and a few pills. Tonight she would wash away memories of Hunter, strangle the frantic cries within, maybe even find sleep.

⁂

Sleep had taken Hunter down hard. At three a.m., sleep released him abruptly to the distinct sensation of movement in the darkness. With an outraged scream, he leaped to a fighting position beside the bed. His fist struck only the wall. From beside him came a jarring bang. In anger he screamed again and hit the light switch. He was alone.

Shaking and breathing hard, he looked around. Okay, the bang had only been the croquet ball crashing to the floor after his fist hit the wall. It was bound to happen eventually, so precarious was the ball's perch on two nails.

But there had been another sound alongside his own scream;

he was certain. The room appeared undisturbed. He checked the door. It was pulled shut, but the latch had not caught. Someone had been in the room.

Dreading what he would find, Hunter opened the drawer of his dining chest. Yes, there lay the gun, right where he had placed it four nights ago and exactly where it had not been the previous morning when Jack Franklin had searched his apartment.

Okay, cool. He was a twenty-year-old kid who was being set up by a professional killer. At the moment, it didn't matter why. Jack Franklin sure wouldn't be asking why. What to do about it was what mattered.

His first instinct was to smuggle the gun out on the water in the skiff and drop it in a deep channel. Unfortunately, he was already being watched by the Feds. He would like to ask somebody why his every move was being monitored, yet no one seemed to notice his apartment being robbed. And then un-robbed.

His second instinct was to put it back in his grandfather's desk and pretend he knew nothing about it. No longer did he want to kill his father anyway. He just wanted him gone. To do that, however, would involve Granny Jen. Unthinkable.

Call Grayson Tucker. Now there was a pleasantly innocent thought. Grayson would, no doubt, believe him. Grayson would not, however, be able to protect him from the simple fact that he was in possession of a probable murder weapon. Hunter would bet his apartment that if any fingerprints were on the gun, they were his own. He decided not to wipe the pistol clean, however. If the gun were ever found, his only salvation might be in other fingerprints found on it.

Hunter switched off the light. Somewhere in the darkness, eyes were watching for his next move; he could be certain of that. The Feds couldn't possibly know he had the gun. He guessed he had a few more hours before Jack Franklin saw the pictures Grayson found. Without the gun, Jack could question him from now until doomsday, but Jack couldn't touch him. With the gun, Hunter was hung. No matter how pitiful the rest of the evidence was, Jack Franklin wanted his neck too much not to stretch it.

Quietly, Hunter opened every window in the room and switched on the air conditioner. Perhaps whoever was watching would assume he had gone back to bed. In the darkness, Hunter located a few items and opened the door of his one tiny closet. With his only kitchen knife, he sliced into the wall board and bent back a section just large enough to slide the small pistol through. A solid thunk told him it was secure. With his hands, he pieced back the wall and patched it with wall putty, then smeared a little paint over it with his fingers. Hopefully, since he had sloppily painted the closet to start with, this mess would not attract attention.

Feeling like a criminal, Hunter sprawled across his sofa to await whatever would happen. In the dark, he couldn't be certain how well he had cleaned up the closet floor or his hands. If he were caught, he would be in worse trouble than if he had called Grayson. But maybe, just maybe, he would slip through this mess long enough to figure it out.

At four a.m., Jen Kittrell woke up fearless. Soft light touched the room from the hall nightlight. Footsteps had awakened her, and now a big man's shadow darkened the hallway. Too big to be Hunter's, it seemed.

"Rob? Rob, is that you?" she called in a clear voice.

The footsteps hesitated, then retreated. The kitchen door closed softly. A younger woman could have run to the window and perhaps glimpsed the intruder as he crossed the yard.

Jen was not young. Reaching beside her, she picked up the cordless phone. One touch put her through to the police station. A flashing blue light seconds later startled her, and she struggled to sit up even as she spoke quickly into the receiver.

The light also startled Hunter, even though he had been halfway expecting it. Jumping to his feet, heart pounding, he arrived at the window in time to see a big man dive into the back seat of an unmarked patrol car. "Kill the light, you idiot; it's me," he thought he heard just before the car sped away.

Granny Jen's light was on. Hunter trotted down his steps and let himself in her back door noisily.

"Granny Jen, it's me," he called.

"I know, Hunter. What happened out there?"

"I'm not too sure." He walked into her bedroom to find her sitting up in bed. Her hand was shaking as she reached for his.

"Did they catch him?" she asked.

"Catch who? What are you talking about?"

"The man who was in here. I called the police, but the blue

light flashed before I was through talking. Surely they caught him."

"Yeah, they did. They did," he whispered, patting her hand.

He never knew until that moment that icicles could form in a man's gut.

"I can't be sure of what I saw," Hunter told Grayson three minutes later. "It was dark. But I would know that voice anywhere."

"You want me to believe that Jack Franklin was in this house?"

"Shh. Granny Jen just thinks it was an intruder and they caught him and it's over."

"C'mon, Hunter. I know you hate the guy, but . . ."

"Look, he was right in front of my apartment, diving into a police car. And somebody was in Granny Jen's house seconds before that. Those are two facts."

Grayson blew out a noisy breath. "Okay. I believe he was here. But he couldn't have been in the house. He must have been investigating the intruder. You said yourself they've been watching the place."

"He was running away."

"Hunter, there simply has to be another explanation. I'll get to the bottom of it. Trust me."

"Yeah, sure." There was nothing else to say. Hunter couldn't make much of an argument from what little he had seen.

"Hunter? Let me talk to Grayson," came from Granny Jen's bedroom. "Alone," she added when Hunter entered the room.

"Did they catch him? Who was it?" Jen demanded when she had Grayson alone.

"Jen, I can honestly say that I don't know what's going on. Please don't worry. Hunter will stay with you tonight, I'm sure."

"Oh, I'm not afraid. But it has to be tied in with these people looking for Rob. In fact, I first thought it was Rob."

"Are you sure it wasn't?"

"He didn't answer when I called. Rob wouldn't have done that."

"Are you sure?"

"You're talking like somebody who knows he didn't catch him," Jen said.

"Jen, you're too smart. All I can say is that a patrol car picked up someone, but I don't know if it was your intruder. You try to rest now. Hunter can help me look around and see if anything's missing, then I'll get out of here and let you sleep."

"Sleep? It will soon be time to get up."

Grayson went out shaking his head.

After Grayson left, Hunter sat on the porch and drank coffee. From here he could watch his own apartment and hear Granny Jen if she called.

She didn't call. There was a crash from her room at about six o'clock. Hunter ran to her, expecting to find her on the floor. A lamp was on the floor. She was still in bed.

"Granny Jen, what happened?"

She shook her head and smiled a sad, sweet smile.

"Oh, no. Please, no," he sobbed.

She closed her eyes while he dialed the paramedics, her face gray, still shaking her head, still smiling.

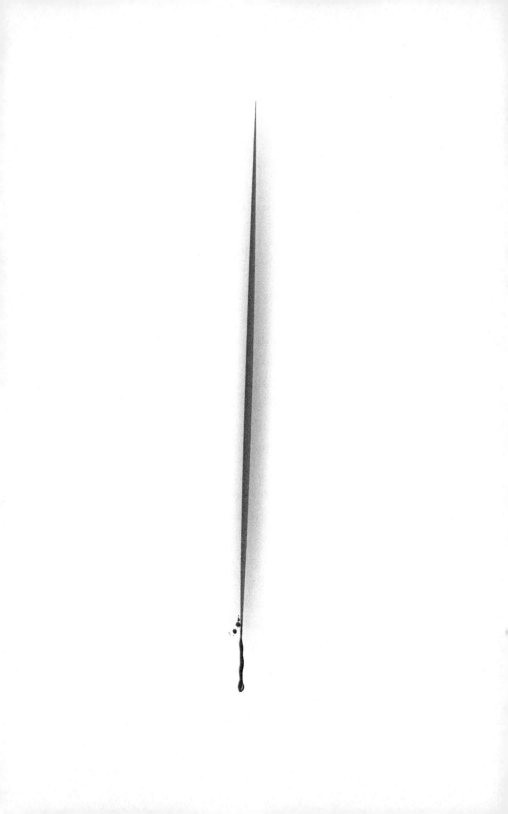

SIXTEEN

"Franklin! Jack Franklin, get out here." The voice was angry and challenging, causing people on the boardwalk to stop and stare. "I said get out here before I come in there and drag you out."

"Kittrell, what the hell do you want?" Jack's voice was cool and controlled as he stepped out on deck of his yacht, buttoning his shirt.

"Get down here and talk to me face to face." Hunter stood on the ramp, feet apart, fists clenched, voice shaking with anger.

Jack dismissed him with a wave of his hand and started back inside.

With one leap, Hunter swung himself up and stood on Jack's deck. "Face to face. Me and you," he said.

"Get off my boat before I have you arrested for trespassing."

"At least I do my trespassing in broad daylight."

There was silence.

"You know what I'm talking about. Last night. I saw you."

"I was investigating an intruder. He got away." Jack's smooth voice showed his training.

"Yeah. I guess that's your story and you're sticking to it, huh? But the truth, Franklin. You and I know the truth."

"You know nothing. Now get off my boat."

"Not until I'm through with you. You nearly killed my granny."

"Oh? There was harm done to your granny? I do need that for my report."

"Drop the phantom intruder act. Between that bogus search yesterday and your breaking into her house, you gave her heart failure."

"I'm sorry to hear about your granny. But these things happen when people get old. You can't blame . . ."

"You! You caused it, and I am blaming you. And I'm telling you, man to man, to stay away from her. If you want to question me again, do it in Grayson's office."

"And I take it you're expecting me to want to do this for some reason?"

"And if you plan to search my apartment again, do it now before she comes home from the hospital."

"Oh, that's funny. Very humorous." Jack's eyes narrowed. "I have a job to do, Kittrell. If you're so worried about your granny, maybe you'd better put her in a rest home."

Hunter's eyes shot pure hatred.

"If you're not off my boat in three seconds, I will throw you off."

Hunter raised a fist in his face. "I'll beat you, Jack Franklin. You hurt Miki or come near my granny, and I will beat you till you beg to die."

"Hunter!" Grayson Tucker's voice carried across the water.

Hunter flinched but kept his eyes on Jack.

"What are you doing?" called Grayson.

"Nothing. I'm outa here." Hunter bounded off the yacht and walked away without looking back. A man at a neighboring yacht shook his Bloody Mary with extra vigor as Hunter passed, and then the harbor was quiet again.

Grayson approached Jack's yacht slowly, a manila folder in his hand.

"What is it, Tucker? I haven't had much sleep."

"So I've heard. I need to ask you about that and go over this evidence from yesterday's homicide with you. Now, though, I think it will be better to do it later, in my office.

"Don't waste my time. Just hand me that evidence." Jack reached down for the envelope.

"Eleven o'clock. My office." Grayson turned on his heel and left.

Jack was laughing when Miki stepped on deck.

"What's so funny? That was awful about Hunter's granny."

"He's cracking." He put his arms around her and kissed her full on the mouth. "And when people crack, they make mistakes. I'll catch that boy at something sooner or later. It's quite amusing, from my perspective."

"Jack, don't make fun of Hunter. He's just, he's just . . ."

"He's just a stupid, bull-headed, cocky little bastard who needs to be taken down a notch. And I will do it quite legally, my dear, because he is cracking, and I will catch him."

Miki cursed softly and turned toward the cabin.

"Where were you last night?" he asked in a careful voice.

"Here."

"Don't lie to me. Never lie to me. I looked everywhere for you."

"I was on the top deck." She gestured to the deck behind the flybridge. "I saw you leave."

"Why didn't you call down to me?"

"I thought you had gotten a call, an investigation or something. I didn't know you were looking for me."

"Of course I was looking for you." He reached and touched her hair. "I care for you. Get it through your head; I'm not your stupid boy. I'm a man. I looked everywhere."

She grabbed his hand and pulled it away from her hair. "You broke into Granny Jen's house to look for me, didn't you?"

"Don't be ridiculous. The old lady was lucky I happened by when I did. Put that thought out of your head." He held her and kissed her with heat.

She turned away from him. He pulled her close again.

"What were you doing up there?" he asked.

"Your booze. Sleeping pills. A joint. Attempting sleep."

"And did you sleep?"

"Not really."

His hands were not sweet like Hunter's, not warm. They burned their way across her skin, searing her, claiming her. "I have a little something in my briefcase that will help you," he whispered. "I'll let you have it this once. You need sleep badly. You're becoming paranoid, and the one thing I need from you is trust. Show me you trust me."

She nodded and let him kiss her, a deep, experienced kiss, and she kissed him back and drew him into the cabin.

"I'm going to be all right, Hunter," Granny Jen whispered without opening her eyes.

"I know, Granny Jen. I know." He had pulled a chair as close to her hospital bed as he could, his hand now enclosing her arm gently around the tubes.

"You go on home and sleep. Winnie will be here soon."

"I'll wait until she gets here. Make sure she doesn't boss you too much. You know how your prissy daughter can get."

Granny Jen smiled but did not open her eyes. After a bit, she whispered. "I'm going to see you graduate, Hunter. I've made up my mind."

"I've never doubted it."

"But I may not live to see you marry, if you don't get serious."

"Shh. You just rest."

Another silence, and then she said, "Marry your soul mate."

"Shh." Hunter leaned his head on his free hand. When he thought she was asleep, he rested his head on the bed beside her arm.

"Hunter, get up," spoke a precise voice. "You don't need to wallow your grandmother like that."

"Hello, Aunt Winnie. Nice to see you, too."

"Don't be facetious. How is she feeling?"

"I'm feeling fair," said Granny Jen.

"When was the doctor in last? How did he say she is?" demanded Winnie.

"He said I'm not dead or deaf."

"Mother, please be still and rest."

"Hello, Winnie, nice to see you, too," quipped Granny Jen, her voice weak but full of humor.

"Mother, it's not necessary for you to become a comedienne now."

"Aunt Winnie, what have you done to your hair? It looks so—so youthful." Hunter squeezed Granny Jen's arm as he said this.

"Really? Do you like it?"

"Yeah, sure."

"Well, come give me a kiss, Hunter. What were you doing at Mother's at six o'clock this morning?"

"I live there? Hey, I know. Why don't you find the head nurse and see what she knows about your mom?"

"I'll do that. Be right back, Mother." She clicked out in practical heels.

"What do you have against the head nurse, Hunter?" Granny Jen's voice cracked with humor.

"Get well quick, Granny Jen. Real quick."

She smiled and nodded.

"Should I stay? Maybe I can protect you from a major priss-out."

"No. Go on," she whispered. "I'll pretend I'm asleep."

"Good deal. You rest. Really." He kissed her on the cheek and left quickly.

"Oh, man, Amy, I forgot about you," said Hunter when he returned to his apartment to find her sitting cross-legged on his sofa. "How long have you been here?"

"Just a couple of hours. No problem. Where's Granny Jen?"

"The hospital."

"Hunter! What happened?" She stood and crossed the room toward him.

"Heart failure. About six this morning."

"I'm so sorry." Amy's voice was sympathetic. "How is she?"

"She's okay. They're changing her medicine. She'll be better for a while."

"A while?"

"Yes. Just for a while." His voice was quiet.

Without a word, she hugged him. He looked out the window as she wiped her eyes on his shirt sleeve.

"Has anybody been around?" he asked.

"No. I haven't seen a soul."

"Not in the yard? Not parked on the street?" he persisted.

"No. Why were your windows open with the air conditioner going?"

He walked to his closet and inspected his patch. It looked like sloppy work, but it didn't appear new or smell of fresh paint.

"Hey, where's my breakfast, woman?" he demanded, closing the closet door.

"Does this look like Meals on Wheels to you?" Amy's hands were on both hips, her pretty mouth quirked to one side. "And you didn't answer my question about the air conditioner being on."

"Look! You brought me a teddy bear." Ignoring her question, he dived on the bed and grabbed the fluffy brown bear. He rolled on his back and laughed as if he didn't have a care in the world.

"You are so weird! I've got to go pick up lunch before I go to work."

"Lunch? Bring me back some. Please?"

"Oh, Hunter," she said in an aggravated voice.

"The bear will starve. Honest, he will. See how pitiful he looks?" Hunter held up the bear and made a puppet of it, imitating sadness.

"Oh, all right. When is it going to be payback time?" asked Amy.

"Soon. Anything you want. Just ask. Right, Bear?" The bear nodded.

She started for the door.

"Amy?"

"What?" She gave the word exaggerated irritation.

"What is a soul mate?"

"Now that's a real good question, Hunter. You and Bear will just have to figure that one out for yourselves." The bear waved good-bye as she turned to go, and she gave a quick wave over her shoulder.

When she returned with lunch a few minutes later, Hunter was sound asleep on the bed, the bear cradled in his arms. She studied his sleeping form for a long moment, put the food on the kitchen counter, and left quietly.

* * *

"No, I didn't inform my people that I was in the vicinity," Jack was saying to Grayson Tucker. "I was restless—couldn't get those murders off my mind. Couldn't stop thinking that Rob Kittrell has to turn up soon."

Grayson drummed a pencil on his desk. "Why? Why does he have to turn up?"

"I don't have to tell you what my sources say."

Grayson's face twisted, but he didn't comment. "And so you

hung around in the yard while this intruder was in the house?"

"Of course not. I saw the man enter the house, and I was on my way to alert the guy on stakeout when the intruder came running out of the house."

"Why didn't you alert Mrs. Kittrell?"

"And create a hostage situation?"

"Could have been her grandson."

"It wasn't."

"So you got a good look at him?"

"That's enough, Tucker. I don't have to answer to you."

Grayson let a long moment pass as he stared Jack Franklin down. "I'm investigating a breaking and entering at the home of a citizen. A citizen in my town, Franklin. You're an eyewitness. I want to know if your description matches Mrs. Kittrell's."

Silence.

"Well? What did he look like?" Grayson demanded.

"You're bluffing."

"Could be. But you saw him clearly enough to know it wasn't Hunter. Mrs. Kittrell knew it wasn't Hunter. So who was it?"

"Okay, I thought it was Rob. I was going for backup to arrest him. I knew the old lady wasn't in danger. And I didn't get a good enough look at him when he ran away to say for sure who it was."

"And your partner—the one who picked you up—he could identify him?"

"No. The idiot was looking at me, thinking I was the guy he had seen going inside."

"Interesting," said Grayson.

"No, just stupid. He's back on a desk today."

"And why wasn't Mrs. Kittrell in danger?"

"Huh?" Jack's voice was abrupt.

"If Rob Kittrell is as desperate and dangerous as you say, not even his own mother would be safe."

"No more, Tucker. I've humored your hometown investigation long enough, and I don't have to answer to you regarding mine." Jack's eyes narrowed. "Now you give me Mrs. Kittrell's description so I can continue my own investigation."

"Well, you know what? You've slung a lot of bull here today, but you got one thing right. I was bluffing."

With a curse, Jack reached for the manila folder and methodically went through the contents. Grayson watched him, not offering an interpretation. Jack took a long time to do this. Occasionally, a laugh would come from low in his throat.

After watching his every move carefully, Grayson finally asked, "Precisely what part of this do you find humorous?"

"Probably the parts you don't. I suppose the coroner's report is not in yet?"

"The coroner takes time. You know that." Grayson tapped his fingers on the desk.

"I need it today."

"Do you now? And what might this sudden rush be?"

"You'll find out when you need to know," said Jack.

"I need to know now." Grayson's body language remained laid-back Southern, but the deep creases around his eyes revealed the strain of the summer.

Jack chuckled, enjoying the control. "I have sources."

Grayson stopped himself before cursing Jack and his sources. Instead, he prompted, "Go on."

"You expect me to reveal my information to the hometown

hick police?"

"Now."

Smiling arrogantly, Jack said, "I'm obtaining a search warrant. If my source is correct, we'll turn up the murder weapon."

"Where?" Grayson asked.

"Oh, that's the amusing part. That Kittrell boy's apartment."

Grayson stared at Jack for a very long time.

Finally, Jack stated carefully, "You have a problem with this."

"You are maliciously harassing one of my citizens, and you ask me if I have a problem?"

Jack stood abruptly. "This attitude is about what I would expect from you, Tucker. These are my copies, I assume?"

"Assume this, Franklin. I'm going to be watching you."

The smile returned to Jack's face. "Yeah? And why might that be?"

"I always watch snakes."

Jack's handsome face was stone. "Good for you, Tucker. Go ahead and watch. Then you can weep when I come up with the killer while you're still looking for your balls."

"Don't go near that boy unless I'm with you."

"I don't need your permission to do my job."

"That would be true," Grayson drawled slowly. "If you were doing your job."

Jack turned his back and headed for the door.

"One more thing, Franklin."

"What is it, Tucker?" Jack paused without turning around.

"Hunter Kittrell reported a pistol stolen just yesterday. If you go through with this search and if you turn up the same weapon, then you will reveal your source to me and to a judge."

Jack's foot kicked the doorsill on his way out.

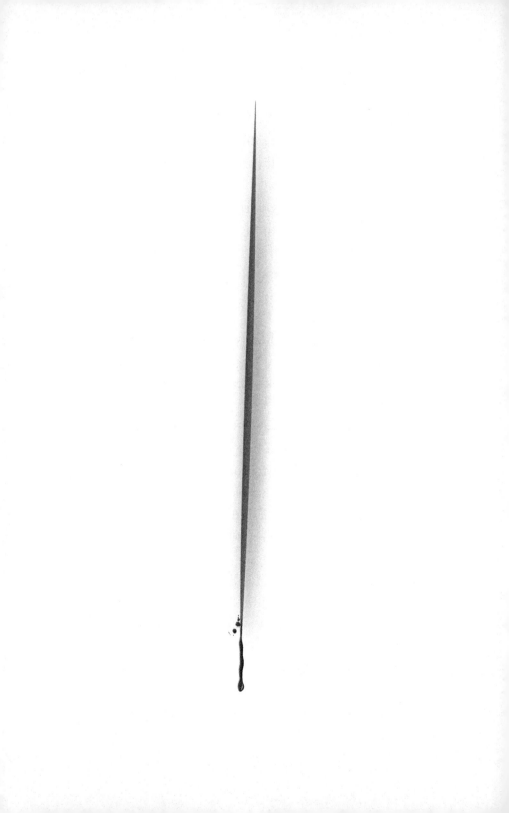

SEVENTEEN

"Open up!" The sound of a fist hammering his door jerked Hunter from dead sleep to groggy reality.

"It's not locked," he called thickly.

Two big men walked in, heavy feet on hardwood. The tromping stopped at the foot of the bed.

"Bring on the Nazis," said Hunter, rolling himself to a sitting position, still clutching the teddy bear.

"What's in the bear?" were the first words out of Jack Franklin's mouth.

"More heart than you've got," was Hunter's response. He watched impassively as Jack ripped open the bear and raped its insides with his big hand. Then, when Jack handed the gutted bear back to him, Hunter dropped his head into his hands and sat staring at the floor. He did not watch as Jack searched every inch of his room and its meager furnishings, not even glancing up as his closet was raided or as Jack opened and closed his dining chest drawer.

Grayson kept his eye on both Jack and Hunter. Finally he asked, "Is something wrong, Hunter?"

"Oh, yeah. Big time wrong. Granny Jen had heart failure this morning, compliments of your friend there. I haven't eaten since yesterday. And I only meant to sleep an hour. I've probably lost my job on top of everything."

"Save the dribble, Kittrell. Tucker, come help me pull this piece of junk away from the wall again," Jack said, indicating the dining chest.

Hunter's heart stopped. At the edge of his mind trembled a half-memory from the night before, a definite sound he had heard at the moment he woke up.

"Jack, we moved every stick of this furniture yesterday. What you're looking for today is not behind that cabinet. Now move along and let's get out of this kid's hair."

Jack cursed Grayson, grabbed the drawer of the dining chest a second time, and dumped its contents on the floor. Grayson stepped his big body in the way, even as Jack reached toward the scattered items, and said, "Enough. Get out."

"You have no authority . . ."

"Get out."

Jack was gone with a curse and a slammed door.

"I'll get that in a minute, Mr. Tucker," said Hunter as Grayson bent to return the papers and objects to the drawer.

"You eat something, Hunter," responded Grayson. "You'll feel better."

Hunter went to his kitchen counter, opened the cooler Amy had brought, and began pulling containers out. When he had the counter scattered with food, Grayson commented, "Looks like you've got a regular buffet here."

"Amy," Hunter laughed as he grabbed a fork and dug in.

"This has your name on it." Grayson handed Hunter an envelope from among the papers he was returning to the drawer.

Hunter took the envelope and continued eating, studying the handwriting.

Grayson had lifted the drawer and was fitting it back in the cabinet when Hunter said, "Wait. What does that say underneath?"

Looking at the underside of the drawer, Grayson read, "J. Hunter, 1848."

"Cool," was the only response.

Grayson helped himself to a soda and stood as Hunter devoured his meal. When the young man slowed eating and sighed deeply, Grayson asked, "Where's the gun, Hunter?"

There was a slight squint, just enough.

"You have it, don't you?"

"If I do, I'm hung."

"Without it, it will be mighty hard to hang the killer."

Hunter nodded and looked away.

After studying him a few seconds, Grayson said, "Think about it," and plodded wearily down the steps.

The Cat grew restless. Beaufort was steamy, boring, sometimes stinky. Tourists were in the way. The games he invented to amuse himself grew stale. His next mark, the fourth on his list of low-life drug pushers, was taking his sweet time coming down the waterway.

Still, he had an interesting diversion. His network was luring in one mark, the next-to-last on his list, even now. This meant number four and number five could potentially be executed the same day. And, as an added bonus, he was about to move in on a small-time dealer working out of a house on a side street just at the edge of the historic district. Planning the scenarios, working out the logistics of making all three executions happen within a short time frame, provided a very satisfying rush. After that, just two more weeks and he would be done with Beaufort. He must wait until August for his final, most brilliant execution.

➤ ➤ ➤

Hunter lay sprawled upon his sofa and contemplated the rising moon through his blue window. He wanted to go fishing, but he felt paralyzed by the events of the last three days, as if leaving his house might bring on another disaster. Puzzling over today's near-miss was driving him nuts. After Grayson left, Hunter had moved his dining chest and, yes, he had found a single packet of white powder, no doubt cocaine. It had taken him two seconds to feed it to his ancient toilet. Now, here was the puzzle: Jack Franklin had not brought a drug dog with him. Did that mean he didn't know about the cocaine, or did it mean he was so certain of finding it that he'd thought a dog was unnecessary? And why had cocaine been planted along with the gun? Was someone just out to get him in general or was that particular combination of weapon and drug supposed to trap him as the Kitty Killer?

And who was the killer? Franklin and Tucker were both looking for Rob Kittrell mighty hard. His stony hatred toward his father simmered alongside his confusion over his father's role in the harbor murders until Hunter thought he would explode.

With soft moonlight glowing through the blue glass panes, Hunter's window mocked him. It had not kept its promise; the father who had gone out had not come back. No longer did Hunter even want him back nor did he want him dead. He just wanted his father to be gone, period.

Hunter switched on a light and reached for the envelope Grayson had found in the drawer. He studied it, turned it over and over, and even sniffed it. It was a simple white envelope, slightly scuffed at the corners, fat from the folded pages inside. In an unfamiliar handwriting were the words: *For Hunter*. He did not open it.

After staring at the envelope for several more seconds, Hunter struck a match and touched the flame to it. The flame spread quickly, destroying the envelope and its contents. When the flame nearly touched his fingertips, he dropped the last inch of scorched paper into a dish and watched it turn to cinder. He felt pretty certain that it was a letter from his father. He wasn't sure how old it was, but it was about eighteen years too late. A letter was not going to change anything.

Miki had dumped him, Granny Jen was in the hospital, his father was worthless as dirt and probably a criminal, and now somebody wanted him in jail. Right now, it seemed all Hunter had going for him was Amy. When he had gone down to the waterfront tonight to wait for the ketch to dock, expecting to be fired, he had found a sympathetic boss. Amy had settled every-thing with old John at noon. Hunter had to admit: Amy was a great friend.

A light step bounced up his stairs. In his mind flashed an image of Amy: a sparkle of blue eyes, surprise of dimples, delight-ful tangle of curls. He could almost smell the perfume she wore, something pleasant and warm, faintly vanilla. With a chuckle, he turned toward the door. Miki stood in the doorway, willowy against the moonlight.

"Hey, Babe. Whatcha want?" he asked.

"Hi, Hunter. Are you okay?"

"Sure."

"I need to tell you something."

"Well, come on in and sit on my lovely sofa and enjoy my superb decorating."

"No, I can't stay." She stood just inside, her hair up, elegant in a perfectly-fitted silk dress.

"You look fantastic." He stood up and walked toward her, watching her face carefully.

Her smile was vague, distant. Hunter thought that she no longer looked like a funky rich lady from the yachts. She just looked plain rich, and he felt outclassed.

"I have something to tell you," she repeated.

"Okay."

"Jack is out to get you."

"No!" He copped a pose, hand on his hip. "You're making this up."

"Don't joke, Hunter. He says he's going to catch you at something."

"Why are you telling me this?" asked Hunter.

She shrugged. "You know. We were—us."

"But we're not us anymore."

"Things change. We always knew it wouldn't last."

He let that pass. "So are you happy?" He touched her face, but she would not look into his eyes.

"I don't know. Sure. It's something different. Look, I've got to go." She backed away.

"Are you afraid of him?" He searched her face for the truth.

"Of course not." She turned away and opened the door. "Don't start that again. I need to go back."

"Miki."

"What?" She started down the steps.

Hunter followed her out the door. "Please don't let him take you away from here."

"He's not going anywhere. He's working. Look, I'm not coming back to see you. And you stay away from me, okay?"

"No."

"I mean it." She was halfway down the steps by now, and he stood on the landing. "I've said all I came to say. Good-bye."

"No."

"Please." She looked up at him. Even in the moonlight, her face was perfect: high cheekbones, full, sensuous lips.

"I already told you." Hunter kept his voice low and even. "If I want to check on you every day, I will."

"Don't expect me to speak to you." She started toward the

street. "Oh, by the way, how's your granny?"

"They say she'll be fine. She may come home in a couple of days. Come by and see her."

"No. That's not a good idea. 'Bye, Hunter."

He watched her go until her elegant figure was lost to the night's shadows.

$$\bullet \quad \bullet \quad \bullet$$

Miki took her shoes off and walked quickly down Beaufort's cracked sidewalks. She had only a few minutes before Jack returned. Guests were coming by for a late nightcap. Jack expected her to be poised, polished. Tonight she needed something to help her be those things, and she knew a house at the edge of the historic district where she could buy just what she needed.

As she neared the house, she slowed her pace. The house was familiar by moonlight, but she had never approached it this early, only ten-thirty. The front light was off.

There was a light in back, however. This frightened her a little, as she had guessed the heavy deals took place there. Still, she knew what she wanted. Maybe Gus, the dealer, would have his wife take care of her in the front.

Cement steps led up to a wooden porch. Warped boards creaked in the stillness. Her light tap sounded ponderous to her ears. There were no answering footsteps, no scuffle of hiding. Nothing.

The paneled front door was open. Looking through the screen door, Miki could see a sliver of light coming from a doorway at the back of the small house. She guessed the room to be the kitchen.

She knocked again. The sliver of light opened a substantial crack. Good; they heard her. The screen door creaked rustily as she stepped inside. From beyond the crack of light came a low, male laugh, then the murmur of voices.

Miki stood just within the doorway, in the living room of the house, unsure whether to call out. Something silky brushed her leg. She jumped, and a kitten skittered sideways, tail up. She bent and picked it up, stroking its fur, and decided to leave.

Just as her hand reached back to open the screen door behind her, her eyes caught the silhouette of a man moving beyond the crack of light, casting a shadow on the floor. Her angle did not allow her to see clearly into the room, but the silhouette seemed to belong to a big man, bigger than Hunter, definitely bigger than the wiry Gus, whom she had come to see.

There was a grunt and a strangled cry from within the room that was too deep and awful to be a scream. She heard a door slam, a heavy sound; perhaps it was the back door of the house. And then Gus tumbled into view through the kitchen door, light following him, his body flailing and falling into the living room just eight feet away from her. His eyes were wide and staring straight into hers with a wordless scream of horror. She saw blood on his face, blood on the door, blood crashing with his body to the floor, blood on his hand that reached toward her.

She choked on the scream that caught in her throat, paralyzed by terror. One step at a time, she backed out the door, still holding her shoes, unable to look away from the blood. The screen door banged as she stepped onto the porch, and she ran, dropping her shoes in the middle of the street, rocks hurting her bare feet. Glass cut her foot, and she gasped in pain, but still she ran. Strands of hair fell from the elegant twist; sweat soaked her silk dress. She ran four blocks to the waterfront and kept running, her feet hammering the boardwalk, and she did not slow down until she reached the ramp. She was still clutching the kitten. Neighbors looked at her curiously. Jack would be home any minute. Guests would arrive very soon.

She did not remember dropping the cat on deck as she hurried into the cabin. Washing her hands over and over, she could only think of blood, and she would not look in the mirror as she rinsed her face. A mew from the kitten caused her to look up, and she saw that blood had tracked behind her across the salon and the stateroom carpet. She screamed, high and out of control.

And then she put a hand to her face and waited for what she knew would come next. "Miss Stone? Miss Stone, are you all right?" a neighbor called.

"Yes, Mr. Fearington. Sorry. I cut my foot, but I'm okay now."

The kitten mewed again, and Miki dropped to the floor and inspected her foot. A nasty gash, blood still flowing. Sobbing, she washed the cut, and sat on the edge of the bed, pressing a cloth to her foot.

She was still there when Jack walked in and dropped her shoes on the bed, his masculine cologne heavy in the small cabin. "You shouldn't have been there," he said. The light was dim, and his handsome face was stone in shadow.

"What?"

"You should never, ever have gone there."

She stared at him dumbly, feeling herself shrink.

"I was on stakeout. We were about to go in when who should saunter up on the porch but my own little darling? My own beautiful, elegant, dressed-up, dope-head of a darling."

"Don't . . ."

He held up a finger. "Do you realize," he said as he leaned closer, his breath tobacco and mint, "do you realize I almost had him in my hands?"

She shook her head, barely.

"Almost. One signal from me, and my partner would have gone in the back door, BOOM, and I would have gone in the front, BANG, and I would have had the Cat in my *hands*. And maybe your little pusher friend would be alive now. In jail, but alive."

She stopped breathing.

"But no. There was my little darling by the door, and I couldn't do a damn thing. Not one thing." His voice stretched in anger.

Miki wasn't sure if the mewling she heard came from the kitten or her own horrified soul.

"So there's the damn kitty," he said. "We looked that house over for the blasted thing. I knew there had to be one."

A sob rattled in her throat.

"Oh, now, don't cry. Two minutes and our guests will arrive."

"No, I can't."

"Yes, you can and will because you owe me that much. And because you're learning from old Jack what it takes to be a woman. You do want to leave that waif of a girl behind, don't you, Miki?"

She didn't respond.

"Let's see that foot . . . unfortunate. Yes, it could probably use a few stitches." After rummaging through a compartment, he applied antiseptic and pressed a large bandage to the cut, his hands firm and businesslike.

"That will hold you for an hour or so. You may keep your foot propped up. But you will smile, and you will charm these people, because that's what I expect. You know, you could have been busted tonight, or caught in the crossfire, if I hadn't been there." He moved around behind her, his weight settling on the bed. "You do see what you owe me."

"I feel faint, Jack. I can't . . ."

"Of course you're faint. You've seen too much to take in." Deftly, he began taking the remaining pins from her hair, smoothing the tangles with his fingers. "Tell me what you saw. Exactly."

"It was dark—ouch."

"Shh. This has to hurt if I'm going to get rid of these knots in one minute. Tell me, exactly."

"Honest. I couldn't see much. But I think the man was big."

"Big? You mean, tall, like your Kittrell boy?"

"No, big. Broader. Like, like a grown man."

He chuckled low. "You see, there is a difference. You have learned something from your Jack."

"Don't joke. Gus is dead." And she began to sob, gasping and shaking.

"Stop that. There's no time for that now."

"There was blood, Jack. Blood all over. Everywhere." Her voice was anguished.

"And it was horrible, and you shouldn't have been there, but you did see it, and now you're going to have to suck it up."

"But why?"

"Because no one besides me knows who these belong to." He tapped the shoes. "You were at a murder scene, which happened to occur in the middle of a failed drug bust. How do I, the senior agent, explain your presence? I can't. So you must act as if nothing is wrong. I mean tonight, tomorrow, and the day after that. We will smile and converse with our guests for an hour or so. They will think you cut your foot on the beach. The emergency room doctor will think you cut your foot on the beach when he sews it up. If you must cry, it will be later, when we're alone."

Footsteps tromped on the wooden ramp. Miki looked toward the deck and let out a sob, her eyes unfocused from the horror she had seen.

"Let me see your *best* smile," Jack demanded.

She smoothed her face with her hands, wiping the tears and distress from her cheeks. Dutifully, she spread her mouth into a smile.

"Have you not been listening to me? Your *best* smile." He took her face in both hands, his thumbs lifting the skin at her temples, his eyes demanding that she obey.

Drawing in a deep breath, she let it out slowly and looked into the mirror. She was an actress, playing a part, and she rearranged her features from those of terrified girl into those of a beautiful woman: classic smile, chin lifted, eyes glittering unnaturally.

"Better. Now, twist your hair back up and come on out on the deck. Your glass will be beside mine, straight orange juice, no alcohol. Don't give me that look. You said you felt faint, and the OJ will help."

He stopped in the doorway, his back to her. "How sure are you it wasn't the Kittrell boy you saw?"

"Jack."

"Tell me."

"Okay. I had just left Hunter's house. I only stopped by for a minute, honest."

"Yes, I know. I just wanted to see if you would tell the truth."

"You were following me?"

"No. We've been following him. Thanks for your honesty." And his voice rose, gracious and charming, as he greeted his guests topside.

With trembling fingers, Miki twisted her hair, scattering pins. The tears rose and poured down her cheeks. Opening a bedside compartment, she pulled out Vodka and drank deeply from the bottle. Composure, or at least a cold mask, settled once again over her features. Then she wadded her hair, secured it with an elastic band, and joined Jack's guests, hair and face half-hidden under a smart, red hat.

EIGHTEEN

Jack stepped off his yacht early the next morning to find Grayson Tucker sitting on the nearest boardwalk bench, legs crossed, arms folded across his chest. He looked relaxed, Panama hat pulled low against the rising sun.

"You don't waste time, do you, Tucker? Might as well give you last night's details, I guess."

"Mmm."

"There's not much to tell. We got there a couple of minutes late for a bust. Just a couple of minutes, and we would have had him."

"Mmm."

Jack studied him. "What is this, pout time because you weren't called? It was pretty much a rerun of the other homicides. You've read the report, I'm sure."

"No cat."

"No, but I have a theory."

"Let's hear it." Grayson scratched his ear and refolded his arms.

"The door was open, and the screen not latched. Maybe there was a cat, and it ran away."

"Which door?"

"The front," said Jack.

"So you think the killer ran out the front?" asked Grayson, shifting his position on the bench. He looked up at Jack, squinting into the morning sun, the creases deep around his eyes.

"Could be. I'm going back now to look it over in the daylight."

"Where were you?"

"What are you implying?" Jack asked, his voice cold.

"How long did you watch the house before going in? How many minutes behind him do you think you were?"

"It's all in the report. Read it, Barney Fife," Jack growled.

"I did read it, and I just can't figure out how you managed to miss somebody running out the front. Had to be a matter of seconds."

"Timing is everything. In this case, it was against us."

"Mmm."

"Look, I'm as sick as you are over this. I was *this* close to having him in my hands."

"Seconds," said Grayson, still squinting up at him.

"Hell, I can't talk to you. I'm going to work." Jack dismissed Grayson with a wave and started to walk away.

"So you're going to search Hunter Kittrell's place again?" asked Grayson.

"Huh?"

"Well, there's been another murder. According to you, Hunter or his father is involved. Now would be a prime time to search, if you're going to."

"That's been a dead end twice." Jack's eyes narrowed as he spoke.

"Oh? Hunter had a knife in his kitchen. Straight, thin blade just like the coroner said was used in the first three murders. I didn't see you take it for evidence either time you searched his apartment."

"Well, you confiscate it if you're so smart," Jack snapped. "I'm headed in other directions today, like the crime scene, where one would assume you'd want to be, instead of here harassing me."

"I'm guessing something happened to change your mind about Hunter."

"The boy barely left his place at all after we were there, if you must know."

"And nobody visited him? Maybe dropped something off with him?"

"You're losing your mind, Tucker. I can conduct this investigation alone while you try to find what brains you ever had again."

"Good." Grayson pulled dark sunglasses from his pocket, put them on, and kept his seat.

Jack stalked away without a backward glance.

Hunter slept later than usual. When he let himself in Granny Jen's kitchen, hair tousled, shirt off, drawstring pants low on his hips, he was startled to see Aunt Winnie in her robe, sipping coffee.

"Oh, hi. I thought you spent the night at the hospital," he said, reflexively pulling up the pants.

"She was sleeping well, so I came on in sometime after midnight." She eyed him sideways, "Your light was still on."

"Yeah. Couldn't sleep. I worked late on some drawings."

"Good for you." She sipped her coffee. "You know, if your music hadn't been quite so loud, you might have heard me come in."

"Oh, sorry. I'll keep it down tonight." He sliced a banana over his cereal, avoiding her eyes.

"Mother may come home this afternoon."

"Great."

"She'll be in a wheelchair for a few days. I'm going to need some help around here."

"Sure." Hunter chanced a glance at Winnie. Even though she was still in her robe, her dark hair, peppered with gray, was smoothly brushed into a short, neat bob.

"Who's been doing your laundry?" she asked.

He eyed her suspiciously. "Eloise? You know, Granny Jen's maid?"

"Well, I let Eloise go this morning. She had become sloppy in her work."

"Okay," he said carefully.

"So you see what I'm saying."

He smiled, slow and easy. "I'll tell you what. You do the laundry, and I'll do the cooking."

"Such a charmer. Just like your daddy."

He stared at her, cereal forgotten.

"Why are you looking at me like that?" she asked.

"Tell me about my father."

"Why? You've never asked about him before."

"I have a sudden burning need to know," said Hunter. "Have you seen him? Heard from him?"

She studied him over her coffee. "Rob and I weren't close.

There was the age difference, you know."

Hunter studied her in return. He'd never thought about it, but she must be, what, fifty-five or older? Her grandchildren would be nearly teenagers by now.

"Surely, in all these years, he's called you," Hunter persisted.

She hesitated before answering, "No. But he did call Donnie a few times."

"Uncle Donald? He never told me that."

"He would tell you now, I think. Now that you're old enough."

"Old enough for what?"

She shrugged and set her coffee cup down. "Rob did ask about you. You and Mother."

"So, he knew I was alive. Why didn't he ever send a birthday card? Or you know, like, graduation money?" His voice was carefully indifferent.

"I can't answer that. There was certainly no excuse for what he did." She was silent.

"So, how's Uncle Paul?"

"Don't change the subject. I'm thinking how to say this."

"Just spit it out. It's easier."

She laughed shortly. "Well, the last time he called was just before Donnie got sick. Seems he was in trouble with the law and wanted Donnie to hide him."

"Did he?"

"No. Donnie begged Rob to turn himself in."

"Why? Why wouldn't he help him?"

"This is difficult, I know. What your father needed was a chance to start over, make things right. He didn't need to perpetuate the life he was living."

Hunter wasn't even aware he had closed his eyes until he felt Winnie's hand on his arm. "Many people love you, Hunter. I know that doesn't make up for your father, but it matters. You're turning out okay."

"Yeah. I guess." He stood abruptly. "Hey, I've got to go. Granny Jen must wonder where everybody is this morning."

"Wait, Hunter. Have you heard from your mother lately?"

He sighed. "She's left me several messages on my cell phone. She's mainly pissed off that I managed to find a dead body." He started out.

"She's just very worried about you, I'm sure," said Winnie. "You should call her back."

"No thank you. She's pissed off, just like usual, and I don't want to hear it. See ya."

"Wait. Doesn't she usually come down around your birthday in August? This is a big one coming up, isn't it? Twenty-one?"

"Maybe if I'm lucky, she'll forget."

* * *

"That's him. Sitting on that bench." The morning quiet of the waterfront was interrupted by a crisp voice.

Grayson flinched but kept his seat on the bench, arms still folded. He stared at the water, his eyes hidden by the dark glasses.

"Mr. Tucker! Chief Tucker! When are you going to make an arrest?" The man who belonged to the voice rushed to stand in front of Grayson, breathless as if he had chased Grayson to the bench. His extended arm held a microphone in Grayson's face, and he adjusted the pack on his back, impatiently waiting for a response. A cameraman joined him, hovering to Grayson's left.

Grayson sighed and slowly looked up at the reporter. He had been expecting this. In the two days since Doug Sanders' murder, he had managed to avoid the infestation of national news media while his harassed staff handled the reporters as best they could. With one more murder to feed to the public, Grayson had known the media sharks would be circling today.

"Five murders in your town. People are in a panic. They're not safe inside their own homes. What are you going to do about it, Chief Tucker?" The voice was insistent; the microphone was stuck more emphatically under Grayson's nose. When Grayson did not quickly answer, the man demanded, "Give us your statement."

"You're standing way too close, kid," Grayson drawled. He held the reporter's eyes until the man eased the microphone away a half-inch. Grayson motioned with his hand, and a second camera crew, which had been fast approaching from his right, rushed up. A uniformed police officer joined Grayson from behind. The first reporter grudgingly backed away another inch.

Grayson cocked his head to one side, still looking at the first reporter. "Where are you from, kid?" he asked.

"Philadelphia." The clipped voice was impatient. "Chief Tucker, surely you . . ."

"Do you see this officer?" Grayson's Southern voice was conversational.

"Mr. Tucker . . ."

"This man has barely seen his children in five weeks." Grayson tormented the antsy reporter with deliberately slow words.

"Why do you think the killer picked Beaufort?" the reporter persisted.

"*I* have slept very little in five weeks." Grayson raised his eyebrows at the reporter, daring him to interrupt again. "This is our home, and the people you have labeled panicked are our friends and families."

"Exactly." The second reporter moved closer. "These people are expecting . . ."

"These people are expecting something I can't give them," said Grayson quickly. "Beaufort is a small town, and I have a small department." He looked from one camera to the other. "Here is my statement. Get it down right, because I will not repeat it."

The reporters waited, cameras rolling.

"This killer is a professional, and he knew how to kill before he ever came to Beaufort."

"So you're sure the killer's not a local?" the first reporter interrupted.

Grayson raised his eyebrows at the man once again. The man backed off, but the second reporter moved in.

"How can anyone kill five times and not get caught in a town this size? Where is he hiding, Chief Tucker?" Once again, two microphones were stuck in Grayson's face. Grayson stared both reporters down. A third crew rushed up, the camera guy still chewing his breakfast.

"What do you think about the reports . . ." the third reporter began.

"I have one thing to say and one thing only," Grayson drawled in his deep voice. "The State Bureau of Investigation is handling this case along with the DEA and FBI. These agencies have highly specialized crime labs and investigators who are trained to track down professional killers. They will find this killer very soon. My department will do all it can to protect the town's citizens. It would be very helpful if you reporters would stand back and let us do our jobs. That is all I have to say."

"Are you doing your job now, Chief Tucker?"

"Are you saying the investigators know who they're looking for?"

"What, in your opinion, is the profile of the killer?"

"Are you investigating the shooting of the tourist as a separate case?"

"Have you taken anyone in for questioning?"

"What do you know about the reports that a former resident with drug connections has been seen in the area?"

Grayson held up a hand. "You have thirty seconds to back away from me fifty feet or this officer will arrest you all for impeding an investigation." The reporters hesitated. "Thirty seconds," Grayson repeated. All three crews stepped back one step. The officer behind Grayson moved his hand closer to his gun. "And let your cohorts know that we will arrest anyone who hinders us from doing our jobs." When the reporters hesitated again, he added in a deep Southern drawl, "And ya'll don't even want to know where my good friend the judge will put you if you don't comply." Hastily, the reporters retreated.

When they were a safe distance away, Grayson asked the officer in a low voice, "Who in this town has been talking about Rob Kittrell?"

The officer shook his head and shrugged.

"Find out," said Grayson. He refolded his arms and stayed on his bench.

❋ ❋ ❋

Around lunchtime, Jack Franklin returned to his yacht. There sat Grayson, arms still folded, on the same bench. "Are you still here?" Jack demanded. "You know, people are going to start talking—a town full of homicides, and the chief of police sitting on his can."

"Good," said Grayson, nodding his head.

Jack glanced at the camera crews hovering fifty feet away and walked to his yacht, frowning.

A while later, Hunter walked by, dressed for work. He gave Grayson a wave, then walked boldly up to Jack's yacht. "Miki!" he called.

Jack stepped on deck. "Be quiet, boy. Miki's asleep. By the way, you're trespassing again, right in front of the law."

"I want to see her. I need to know if she's all right."

"Actually, she's not all right. She cut her foot at the beach, and we were in the emergency room nearly all night. She's sleeping in today."

Hunter backed away, dodged a reporter who tried to speak to him, and approached Grayson. "Uh, Mr. Tucker, can I ask you a question?" he asked.

"Sure."

"Have you seen Miki?"

"The blonde?"

"Yeah."

"Not today," said Grayson.

"Well, maybe he was telling the truth." Hunter glanced at Jack's yacht.

"That she cut her foot at the beach?"

"Yeah."

"Do you find that odd?" asked Grayson.

"I don't know," Hunter shrugged.

"Does anything about that strike you as odd?"

"Now that you mention it, she was all dressed up last time I saw her." Hunter kept his voice low, aware of the reporters.

"What time was that?"

"I don't know. A little after ten. She stopped by my apartment."

"So how long did she stay?"

"Two minutes maybe."

"Would you say she left before ten-thirty?" Grayson asked.

"I guess. Why?"

"She was all dressed up when I saw her, too. About ten-forty-five. Running to beat hell right across there. You can see tracks of blood."

Hunter stared at him, silent.

"Last time I looked, the beach was over yonder." Grayson gestured loosely, took off his hat, ran a hand through his thinning hair, and put the hat back on.

"Huh." Hunter shifted his feet. "You know, I've got to get to work."

"She was carrying something furry."

"Furry?" Hunter asked.

"You didn't give her a cat, did you?"

"Uh, no."

"Mmm." Grayson looked out at the water. "Hunter, you need to lay low," he said in a quiet voice. "When those reporters figure out who you are, they'll be all over you."

"Sure. I can do that," said Hunter, and he sauntered past the reporters toward his job aboard the *Pirate's Lady.*

Grayson watched him go, noting the smooth way Hunter swung himself onto the deck of the ship, the easy way he went about his duties. Within days, Grayson knew, investigators planned to haul Hunter in for questioning about Doug Sanders' murder. Grayson was sure Hunter knew how much trouble that one dead guy had gotten him into, but Hunter would never know that Grayson was the only reason the SBI had not questioned him before now. The police chief had personally guaranteed that Hunter was not going to run. He had not yet told the state investigators that Hunter was probably hiding the murder weapon. The gun wasn't going anywhere, and Grayson figured the kid could use a break for a few days. Now that reporters were already asking about Rob Kittrell, though, Hunter's break was bound to be short-lived.

> ⟶ ⟶ ⟶

"Granny Jen! It's really you," exclaimed Hunter as he stepped onto the porch for breakfast the next morning.

"Yes, I got home late yesterday evening. Sorry I couldn't stay up until you got in from work last night. Winnie made me go to bed early."

"Mother, you needed your rest," called Winnie from the kitchen. A rank fishy odor drifted from the kitchen to the porch.

"How do you like my new wheels?" asked Granny Jen, patting the arm of her wheelchair.

"Mega-cool. We'll go pop wheelies around the neighborhood later," said Hunter.

"No, you will not," Winnie argued from the kitchen.

"Honestly, I feel better than I have in a few weeks," said Granny Jen. "But they want me to take it easy a few more days. Maybe one evening when you're off, you can stroll me down to the waterfront."

"Absolutely not," said Winnie. "People are getting killed down there."

"Aunt Winnie's right, Granny Jen. Things are a little tense at the harbor these days."

"I just don't understand why they can't catch this guy," said Granny Jen. "They've got the SBI and federal agents all over town."

"He's slick," said Hunter.

"Mother, you shouldn't even let yourself think about that," came from Winnie.

"And I'm worried about your Miki," continued Granny Jen without missing a beat. "Everybody in town knows that Franklin guy is an agent. Surely the killer knows it, too. Franklin and Miki could both be murdered in their bed."

"Mother . . ."

"And what's this all about?" she demanded, pointing to a front page photo of Grayson sitting on the bench at the boardwalk. "The editor seems to think Grayson has taken a vacation from investigating."

"Uh," Hunter recovered slowly from open-mouthed shock at her words, "actually, I think he may just now be starting."

"He'd better be. Look, there's Jim Harrison sitting next to him and Ila Hutchens just walking up in the picture. If he keeps sitting there, the whole town will get up a lynch mob."

"This conversation is too upsetting for you, Mother," said

Winnie as she marched in carrying two steaming plates. She set the plates in front of Hunter and Granny Jen and marched back to the kitchen.

Hunter and his grandmother stared at their plates.

"What is this, Aunt Winnie?" Hunter finally asked.

"Heart food. Creamed codfish over toast. Steamed asparagus."

"Oh." He speared a limp wad of asparagus and held it at eye level above his plate, a mixture of disbelief and disgust claiming his usually impassive face.

"For breakfast?"

Granny Jen began to sputter.

"I thought I was going to do the cooking, Aunt Winnie," Hunter called.

"I decided I could manage. You have your job to attend to," Winnie answered back from the kitchen.

"Oh, but I insist," he said, and Granny Jen hooted in laughter.

＊ ＊ ＊

Hunter stepped off the *Pirate's Lady* that night to find Amy waiting for him. "Hi. Have you come to collect?" he asked.

"Collect?"

"Whatever it is I owe you."

"Oh," she laughed. "I just thought I'd see if you wanted a ride to the beach."

"Why aren't you there already?" asked Hunter, starting down the boardwalk.

"Dad had me going over his accounts. I'm just now getting off work," Amy said.

"Bummer. There's something I've got to do first," said Hunter. "Come with me."

Amy hung back. "Well . . . there's not much time before Mr. Tucker's curfew."

"It won't take long. Come on." He walked quickly along the boardwalk, and without hesitation, started down the ramp toward Jack's yacht.

"Hunter, are you crazy?" asked Amy.

"Yeah. C'mon. Maybe they won't run me off as fast if you're with me." Hunter motioned for her and waited until Amy caught up before he approached the yacht.

"Hi, Miki," he said softly to the figure on the deck.

There was a slight movement, no response.

"How's your foot?"

"Hurts."

"I'm sorry," Hunter said. "You feel like going to the beach with us?"

"No, she doesn't," Jack's voice spoke from behind him. Without turning, Hunter realized Jack had stepped off a neighboring yacht and had moved behind him, blocking his exit.

"Miki?"

"No, Hunter. I told you to stay away from me."

"There, that's all I need," Jack said. "I'm taking out a restraining order on you tomorrow."

"Jack, that's really not necess—" Miki began.

"Evidently it is. Kittrell here can't seem to get it through his head that this is private property, and you don't want to see him."

Hunter didn't turn around. "Where did you cut your foot, Babe?"

She gestured loosely and gave him a beseeching look.

"I told you where yesterday," Jack said sharply. "If you kids didn't leave your garbage on the beach—step back, Kittrell."

Hunter had whirled abruptly while Jack was speaking, his face two inches from Jack's.

"Hunter, let's get out of here," Amy said softly, pulling his arm.

Jack gave them both an appraising stare. "Why do you keep chasing my Miki? Isn't this girl's piece enough for . . ."

There was a solid smack of flesh striking flesh, and Hunter found his right arm in a vise-like grip. More quickly than he could think, he had thrown a punch, and even more quickly, Jack had caught his arm before his fist made contact.

"I just did you a favor, Kittrell." Jack's voice was low and distinct, his grip hard. "If you had touched me, I would have had to decide whether to arrest you or just kill you."

Feeling a tug from Amy on his left arm, Hunter stepped back, and Jack released him. Without another word, Amy and Hunter walked away.

"Damn," he said when they neared Amy's car.

"Shh," Amy warned.

"*Damn!*" Hunter said more loudly. "I never saw anything like it. Unbelievable reflexes. His face never changed expression. Did you even see his hand move?"

Not answering, Amy got in her car, and Hunter followed suit. "And he lied through his teeth! I know Miki cut her foot somewhere besides the beach."

Amy put the key in the ignition but didn't start the car. When he looked at her, there were tears brimming in her eyes.

"Oh man, Amy, what that jerk said about you. I'm so sorry."

She waved his remark away impatiently. Grabbing a ballcap off the dashboard, she put it on, tugging her thick ponytail through the back, collecting herself.

"You've been in the middle of my messed-up life all summer," he finally said.

"No." She shook her head quickly, ponytail flipping. "I think you're just now getting your act together. Miki is the messed-up one. I feel so sorry for her I could cry. She looks so lost."

Hunter stared at her in silence.

"And I think she's in a dangerous situation. That man is mean and trained, Hunter. He threatened to kill you."

After a pause, Hunter said softly, "So you see why I can't let her go, no matter what he threatens?"

"Absolutely! I think she desperately needs to know someone cares for her, because I don't think she cares about herself anymore."

"How did you get all that this quickly?"

Amy smiled as she started the engine. "Maybe I have a heart like Granny Jen's." She looked Hunter in the eye. "But you've got to stay away from him. There's no telling what he'll do to you or Miki if he sees you come back."

When she reached for the gearstick, Hunter's hand closed lightly over her arm. Softly, he said, "When I do get her away from him, I don't think she and I will ever be—you know—again."

He caught a quick flash of dimples before she looked away.

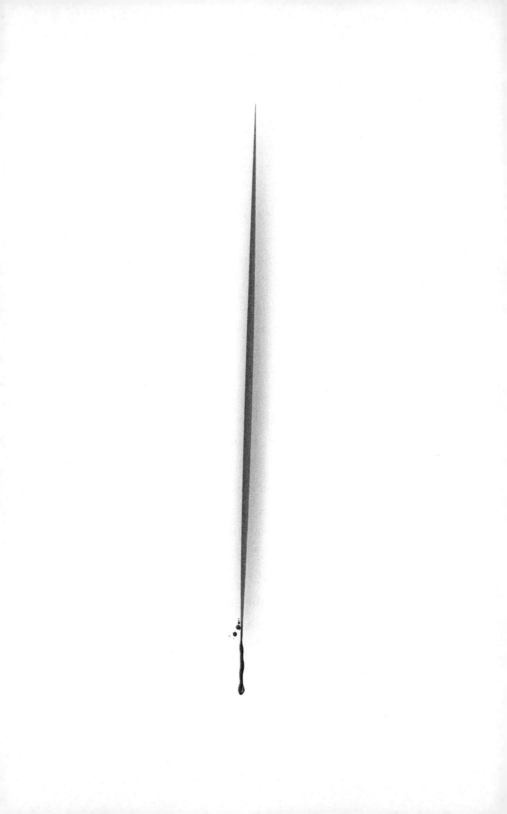

NINETEEN

She moved easily through the crowd, enjoying the stares. Polished perfection. The men who stared had wealth, influence. They may have wanted her, but they would never touch her. The women who stared envied her. Or hated her.

Joining Jack at the bar, Miki put a smooth hand on his arm. His smile was approving. It gave her a rush, being with Jack in a crowd, being his woman when a roomful of attractive women sought his attention. Deep creases marked his cheeks instead of dimples, giving his face a distinctly masculine, adventurous appearance. The lines around his eyes crinkled in amusement at the women with whom he flirted. Man or woman, anyone who stepped into his space felt the crackle of excitement that emanated from his presence. He was dark, handsome, a man in his prime. She was beautiful, elegant, all any man could desire. Together, they turned heads.

Everyone on the waterfront now knew his occupation. So he wasn't the wealthy owner of that sleek yacht in their midst. It didn't matter. He seemed even more exciting, dangerous. They all waited to see him crack the case no one else could.

In particular, one pair of eyes followed the couple's every move, expectant.

* * *

Hunter knocked on the door of the brick ranch home that sat several blocks away from the waterfront. The door was opened by a woman, whose broad face broke into a wide smile when she saw him on her doorstep.

"Well, hello, Hunter. How are you?"

"Okay, Eloise. I hate to barge in on you like this, but . . ."

"I've been expecting you." Eloise sized him up wisely. "Is your Aunt Winnie getting the best of you?"

"She thinks people actually eat codfish."

She laughed a rich, melodious laugh and waved him inside.

"I'm sorry about her firing you."

"Oh, she hasn't fired me. I'm just taking a paid vacation." In answer to his raised eyebrows, she added, "Jen and I had already discussed what we'd do when Winnie came in and put me out."

"You can't get much over on Granny Jen," he said lightly, maybe too lightly.

"Not a thing." She paused. "Your granny's going to live until the Lord calls her home, Hunter. Don't worry about her. She's in good hands."

He sighed and looked away.

"So which of my famous recipes do you want?"

"All of them."

She laughed again, warm and low. Eloise had cooked and cleaned for Granny Jen three mornings a week for many years. Her fried chicken and roast beef were legendary. "You know I don't tell my secrets to just anybody."

"This is life and death. We're talking asparagus for breakfast."

"A little greenery won't hurt you, young man."

"Please, Eloise. All I can do is cook fish. Aunt Winnie will fire me in two days."

"Lord, what a smile. Sit yourself down here at my table first and eat some home cooking. Then I'll tell you my secrets."

She served him fried okra, crisp and peppery, butter beans, sweet and creamy, and barbeque, the Down East kind. "It takes hot oil, corn meal, and plenty of pepper to make this okra, Hunter," Eloise told him. "And cook your butter beans with real butter, a pod of okra, and a teaspoon of sugar. And no more than a spoonful of sugar in your barbeque sauce. Use plenty of vinegar, black pepper, red pepper, and hot sauce. You want it to bite you back."

He laughed and nodded his head.

"You just have to roll up your sleeves and try it, Hunter. The main thing is to clean up the mess you make or your Aunt Winnie will fire you in one day."

"Can I call you if I get stuck?"

"I've cooked my daughter's supper over the phone many a time."

He stood to leave. "Do you have a map to the grocery store?"

She swatted him lightly on the backside. "Get out of here."

Impulsively, he hugged her. "Take care, Eloise."

She hugged him back, then tightened her grip. "Hunter, there's something I should give you. I think it's time."

He stiffened and made his face impassive.

"You're afraid of anything to do with your father, aren't you?"

"If only you knew."

"I do know, more than you think." She rummaged through a drawer. "Your Uncle Donald left this with me. It's a phone number where your dad can be reached."

He stared at the paper without moving.

"Here, take it. I already called and told him his mother is failing. I don't need it any longer."

"You—you talked to him?"

"No, no. It's one of those fancy answering services."

He laughed shortly. "I think he's on the lam, Eloise."

"Maybe, maybe not. But Donald said he would always get the message, no matter where he is."

"Huh. Why are you giving me this now?"

"It's time. Maybe you'll have sense enough not to throw it away."

"Maybe." He folded it carefully and pocketed it. "Don't expect me to thank you."

"Someday you will."

The Cat moved quickly. The time for restless waiting was past. The night of reckoning had come.

He entered the water without a splash, swimming effortlessly, his motions smooth and efficient. Beaufort Harbor's first underwater drug deal. His mark was excited about it, he had been told. Excited. Yes, death was exciting.

Moving away from the docks, he swam beneath several yachts toward the deep open water of the harbor. Bubbles rose in rhythmic bursts from his regulator. He had always found the sound mesmerizing. Inhale, exhale. Life and death in a simple breath.

The water was inky, and he swam by compass, not illumination. For a week, he had practiced his approach, flippers moving efficiently, mapping the coordinates, counting the strokes. Surprise was all he had. Strength and quickness were not as certain in the water as they were on land. And his time was limited.

He would deliver two executions tonight.

Ahead, he caught the signal flash. Yes, his mark was in place, periodically flashing his light, watching in the opposite direction. The mark had been told to position himself at a depth of twenty feet, in the center of the channel directly in front of a certain restaurant, and to watch for his buyer to approach from the opposite bank. The Cat had approached instead from his right at a depth of thirty feet and was now directly behind him, rising slowly to match his depth.

As he came nearer, The Cat adjusted his breathing, matching it to the bubbles he detected rising from the lone figure. Ten feet separated them. Eight. The mark was still facing the opposite direction. Knife in hand, The Cat approached carefully, and with one quick slice, the main hose from the air tank was nearly severed.

But this man was quick. Even as he reached for his alternate regulator, he made a grab behind him, his hand closing over The

Cat's own air hose. One yank, and the regulator was torn from The Cat's mouth.

And this man was no fool. As he backed away, he shone his wrist light straight into The Cat's eyes. The Cat smiled evilly at him, bubbles streaming from his mouth. Recognition. The man hesitated; The Cat did not. The knife flashed in the beam of light and made contact, but not fatally. Red spurted into the light. Another strike, and the man's alternate hose was cut.

Kicking madly, the man rose toward the surface, bubbles exploding from the severed air lines, blood spreading in the illuminated water around him. Calmly, The Cat replaced his regulator and followed. He let the man almost breathe air. Just within reach of the surface, he yanked the man's leg, pulling him under. The man kicked, deliberate hits with his flipper against The Cat's airline, ripping the main hose loose. No matter. The man's strength was ebbing, the blood flowing, the last silent bubbles escaping from his open, horrified mouth.

The Cat yanked him down once more and pinned him from behind with his legs and left arm. Hopelessly struggling, the man clawed with one free hand, fingers digging flesh. Lungs screaming for air, The Cat plunged his knife at last into the throat, a satisfying spurt of blood and air signaling the end. With one final slice of the knife, the man's buoyancy vest was ripped, and the body sank to the depths of the harbor.

Breathing at last, The Cat moved away, tasting his greatest high yet.

He was eager for the next execution.

Hunter spoke into the phone, feeling foolish, maybe a little clandestine. "Uh, this message is for Rob Kittrell. From his son. Hunter." The voice on the other end instructed him to wait for the tone. Two more seconds to think about hanging up.

"Uh, Dad, whatever you do, don't come to Beaufort. The place is crawling with cops, and they're all looking for you. Granny Jen—your mom—is a little better right now."

He breathed through a long silence and nearly hung up. "By the way, I know you don't care, but I'm going to be an architect. A damn good one." Click.

Ice. Parties reminded him of ice. You could leave for an hour and return, and the people would be frozen in the same positions. Same conversations. Same laughter. Same ice clinking in glasses. Icy courtesy.

And nobody really knew you had gone. That was the funny part. People got on an ego high, each on his own stage, posing for the same spotlight, and nobody contemplated your absence. Oh, someone might come looking for you and soon give up, assuming you were in another room, with another group, outside, in the bathroom. Somewhere. When you walked back into the room, smiling, they would know for sure. Of course, you had been *somewhere*.

In this case, Jack had been in a private room with Miki and Bob Schneider. Bob had been watching Miki all evening, drooling. At just the right hour, Jack had introduced them, had found a private room for conversation.

Bob had a nice little import business. He moved items into the country from all over the world. Most of these items wound up on people's curio shelves and mantels. Souvenirs, bric-a-brac. Sometimes his merchandise went up people's noses.

This particular yacht club set would have been truly shocked to know that about Bob. Jack wasn't. And Jack knew something else about Bob. Bob was a big fan of Vanessa Singer.

Miki enjoyed being Vanessa for Bob. She didn't mind when Jack leaned over and whispered, "I've got to talk with a guy before he leaves. I'll be back." She was just beginning to tire of the act when Jack returned, smiling approvingly. Jack and Miki rejoined the party. Charming couple.

Very late, on their deck, Jack touched her cheek. "You were great tonight."

"It was fun. I get a kick out of doing that sometimes."

"Have you always wanted to act?" asked Jack, lighting a cigarette. His eyes studied her intently.

"I always have acted, Jack," she said wearily, reaching for his drink.

"In what way?" he asked. She looked away and sipped the drink. His voice was insistent. "Tell me, Miki. I want to know."

Her voice was bitter. "I acted like my mother wasn't a slut; I acted as if I didn't care my father never showed up for my dance recitals; I acted like life was more than just something to get through." She stopped abruptly and looked away, biting her lip.

"Shh. I didn't mean to upset you." He leaned over and kissed her arm. "Look at yourself now, Miki. You've got it all. You've put that girl behind you, and you've learned how to be a woman." He touched her face and made her look at him. "When you're Vanessa Singer now, it's more than just a role for kicks. You are beautiful and exciting and *desirable*," he whispered. "To become that which you imitate is acting to its highest degree. I was very proud of you tonight."

An irritated expression crossed her face. "Is there something you want, Jack?" she asked.

He laughed a pleased, self-satisfied laugh. "My Miki. You know me so well." He kissed her on the lips. "Yes, there is something. It involves Bob Schneider."

She looked at him suspiciously.

"First, tell me what Bob said tonight about his business."

"Like what?"

"Anything I might be interested in knowing."

She cursed. "You think that little guy's a drug dealer?"

"His business may allow him the opportunity to trade certain products without actually getting his hands dirty."

"What, you're trying to catch him at it?"

"We know these products come and go from his warehouse. That's enough to put him in prison. What we lack is concrete evidence that Bob himself orders and distributes those goods."

"Does it make a difference?"

"Not to Bob. He'll still go to prison, even if he claims he knows nothing of the goods, even if we subpoena his records and find no trace of illegal activity. We'll move in early tomorrow, and I'm confident we'll have the evidence we need to charge him with possession."

"So it doesn't matter."

"In the big picture it does. If we have some proof, no matter how little, that old Bob knows exactly what illegal goods he's moving, we can push his buttons a little harder to reveal his sources, his distributors. You see, it's more difficult to do that when the person you have in custody keeps saying, 'Duh, I don't know how that cocaine got into that shipment of glassware. I'm just an honest businessman. I'm the victim here.'"

Miki laughed at his imitation. "You should have told me you wanted me to ask questions. I wondered why you wanted me to entertain him of all people."

"No, no, I didn't want you to ask questions. Just gain his confidence. Even though he's new in the harbor, he may very well know who I am. And he thinks he knows who you are, my dear."

"You think I pulled off being Vanessa?"

"He saw what he wanted to see. Other people tonight may have noticed the resemblance, the way you wore your hair, the way you walked. But they knew they were looking at Miki Stone. That's why I got you alone with him, where you could be Vanessa Singer without someone walking up and saying, 'Good evening, Miss Stone.'"

"So?"

"So he's coming over in a few minutes for a nightcap."

"A nightcap? The sun will be up soon." Miki looked out at the harbor and sipped her drink. The dark water swirled heavily on the rising tide, blurring the reflected lights from nearby yachts. "Can't we do this another time?"

"He'll be in jail by noon. Weren't you listening?" Jack leaned toward her, his voice impatient. "I have only this one chance to trap him into implicating himself."

Miki sighed and closed her eyes. Perhaps Hunter was right. Jack had wanted to use her from the start. What difference did it make? She had used Jack herself. And she did owe him for keeping her out of trouble the night Gus was killed. In a soft voice she asked, "What do you want me to do?"

"I want Vanessa Singer to ask him where she can get her hands on cocaine."

"What?"

"The harbor is swarming with narcs. Say you're cut off from your sources in Hollywood. Your local source was iced."

Miki winced.

"Don't imply he has any on him. Just ask if he knows a source." Jack looked at her appraisingly, anticipating her response. "He's the new guy in town. Innocently ask if he has connections no one else in the harbor does."

Fear replaced the composure in her eyes. "Jack, I never went to Gus for cocaine, I swear. Just pot and pills."

"Shh. I know that. You'd be in jail yourself if you had." He smiled, satisfied with himself.

"You asshole."

"No. I'm a damn good agent." He reached for her, the pressure of his hand insistent on her neck. "Help me be a better one tonight."

She looked at him icily.

"Please, Miki."

"Won't he think it's strange that Vanessa Singer would live with a narcotics agent if she did coke?"

"Not if she was as fooled by him for two months as everyone else was." He smiled at her, charming her. "Tell him that. Let that be part of your story."

"You've got it all figured out." Her voice was brisk.

"Possibly. Do this for me, Miki." He took her hand, a beseeching gesture. "I could use a break this summer. These murders are giving the agency a bad name."

"What if I fail?"

"Fail in what way?"

"Choke up," she said, her eyes bright as she anticipated her role. "Or don't get him to tell me anything."

"No harm done. We'll still have him on possession. The only way you can fail is if you push him too hard, make him nervous, or make him run."

"I won't, Jack. I promise." Miki put her hand on his arm.

"You love this, Miki; admit it. You love the excitement and glamour of being part of my life."

She smiled coolly and admitted nothing.

He disappeared for a minute and returned with a digital voice recorder.

"I'm putting this in the bottom compartment of the humidor. When I leave for a walk, get the box and offer him a cigar. Whether he takes one or not, he won't think it's unusual that you leave the humidor on deck for a few minutes while you talk. I'll return very shortly and put the humidor up, as any cigar aficionado would."

"How much time will I have?"

"About six minutes," he said, his voice businesslike. "It's okay if you act urgent. Tell him I walk the boardwalk every night before turning in and will be back very soon."

"Okay, James Bond. Do I get a kinky name like in the movies?" She was smiling as she said this.

"Sure, Miss Galore. But if I were James Bond, you would have a video recorder that fits on the end of your hairpin right there." He kissed her.

"If I pull this off, will this make up for—you know—the other night? When I messed up your bust?" she asked.

"All will be forgiven and forgotten. Grayson Tucker thinks something strange went down that night, but he'll never know what."

"Then let's do it."

A smile cut across his handsome face, and his eyes held hers a long moment before he kissed her once more.

The Cat didn't mind waiting until nearly dawn. Performing two executions in a six-hour period was a brilliant success.

Bob Schneider was surprised to see him. He complained of the late hour but invited The Cat on board.

The Cat was charming. "I apologize for the intrusion, but I have something very important to tell you."

Bob sighed. "Have a seat then. Would you like a drink?"

"No. You go ahead. You'll need one. Make it good and stiff."

When Bob turned around, he was startled to see The Cat cutting into an orange with a straight-blade knife that looked like a utility knife. "Breakfast," was the only explanation given.

Bob sat across the small table and watched juice stream from the orange with the slow fascination of a man just ending a night of cocktails. "So what's so important?" he finally asked.

"I've heard that the feds plan to arrest you before noon."

Bob swallowed hard and set the glass down, gripping it with both hands. He stared at The Cat.

The Cat slid an orange slice into his mouth, smiling slyly, the knife sharp against his lips. "You've made a mess of things, Bob," he said, his voice Southern with a local accent. "There's only one way to deal with this kind of mess."

Bob glanced right and left, as if considering his best option for escape.

The Cat sprang, his entire weight pushing against the table, and the bolts he had loosened earlier came away from the floor. With the force of his forward movement, he crushed the table top into Bob's chest. With Bob immobilized, The Cat plunged the knife into the man's throat. He watched Bob's eyes as the taste of death filled his mouth; he watched the man's private horror with satisfaction. He was strong and Bob was weak, and he wrenched the knife sideways, slicing his throat until the shocked eyes glazed dull and the last choked groan was silenced.

The Cat wiped his knife and pocketed it. Once again, he had touched no surface on his victim's boat with his bare hands. He fed the orange to the fish. Let Grayson Tucker wonder about the juice on the table, in the wound. The kitty this time was in his pocket, dead in a plastic bag. A shame, but The Cat had to be very careful. He left the cat on the floor between Bob's feet.

Two weeks, and he would be done with Beaufort.

TWENTY

"Hey, Kittrell, what's your problem?"

Hunter dribbled the basketball past his friend. "I don't have a problem, Bill," he said and hooked the ball toward the hoop where it bounced off the backboard into Bill's hands.

Bill held the ball under one arm and looked Hunter over. "Let's hear you say that again."

Hunter grinned at him and popped the ball from under Bill's arm into his own hand. "No problem," he said and shot the ball and missed again. "Okay, so I'm off."

"Off?" Bill dribbled the ball behind him, dodging Hunter's attempts to steal. "You were off last week. You've freakin' bombed today."

Smooth and easy, Hunter sprang, stole the ball from Bill, shot, and missed once again. This time he stood looking at the hoop, shaking his head in disgust. On an average day, Hunter was the envy of any kid who cared about basketball. He could reach a zone on the court, shooting hoop after hoop, almost never missing, moving effortlessly. Nobody could stop him. Hunter made the game look easy simply because he didn't care. Today was not an average day.

"You're right," said Hunter. "Let's turn it in."

"I figured all this crap about your father would have you tense," said Bill as they walked away from the court.

"What crap?" Hunter asked, his eyes narrowing.

"You know. In the paper this morning." Bill glanced at Hunter's face. "The paper came late today. You didn't read it, did you?"

"Went fishing and came straight over here. Amy's dad said there were two more murders." Hunter stopped walking and looked toward the harbor where a helicopter was circling, the second one that day.

"Some fool told one of those news freaks that they saw your father on the water. So the news freak reported that breaking news along with the blood and guts murder details. Sorry, Hunter," said Bill. "I thought you knew."

Hunter's gut felt as cold and gray as the sea in November. "I've always wanted to see the asshole hang. Maybe if I'm lucky, they'll do it for me."

"God, Hunter." Bill was taken aback. "Nobody in town's going to believe it. It's just news crap. Man, you're tense."

"Yeah." Hunter's face broke into his familiar careless smile. "I'm a little touchy on that subject is all. Mostly, I'm pissed off at myself. Those reporters have probably been in my granny's face all morning, and I haven't even been there to kick anybody's ass. I'd better get home."

"Watch your back. One of them jumped me while I was pumping gas yesterday, and I'm nobody. They'll tear you apart." They walked on, unable to talk for the irritating racket the helicopter made as it passed directly over them. When they reached the corner where they would part and the noise had become a drone in the distance, Bill said, "What's up with you and Amy?"

Hunter shrugged. "Same as always."

"Except you didn't hunt up another babe when that blonde dumped you. You've usually gone through a couple more by this point."

"Her name is Miki and what's it to you?" Hunter asked, testy.

"I wanna know. I might want to ask Amy out myself. So might a couple of other guys, but nobody wants to cross you. You know, in case you and Amy are getting back together."

"Nobody's stopping you." Hunter turned his back and walked away.

"You wanted to see me, Mr. Tucker?" Hunter joined Grayson on the bench at the waterfront, his T-shirt still blotched with sweat from playing basketball.

"Hello, Hunter."

"Thanks for the escort," said Hunter. A uniformed officer had met him at home. Grayson had another officer guarding Granny Jen's door, turning away reporters.

"Necessity." Grayson shifted on the bench. "Homicides right under our noses in our own harbor. Who would have ever thought Beaufort would come to this?" A news helicopter passed overhead, slinging a spray of water across the boardwalk, the noise deafening.

Several slips in the harbor were empty, and the yacht owners who remained were standing in groups on the docks, frowning and gesturing angrily. Grayson's few officers, the county deputies, and state agents were on every dock, searching the yachts and questioning the owners and crews. More officers kept the news crowd confined to the public boardwalk, radios squawking. Reporters shouted questions above the roar of the helicopter to the people on the docks. Beaufort's quiet waterfront was now bedlam.

"Is this your headquarters now?" asked Hunter, indicating the reporter-free, fifty foot circle around Grayson.

"Something like that."

"Why aren't you investigating?"

Grayson crossed his legs and ignored the question. "Those SBI guys turn out some dandy reports. You should read them. I learned amazing things about those murders. Cozy scenes. No fingerprints. Not one, not ever."

"Maybe the guy has no fingers," said Hunter.

"Maybe the guy always has his fingers on something. An orange. A cat. A glass he brings in and takes with him. He knows he has to keep his hands on something to avoid touching anything of his victims'."

"See? You should be investigating. Quick, before the big news guns start shooting at you." Hunter smiled as he said this, gesturing with his hands.

"You'd be surprised what I learn just sitting here," Grayson said slowly.

"Like what?"

"Oh, you see that seagull squawking over there? She's so

greedy she stole a sandwich right out of a tourist's hand the other day. Then somebody on a boat tossed her a piece of crust, and she dropped the sandwich in the water and went after the crust. Happened right over there."

"Huh."

"And, do you know, last night about nine o'clock, I saw Vanessa Singer walk right across the dock. Right there. In the flesh."

"Oh," Hunter said, choking laughter.

"All duded up, hair piled on top of her head, little butt just a-swingin,' like she was in downtown Hol-ly-wood," Grayson drawled. "What's so funny?"

"Well, Miki pulled that gag the first day we were in Beaufort."

"And you find this humorous."

"Sort of."

"Is there anything else about your blonde you haven't told me?"

Hunter quit laughing. "What's the big deal?"

"I believe Doug Sanders thought your Miki was Vanessa Singer," Grayson said in a low voice. "I think he died because he pursued that belief too closely."

"Oh, man, no way."

"The only person who went into your apartment two days before Doug Sanders was murdered was Miki. It's in the reports."

"But whoever took the gun put it back."

"So you do have it."

Hunter was silent, his face carefully impassive.

"I need the gun, Hunter."

"Whoever put it back planted cocaine at the same time." Hunter's voice was very quiet. "Miki didn't do that. She didn't kill anybody, and she didn't try to frame me."

"I never said she did either."

The silence was uncomfortable.

"What else have you not told me about yourself, Hunter?" asked Grayson.

"Hey, I never smoked anybody," said Hunter more loudly than he intended. He clamped his mouth shut when a reporter looked his way and started a camera rolling.

Grayson made a motion with his hand and an officer moved in front of the camera. "What were you doing with a gun?" Grayson asked quietly.

"I had this bizarre urge to shoot my father when he showed up. I got over it."

"And now?"

Hunter looked away and drummed a rhythm with his hands on his leg.

"Tell me, Hunter."

"Okay. I called him last night. I told him to stay away from Beaufort because the cops were after him."

"Thank you, son. I already knew that."

Surprised, Hunter looked at him.

"It's amazing what all is in those SBI reports. Simply amazing."

With a curse, Hunter stood abruptly.

"You didn't kill Doug Sanders, and neither did Miki. But you need to be very careful what you say and do. This whole mess can still tangle you, Hunter, like it or not." Grayson nodded toward the camera crews. "I can try to keep those guys away from your grandmother, but you're fair game. Watch yourself."

Hunter started away.

"I'm not through with you," said Grayson. "I want you to go with that officer you see coming toward you. I've held the state investigators off as long as I can. They need to question you now about Doug Sanders."

Hunter nodded. He had been expecting it.

"And I still need that gun," said Grayson as Hunter left with the officer.

Jack Franklin sank wearily to the bench beside Grayson, all arrogance gone from his features. He handed over the micro-cassette recorder. "Unbelievable. It has to be somebody inside the department," Jack said. "Absolutely sickening."

"So you've given up your Rob Kittrell theory?"

"Listen to the tape. My Miki had Schneider licking her shoes. We were going in for a bust today, and we would have had the ammunition we needed to pound him hard. But somebody got to him first. They had to have known."

"Maybe Rob's running out of victims, running out of time. Could be coincidence."

"I think the killer wanted Schneider dead before we could put him in jail."

"Maybe Rob knows what's going on in your department."

"Would you get off the Kittrell thing? It took more than a fast knife to pull off that underwater killing. You stay two steps behind this case, Tucker. Catch up."

Grayson took his sunglasses off and stowed them in his shirt pocket. He stared at Jack a long moment before asking, "What do you really want?"

"Okay, you've got me. I'm not just sharing information. I need you."

"For what?"

"To take the heat off me."

"Heat?"

"Look around you, fool. The news vultures have invaded. There's a camera now." He cursed and turned his head. "I put my life on the line to join this investigation. I'll go undercover again, soon, somewhere else."

"You know, I've wondered about that. Why the killer hasn't taken you out while he's at it."

"Maybe he knows I'm ready for him. What I want you to protect me from is the news media. My name can't be mentioned, and my face can't be on camera."

"And you're going to ask this of every person on the waterfront?" Grayson nodded toward a dock where a reporter was leaning over the rail, talking to a boat owner.

"This is a simple request, Tucker. Do your job for once."

"Mmm." Grayson put the sunglasses back on and folded his arms.

🐝 🐝 🐝

"No, Mom. No." Hunter was speaking emphatically into the phone. "You don't need to come down here. *Mom.* I'm not going back to Raleigh with you. It's okay. I'm handling it."

Granny Jen struggled with her wheelchair, trying to exit the room and give him some privacy. Hunter motioned for her to stay. "It was no big deal, really. They mostly asked me questions Mr. Tucker had already asked off the record. I've been expecting it. No, Patrick doesn't need to hire a lawyer. I don't think I'm really a suspect. There's just not enough evidence." He cursed under his breath at something she said. "What I mean is, there's only circumstantial evidence. I haven't done a damn thing, Mom! I haven't been anywhere I wasn't supposed to be." He grew quieter. "I don't know why they took this long to question me. No, nothing else happened. I swear. Look, I've gotta go. No, I mean it. Granny Jen's about to fall out of her wheelchair. 'Bye."

"Hunter." Granny Jen used her rough voice, as if he were a little boy in need of spanking. "You shouldn't lie to your mother."

"So you're an expert wheelchair driver. No big lie."

"I mean about nothing else happening."

"Say what?"

"Save that smile for someone besides your old granny. You've been looking over your shoulder all day."

"Can't a man have a few secrets around here?" Hunter was more pleased that she understood him so well than perturbed at her probing.

"Very few."

"Well here's one thing. I called my father and left a message for him to stay out of Beaufort, on account of the cops. They found out about it. And I have to dodge reporters every time I step outside."

She closed her eyes and sighed. "What else?"

"Something I'll have to keep private to protect a friend." He was hoping the news media would never know about Miki's tenuous connection to Doug Sanders. "Honest, it's nothing I've done."

Her sharp gray eyes appraised him, missing nothing. "I want you to do something," she said.

"What?"

"Call your mother and apologize for the way you spoke to her."

"You should have heard what she said to me!"

"She's worried to death, Hunter."

"She's just pissed. She always thinks the worst of me."

"And that's exactly why I want you to call her. She's had reason to doubt you, particularly this last year, and you know it. Give her reason to have faith in you."

"No. We'll just wind up fighting again."

"Don't fight. I want a favor from her, and it will help if you're on good terms."

"You're kidding."

"I want her to let me have you on Thanksgiving."

He drew in a glad, surprised breath, and then frowned. "Why?"

"Next summer, even if I'm still able to be in this house, you'll be doing an internship, won't you?"

He nodded. He had decided to do that, but he hadn't told her yet.

"Good. I'm glad for you. You're making a commitment to your career, and more than that, to your life. But I'll miss our summers. Maybe Thanksgiving we can start a new tradition."

She said this very matter-of-factly, but Hunter had to look away. "Sure, I'll call her. But I'm just going to apologize and hang up. That's all I can deal with, okay?"

"That's probably all she can deal with, too, Hunter."

TWENTY-ONE

Hunter paced his apartment, restless. He looked out the window. Even this late at night, a news crew was camped out on the sidewalk, waiting for him. He couldn't walk from Granny Jen's door to his own without being stormed by questions: What did he know about Rob Kittrell? Had he seen his father? How did he find Doug Sanders' body? Why did the SBI question him today? So far, Hunter had ignored the reporters.

The gun in his closet haunted him. He thought about walking to the end of his dock and hurling the gun into the water just to see who jumped in after it. But Hunter wasn't about to lose that gun, and he figured Grayson knew it. The gun could hang him; Hunter and Grayson both knew that. If it came down to having no other way out, however, the gun and any other fingerprints on it could be the only thing that would save his hide. The gun could be bane or insurance, and Hunter wasn't giving it up.

Right this minute, with everything in his life going against him, Hunter's most annoying worry was his mother. His family usually came down to see him for his birthday, but after talking with his mother today, Hunter had a feeling she wouldn't wait two more weeks. He wasn't sure he could deal with a visit from his mother right now, especially if she came without his two half-sisters along as a buffer.

He thought about his mother now, sweet and nurturing with her daughters, forever hauling them to soccer practice and swim meets. Her face could change from smiling to tense the minute he walked into the room. One conversation in particular came to mind, the only time she ever mentioned his father to him.

"Hunter, drive Janie to soccer practice for me, please," she had asked.

"Why?" he asked. Hunter had just turned sixteen and had a new driver's license and wheels to go with it.

"Because I have a meeting, your dad's out of town, and Janie's going to be late," his mother answered.

"She doesn't need to practice, he's not my dad, and I have a date," Hunter countered.

"Hunter!" She drew in a breath, controlling her anger. Hunter remembered staring her down, daring her to make him obey. She let her breath out slowly and said in a distinct voice, "You're right. He's not your dad. And do you know what? It's a shame he's not, because you could stand to be more like Patrick and a whole lot less like your father."

"Yeah? Tell me. Tell me how I'm like my father," Hunter demanded.

"Try cocky, arrogant, and rude on for size," she answered.

"What the hell did you marry him for if he was so bad?"

She slammed her hand on the kitchen counter. "I will not have that language in this house. Forget your date. You are grounded."

"Yeah, right." He had walked out of the house, knowing he would be grounded even longer when he came back, and not caring.

Remembering this now, Hunter dreaded her visit. A fight was inevitable every time they were together. He didn't know how to change; he just wished he didn't care so much.

"Thanks for the gourmet meal," Amy said to Hunter the next evening. They stood in Hunter's yard, the reporters thankfully gone for the moment. Hunter had cooked a roast for supper and invited Amy over.

"Hey, it doesn't quite measure up after all you've done, but it's the best I could come up with." It was a mellow evening, the air calm. That marshy odor—mud and shellfish—peculiar to Beaufort, surrounded them, comfortably homey to a native. Overhead, a mockingbird showed off his calls from the old magnolia tree.

"You and Mom will have to give me cooking lessons after I graduate," Amy said.

"Where are you planning to live?" asked Hunter. He noticed the way her hair glinted happily in the glow of the sunset and smiled. Amy almost always made him smile.

"I don't know. It kind of scares me to think about it. And I've only got one more year to decide."

"Lucky you. I've still got my two hardest years ahead, plus an internship. For a guy who likes to take the easy way out, I sure managed to pick about the hardest career to get into."

"Hey, it'll be worth it," she said.

"Yeah, but you know, I think I wanted to fail. I wanted something so hard that I knew I'd never finish it, and I could just drop out and say, 'See? I couldn't cut it. I'll never be worth anything, so just leave me alone.'"

"And now?"

"So much has gone down this summer, I've decided, by damn, I'm gonna do it."

"Shh."

"I'm gonna do it, and it won't be to please my dead uncle or my mom or my step-dad or even Granny Jen. It's because I want to be an architect, and I'll be a damn good one. And don't shush me, Miss Perfect."

She grinned at him. "You'll miss me and Granny Jen trying to make a good boy out of you after this summer." And then she sighed as it hit her that this would be their last summer together.

Hunter sighed and hooked his left thumb in his belt loop. He knew it was their last summer, too. Furtively, he reached behind him and fumbled with the water faucet. A metallic squeak alerted her to what he was doing.

"Oh, no, Mister. You're not getting me wet. Not in this shirt."

"What are you going to do about it?" He pulled a garden hose from behind his back and aimed the spray at her feet, splattering her legs. "C'mon, chicken. You've wanted a rematch since we were little kids." He splattered her again.

"This is a brand-new shirt, Hunter," she laughed.

"So? Take it off." He clucked chicken calls behind her as she ran across the yard toward the other hose, water raining all around her.

She grabbed the other hose and disappeared around the corner of the house.

"What are you doing?" he called.

"Taking my shirt off." His jaw and the hose dropped at the same time, and she jumped into sight, water full-blast in his face, shirt still on.

"Cheat, cheat!" he called, diving for his hose.

"You kids don't need to be wasting water," called Winnie from the porch.

"Just be glad they aren't naked," chuckled Granny Jen.

"Well, I should hope not, Mother."

"Hunter, you soaked my shirt!" Amy yelled.

"Then take it off, cry-baby."

Amy responded with a blast to his crotch.

"Oh, that does it. You're dead now, Girl."

Within seconds, they were both drenched, hair streaming water, laughter bouncing through the neighborhood. A blast from a car horn ended it.

"Uh-oh. We're busted!"

A woman stepped out of a new Toyota Camry, her hair pulled back with a clasp, tall, classic good looks. She had Hunter's nicely defined lips and strong jaw.

"Hi, Mom." Hunter let the hose droop from his hand, water dripping.

"Is this what you do all summer?" asked Karen Baker Kittrell Barton.

"I wish." Hunter rolled up the hose. "You're a little early for my birthday. Where is everybody?"

"The girls are tied up with swim meets so your dad stayed with them. I couldn't wait another two weeks, Hunter. I had to know that you were all right." Mother and son spoke carefully, putting off the inevitable fight. "Hi, Amy," Karen finally said.

"Hello, Mrs. Barton," said Amy. "We've been waiting for a referee. Which of us would you say won?"

"From the looks of things, I'd say you both lost."

"That bad, huh?" Amy asked with a laugh. She put away her hose. "Thanks for supper, Hunter. Good to see you, Mrs. Barton. 'Bye, Granny Jen, Aunt Winnie." She took off at a soggy trot up the street, Hunter clucking chicken calls to her back.

"What was that all about?" asked Karen.

"Oh, just a joke. I wish the girls could have come. I miss their little noisy selves."

"You haven't called your sisters in two months. You must not miss them too badly. And you haven't asked about your dad."

"How is Patrick?" Hunter said, carefully refusing to call him "Dad."

"Working too hard. Disappointed in your grades."

"They're good enough. What's it to him?" Hunter's voice was heating up.

"He wants you to succeed. He's done all he can do, given you every opportunity, helped you get that scholarship."

"Well, you know what? I don't care what he wants anymore. It's what I want that matters."

"And what do you want, Hunter?" Her voice was carefully patient.

"Never mind. You wouldn't understand. I'm going to change

clothes." Hunter walked away.

Karen walked over and sat on Granny Jen's stoop before her former mother-in-law could invite her inside. "Hello, Mrs. Kittrell," she said formally through the screen.

"Hi, Karen. You're looking great."

"I feel great until I get around my son. And did he not get my messages last week? I left several asking him to call me."

"I've been in the hospital."

"Oh, I'm so sorry." She gestured with her long, attractive hands, palms up, bracelets dangling. "There I go again, blaming you for my problems with Hunter."

"You don't really have any problems with Hunter, Karen," Granny Jen said gently.

"Oh, you just don't know. But how are you? You look well."

"I feel pretty good these days. My old heart wants to give up, but I'm not going to let it just yet."

"You always were a fighter."

"Yes, and I'm not giving up on Hunter, and neither should you."

"Trust me; I'm not."

"But you need to step back a little, Karen, and see him for who he's turning into."

"Every time I step back I seem to lose a little more of him," Karen said quietly.

"I know how that feels, and I know how it hurts. But the more you tell him you expect him to fail, the more you make him want to fail to spite you. Just step back. I think you'll be pleased with the Hunter you see." Only Granny Jen could get away with this conversation, and she knew it. Age had its advantages.

Hunter came down his steps, dressed in a dry shirt and shorts. "Do you want some roast beef?" he asked lightly. "I'm chief chef around here now."

"You're kidding," said Karen.

"No, he's really a good cook," put in Winnie.

"Well, sure, I'll try some. And I want to hear about how you wound up in the middle of a murder investigation." Her voice was careful again.

Hunter held the screen door open for her and followed her onto the porch. "It's a big mess, Mom. Trust me. You don't want to hear it."

"Yes, I do, Hunter. How did you manage to find . . ." A look from Granny Jen stopped her. Karen took a seat on the porch with Granny Jen and Winnie. "I've been very worried. I'd really like to know what's going on."

"What if I tell you some day when I get it all behind me? I'm handling it, Mom." Hunter walked inside and came back out carrying a plate. "Here you go, roast beast," he said, using a boyhood expression.

Karen smiled as she took the plate from him. One taste and she said, "Whoo! Cayenne."

"Too much?"

"Maybe just a pinch. Try a little bottled smoke flavor and a little less cayenne."

"Thanks. I didn't think I quite had it perfected."

After a minute, Karen asked, "What happened to the blonde?"

"Her name is Miki." Hunter's voice had a deliberate edge.

"Okay; Miki. Where is she? I thought she was here for the summer."

"I lost her." His shrug was careless.

"You lost her." Karen's voice was flat. "This cavalier attitude toward your girlfriends is a pattern . . ."

"You didn't even like her, Mom." His voice rose with impatience.

"I'm just saying . . ." She stopped. "I apologize. I'm sure it hurts."

Hunter glanced at Granny Jen, who smiled at him and nodded encouragingly.

"So what else have you been up to this summer?" Karen asked.

"Just workin'." He shrugged. "Fishin' a little."

Karen looked at him expectantly. He slouched in his chair, careless smile, not quite meeting her eyes.

"Hunter, for Heaven's sake, tell her what you've been doing." Winnie sounded exasperated. Hunter straightened a little but didn't volunteer any information. Winnie put in, "He's been doing some drawing. Really great, from what I saw."

"You snooped in my room?"

"You didn't bring your laundry down this morning, so I had to go up and get it. And no, I didn't snoop," said Winnie. "I just saw the drawings that were on your table."

"I'd like to see your work," said Karen.

Hunter refused to meet her eyes until Granny Jen gave his arm a little push. "How about when you get ready to leave, I take you up and show you?" he said to his mother.

"I'd like that. So you're trying to get rid of me?"

"No. It's just—you're usually on your way to Grandma Baker's when you stop by."

"You're right; I am. I was trying to tease you."

"Uh, so, how was your trip to the Caribbean last month?"

"Great. You should have come. You were invited, you know."

"But not Miki."

"It was a family trip, Hunter."

"Never mind. I'm glad I was here anyway." He put an arm across his grandmother's shoulders. "I've brought a lot of grief on Granny Jen, but some of what's gone down would have happened anyway. I needed to be here for her." He cleared his throat. "Tell me what all I missed out on. Did the girls enjoy snorkeling?"

They talked until dark, mother and son stepping carefully around a minefield of old hurts, old traps. After years of pushing each other's buttons, it seemed important, suddenly, not to.

She had brought cake for his birthday and money enough to buy tires for his Jeep and jeans for himself. From his sisters, there were scented candles, a new CD, and a huge conch shell from the Caribbean. Hunter was impressed.

"It's getting late," Karen finally said. "I need to get on down to Mama's. Show me those drawings, and I'll let you look at our vacation pictures."

Hunter led the way up the steps to his apartment, dreading being alone with her without the buffer of Granny Jen and Winnie.

"Wow!" exclaimed Karen. "I love this place. When did your grandmother do all this?"

"I did it," said Hunter, a little proudly. "Well, me and Amy."

"And these are your drawings?"

"Uh-huh."

She put on her glasses and examined them closely, not speaking. Hunter could hardly look at the photo album for watching her. Finally, she took the glasses off. "This is most impressive, Hunter."

"I've got a lot to learn."

"But the hours and hours you've put into this! I had no idea of the real talent you have. I'm very proud of you. Your dad will be, too."

"Aw, Mom. We almost had a moment. You just had to drag him into it."

She shook her head, avoiding the fight. "There is a pattern to your work. I didn't realize you had settled on a specialty."

He stood behind her and looked at the drawings with her. "Historic renovation is what interests me, I guess," he said. "Remodeling old homes to keep as much of the original materials as possible and maintain the flavor of the neighborhood. And give the property owner whatever modern conveniences are important to him."

She looked at him in admiration as he spoke. "I noticed this whole set is of the garage and apartment," she said, indicating one of the many folders. "Is your grandmother planning on doing something with this place?"

"She already has."

She looked up.

"It belongs to me now."

She didn't speak.

"Now what's wrong?" he asked.

"I've always been afraid I'd lose you to this place."

"I thought you'd be happy for me."

"Your dad and I thought—well we hoped—you might intern in Raleigh, maybe join one of the big firms there."

Hunter moved away from her and sat on the back of his sofa, his long legs straddling the sofa back, one foot up on the cushioned arm. "I'll have to get established somewhere, get licensed. Charlotte's a possibility, and so is Raleigh. But Beaufort is in my blood. Someday I want to live here."

She sighed and looked around. The dining chest caught her eye. "This piece is still here. Your Uncle Donald showed it to me once. It meant a lot to him because it's signed and dated. Come to think of it, the signature under the drawer is the reason I named you 'Hunter.'"

"Because you were in love with Donald?"

She stared hard at him. "Whatever made you say a thing like that?"

"He told me he wanted to marry you."

She looked the cabinet over, lips tight. "I never really even dated Donald. My parents wouldn't let me." Her voice shook a little. "I was only nineteen, and he was twenty-six. I was only allowed to see Donald where there was a crowd around. But, oh, they would let me date his *brother*." She spat out the word with venom and regret.

Hunter didn't speak, stunned.

There was a strained silence, and Karen turned and faced her son. "Hunter, look at me," she said. He was slouched across the back of his sofa, a study of indifference. When he met her eyes, she held his gaze. "I regret marrying Rob Kittrell, but I have never regretted having you. You were worth it."

He smiled a slow, easy smile, and lifted his chin. "You know what? I already know that. Granny Jen told me."

TWENTY-TWO

Blood. There was blood everywhere. Blood on Gus's face. Blood on the floor. Blood on her hands. She saw Bob Schneider's face, clearly, and he was looking at her in horror, and then blood splattered his face, her face, blood was in her eyes. Suddenly, she was underwater, choking, dying, trying to scream with screams in her ears . . .

Miki wrenched herself from the dream, gasping for breath, choking on her own sobs, trying not to awaken Jack. Reaching beside the bed, she opened a compartment. Her hand came up empty.

"They're gone," said Jack. "I've dumped every last one of your damn pills."

"You don't understand, Jack. I can't sleep. I'm crazy from not sleeping."

"Tell me why you can't sleep."

"Dreams. Horrible dreams. There's blood, and it's all my fault.

Gus—you said if I hadn't been there, you might have saved him. And that Schneider man. You made me trick him, and the next morning he was dead. And I can't get away from the blood and the guilt and . . ."

"Hush. You did absolutely nothing wrong. And no one besides me knows of your connection to either victim. I was surprised when the SBI didn't pull you in with Kittrell, but . . ."

"What?" Miki sat up and switched on a nightlight. "I thought they questioned Hunter about that tourist."

"Right." Jack's voice was smooth, his eyes narrow in the dim light.

"What would I know about that?" she demanded

"And I once thought you were so sharp. My mistake."

"Jack! Tell me." She grabbed his arm, fear in her voice.

He sat up in bed and took his time to light a cigarette. When he finally looked at her, arms folded across his bare chest, his face was smug. "What were you doing with Hunter Kittrell's gun?" he asked.

She stood up and backed away from the bed.

"It's in the reports," Jack continued. "You went to his apartment . . ."

"I wanted to explain to him that I had left him for good . . ."

". . . And you took his gun. You must have. Kittrell reported a gun stolen, and no one else had been in his apartment alone." He took a drag on the cigarette, his eyes contemptuous in its orange glow. "Either he's lying or you took the gun." Jack waited for the truth to surface in her brain.

"I was afraid," she said. She turned her back on him and slid on a robe. The thin barrier of silk seemed to give her courage. "A man kept following me."

"Didn't you think I could protect you?"

"Not every minute." Miki lifted her chin defensively. "Why are you asking me these questions?"

"Where is the gun now?" His eyes dared her to lie.

"I don't know." She hugged the robe around her body.

"How could you not know?"

"My purse. I don't know where . . . I've kept trying to remember if I had it the last night I went to the beach with Hunter. Jack, please, what are you getting at?" She backed away from him.

"The tourist who died was the man who was following you."

She took one more step away, her back against a storage compartment.

"It's hard to tell the exact caliber of the weapon, unless you have the bullet, but Kittrell's missing gun would make a hole about the size of the wound. Very close."

She was moving away from him, edging along the wall.

"You have nowhere to go." There was triumph in his eyes as he stood up. "We're watching Kittrell. Grayson Tucker is watching you. Why do you think he sits day after day fifty feet from our boat? And who do you think has stopped Tucker and the SBI from arresting you?"

She couldn't move.

"Are you sure the gun is lost? If they come in with a search warrant, not even I can stop them from tearing this place apart. And any stash of pot you have . . . well, they'll know it's not mine."

He came toward her, touched her hair. "You have a choice, Miki." His lips possessed hers, and she was choking on his tongue, choking on her sobs. "You are my diamond. Brilliant. *Flawless*. A diamond is only made brilliant through pain, at the hands of the master jeweler."

He released her and began to dress. She watched, not asking where he was going. He did not look at her again. "It's your choice. You can be my diamond. A work of art." He stopped at the door, his back to her. "Or you can let this blood you never touched dull your brilliance. If that's your choice, be gone before I get back."

She watched him go, darkness taking him. In the dim light, she caught her reflection in the mirror, and she made her choice quickly.

Hunter sat beside Granny Jen in church and tried to keep his eyes open. The mood among the congregation was tense. From the few words Hunter had caught, the minister was relating his sermon to the murders. As was his custom when he accompanied his grandmother to church, Hunter made use of the time to redesign one of Beaufort's old homes into a comfortable showplace, open floor plan, very livable. Built in 1824, redesigned for the twenty-first century by H. Kittrell. Over the past three summers, an entire block of Beaufort's historic district had been transformed in Hunter's mind. This was easy for Hunter. The hard part was keeping his eyes open while he worked out the details. He preferred to avoid Granny Jen's elbow in his ribs whenever possible.

A little kid in the pew in front of Hunter squirmed to his knees in the seat and turned around to stare solemnly at Hunter, chin on the bench back, little fingers waving. His mama firmly pulled him back to a sitting position. Hunter wanted to rumple the kid's hair just so the kid would know somebody else wished he were somewhere besides here.

The distraction brought Hunter's attention to his surroundings for a moment, and he realized the minister was wrapping up his message. Good. That should give him just enough time to turn the two front bedrooms into a master suite, complete with a nicely appointed bath.

"The Lord sets before each of us an open door," the minister said.

That sentence caught Hunter's attention. It made him think of the ivy-twined door in his blue window.

The minister continued, "He has promised to watch over your coming and going."

For the first time, Hunter looked up at the speaker.

"The world can throw the worst it has at you." The minister was speaking in a soothing voice. "Certainly Beaufort has experienced the worst that could happen this summer. But as we read a few minutes ago, the Lord will not let your foot slip. No matter how treacherous the path or how dangerous your enemies, he will not let go of you."

Hunter did not look away. The minister seemed to be speaking directly to him. He really wanted to know what this had to do with his window.

"There is a door which leads to trust. You can choose to walk in peace knowing that he cares about every single thing that happens to you, trusting that, in the end, he will work it all out for your good. Or you can choose to walk without him in fear and darkness, not sure that there is anybody there who will catch you when you stumble." The minister looked around at the congregation and smiled kindly.

"The Lord has promised to watch over you, but he won't make you walk through that door. The choice is entirely up to you."

Any further words the minister may have spoken were lost to Hunter. He sat very still, picturing his window with the mountains and water beyond the door. When he felt Granny Jen's elbow nudging him, he grinned at her and winked as he always did when she thought she had caught him napping.

Late the same night, Granny Jen was wide awake, although she was very tired from her trip to church that morning. She sat in the darkness, not daring to reach for the light and disturb Winnie just across the hallway.

Jen had some thinking to do, some worrying, some praying. Hunter's birthday was coming up soon, his twenty-first.

Beatrice Jen Kittrell had a secret, an awful secret, which she had kept eighteen years.

Only a mother would understand her secret, or so she guessed. Her husband had not understood, and neither had her older son. Both her husband and Donald had died and left behind wills with very strange terms, each involving her grandson, Hunter, each man apparently trying to fix what she had done. Winnie, surprisingly, prissy as she was, had understood.

And Karen—Hunter's mother—the one most affected. She never had spoken of it, but she had let Jen have Hunter every summer. That said it all.

Rob had been a difficult son. He had been rebellious, stubborn, arrogant, and charming all at the same time, and Jen had loved him fiercely. Yet there came a time when she knew something was terribly wrong. She guessed drugs, but she didn't know. She suspected that Karen knew.

One evening, while Karen was at work and Hunter was in Rob's care, Jen went for a stroll. She was not young and moved slowly even then. Her walk happened to take her along the tree-lined street where Rob and Karen lived.

The scene she came upon had haunted her for the past eighteen years. There, across the street, was her grandson, walking slowly, looking back over his shoulder toward his home. He was carrying a paper bag in one small hand, and he stopped, looking bewildered as only a three-year-old could. His father was not in sight.

Just then, a man in a parked car rolled down his window and spoke to the boy, and a look of recognition spread over the child's face. He took one step toward the car.

"Hunter!" Jen called. Her grandson grinned at her in delight and started toward her from behind the car. "Stop!" she screamed. A car honked. Traffic separated her from the boy. "Stay there." She made it across one lane. In the time it took for two more cars to pass, the man jumped from the car, grabbed the bag from Hunter, and was back in his car as she scooped up her grandson. Once they were safely on the sidewalk, the car sped away, and Hunter scrambled to get down.

"Daddy!" he yelled to the figure walking toward them, and he nearly broke away from her grasp.

She had Hunter by the neck of his T-shirt, struggling to hang on, watching as her son came closer to his son.

"Hunter, come here," Rob called. There was a challenge in his eyes, an arrogant look that said, *You'll never turn me in.* And there was something else. There was a cold calculation to his features, and she knew that if she let go of Hunter, Rob would run with him. She knew it.

She grabbed the squirming boy into her arms and held on. "Don't come one step further, Rob," she said firmly. "Not another step."

"Let go of my son."

"Don't you think I know what just went down here?"

"Yeah? And what are you gonna do about it? Come on, Hunter."

She held the child even as he wriggled and kicked to get down. "If you touch this child, I will call the police," she said.

He stopped barely an arm's length away.

"I mean it, Rob. You get out of this town, away from this boy, and I won't turn you in. But the minute you come close to this child, I will call the police. And you'd better be leaving now. I'll give you a day's head start before I tell your father what you did. I can guarantee he'll turn you in without hesitation."

"I don't believe you."

"Rob, I love you, but I love Hunter even more. And I will do it, for him. Do you not understand the terrible thing you made him do today, the danger he was in? When you're ready to turn yourself in, you can come back. But don't even think you'll see this child again until then."

Rob wavered. He could have taken the boy from her right there on the street, and she could not have stopped him. But he didn't.

"Hunter," he said softly, "go with Granny Jen. See what Grandpa's doing. Maybe he'll take you fishing. 'Bye-bye. Go on with Granny Jen."

That day, she had turned and carried the squirming boy down the street, her eyes so full of tears that she could barely see to walk. He had called, "'Bye, Daddy," and waved over her shoulder, but she had never looked back. And she never saw her son again.

In the morning, Rob's friend was arrested and on his way to prison for heroin possession, but Rob was gone.

But Hunter wasn't a boy any longer. Very soon, he would be twenty-one. And Rob, through his brother, Donald, knew the strange terms of his father's will. The police had been looking for Rob in Beaufort all summer, but Jen had been fairly certain that if he showed up at all, it would be on Hunter's twenty-first birthday.

On the water, Jack Franklin lit a cigarette and watched Hunter's apartment. He had been doing his job all summer, watching for Rob Kittrell. It was what he was paid to do. But Jack, too, knew about the will, and like Jen Kittrell, he had been fairly certain Rob would not surface before the kid's birthday. Unlike Jen, however, he was damn sure Rob would show up then.

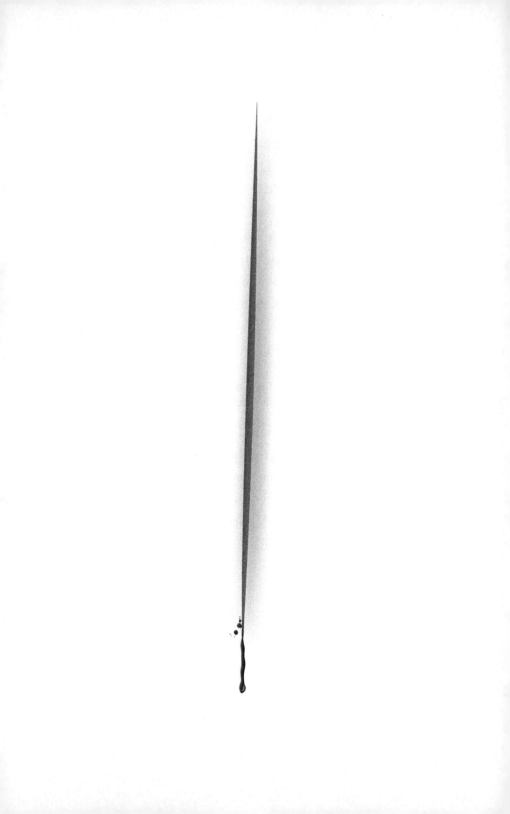

TWENTY-THREE

"Granny Jen, that's not such a good idea." Hunter was groggy the next morning, trying to stir grits and eggs at the same time. In his dreams, he was constantly catching Miki from a great height, and he awoke every morning tired, vaguely sure that something terrible had happened to her.

He no longer held Miki in his arms in his dreams.

"I need to see the waterfront, Hunter," his granny said firmly.

"I promise it hasn't gone anywhere. Everything looks the same. It just feels different. You'll wish you hadn't gone."

"I need to see it."

"Don't you think—"

"It's a nice day, not too hot, and I'm feeling pretty good."

"I was trying to say, don't you think later, after this all blows over, would be a better time?"

"And I'm trying to say today is the day." She gave a determined tap with her cane. Two pairs of gray eyes confronted each other across the kitchen counter. Hunter blinked first. Maybe it was the dull ache in his head. Maybe it was the determination in the old, clear eyes that stared into his. Maybe somewhere in his dream, Miki had not turned her back on him, and his pained heart hoped it would happen today. For whatever reason, he did not argue again.

The day was sharp, Beaufort's midsummer mugginess blown away by a storm the night before. Hunter pushed the wheelchair slowly so that his grandmother could enjoy the view of Taylor's Creek and the lonely sand bank across the water. The sky was brilliant blue with high white clouds far out to sea. An old gentleman called Jen's name from his dock and waved his cap. She waved back.

As they neared the boardwalk, there were familiar sounds: gulls fussing for a perch, the trickle of water from yachts' bilges, motorboats humming by on the creek. The downtown strip looked the same as always, the old buildings hugged together facing the water. Tourists still straggled along the sidewalk, poking in every shop from the ships' outfitters to art galleries looking for treasures. Hunter turned beside the corner restaurant and stopped the wheelchair in front of its weathered porch. When he looked at Granny Jen, her eyes were closed, a poignant smile on her face. Never mind that there were fewer boats in the harbor than usual; never mind that the boardwalk was cluttered with camera crews or that the tourists were pointing with morbid fascination toward the spot where the scuba victim's body had washed up on the opposite shore. There were many better days in her memory.

"Granny Jen," he said softly, "are you sure you want to walk? Just let me push you down the boardwalk."

She gave him a look that hushed him. Carefully, he helped her to her feet. To him, the walk seemed formidable; she was just now able to walk the length of her house again. He did not know that she had a single destination in mind.

🟐 🟐 🟐

Grayson Tucker sat on his bench in the sun. Occasionally, he would fan a fly with his hand. He looked relaxed, a symbol to the town of either frustrated indolence or patient calculation, depending on whose eyes were viewing him. Grayson was aware that a day of reckoning was approaching. Today he was ready to hurry it along.

A familiar figure stepped off one of the yachts, walking quickly up the ramp, legs long and graceful, blonde hair lifting sensuously in the breeze. Grayson knew to the second the moment at which he could catch her eye, and he did so with a simple wave of his hand. Although she looked away and kept walking, she broke stride, knowing she was hooked. After circumventing two news camera crews, she approached him from behind and slipped beside him on the bench.

"Nice day," Grayson commented.

She did not reply. When he chanced a look at her, she was staring at the water, her face set into an impenetrable mask.

"What do you want?" she finally asked in an icy voice. "They'll be moving their microphones over here soon."

"Mighty paranoid, aren't we?" drawled Grayson. "Can't I invite someone over for a nice chat?"

"I don't chat."

Again Grayson looked at her. Even under the unforgiving sun, her features were flawless. Her beauty was ice or steel or some element Grayson was not accustomed to seeing in a woman. She seemed far removed from Hunter and his easy smile.

"Well, Miki, I've just been curious about something."

"How do you know my name?"

"Your name keeps coming up whenever I'm talking with Hunter."

"Well, quit talking to him."

There was a silence. Grayson got the distinct impression she was ready to walk away. "I didn't stop you to talk about Hunter," he said.

"Good, because Hunter doesn't know anything about those murders."

"Oh?" It was a leading question, but she didn't follow. "How would you know that, Miki?" Again, silence. "Who does know about them?"

She whispered a curse, stood, and started away in one quick movement.

"Sit down, Miki. I still have my chatting to do."

Not looking at him, she returned to the bench. Grayson wondered about that, too. Did she think she was a suspect, that he would arrest her if she didn't cooperate?

"I won't take up too much of your time. You know that Jack Franklin is part of this investigation."

"Shouldn't he be here then, instead of you grilling me alone?"

"Grilling? Oh, I've just got a simple question. Easy question. Jack gave me a little tape recorder the day Bob Schneider was murdered."

The cold, haughty look she gave him would have frozen another man to the bench. Experience had taught Grayson that there was often terror beneath a look like that.

"I was just doing my job," she hissed. "I work for Jack, in case you didn't know."

Ten more questions came to Grayson's mind, but he stuck to his point. "I just wanted to ask about fingerprints, Miki. Yours. On the tape recorder and at Gus York's house."

She sprang from the bench even more quickly than he had anticipated. This sudden motion alerted an anxious camera crew.

"See what you've done?" Her voice was more growl than whisper. "I can't have any peace in this town. Now I won't even be able to walk to the market without a camera in my face."

"That's an odd reaction, young lady, to such a simple question. I was hoping for a simple answer."

She stood still and stared at him. There was no simple answer, and she and Grayson knew it.

The vulnerability in her eyes made Grayson look away. He had a daughter of his own, away in nursing school, and there were times when he couldn't help taking his job personally. Where was this kid's father anyway? What was he doing while his daughter was living with a hard man like Jack Franklin, her name hooked to three homicides?

A movement to Grayson's left caused them both to look up. Granny Jen and Hunter were making their slow approach along the boardwalk, two news crews keeping pace and firing questions, one of Grayson's men in front keeping the cameras out of Jen's face. Miki took a step backward.

"Uh, I've gotta go," she said.

"Well, hello, Miki," called Granny Jen in her kind, old voice. "I hoped to see you before you left for school." She moved toward the bench with haste, seeming to sense that Miki was about to bolt. "How has your summer been?"

Miki glanced once at Hunter and looked away.

Calmly, Grayson stood and offered Granny Jen his bench. Before sitting, she waved her cane at the camera guys. "Family business," she barked, and they backed away. Her smile was sly as Hunter settled her onto the bench. It was obvious she loved playing at crotchety old lady when the occasion called for it.

"Come; sit," said Granny Jen, patting the bench.

"That's not such a great idea," Miki said. Beneath the careful sophistication, she looked cornered.

"Hunter's leaving, dear. Come on." She patted the bench again coaxingly.

Miki had no choice. She sat.

"Haven't you been afraid down here all summer?" When all she got was a slight shrug, Jen continued, "I've been afraid for you. Maybe that counts."

"Hunter said you had a heart attack or something." She seemed anxious to turn the conversation away from herself.

"Not exactly. My old heart just tried to give up. I'm still needed here, though, so it will have to keep going."

"Needed." It really wasn't a question.

"Yes. By Hunter, if no one else."

Miki had not been looking at Granny Jen, and now she turned even farther away. Never in her young life had she felt needed. Desired, yes; used, maybe. Never needed.

"Hunter needs you, Miki."

"Granny Jen, Hunter and I, we'll never . . ."

"I know that. I think Hunter knows that. But he needs to see you come out of this okay. I don't think Hunter can ever quite let you go until he sees you safely away from your Franklin man, back at school, taking another try at life."

Miki winced. How much did this old lady know? Miki herself had not yet faced what would happen when Jack moved on to another assignment. "I don't know what I'm going to do about school," was all she said.

"I'm talking about life, dear. Your life," Jen said very gently.

Miki did not look at her. A reporter tried to squeeze past the officer to hear their conversation; all it took was one look from Grayson, and the reporter stepped back.

Jen continued softly, but firmly, "Sometimes we take a wrong turn. We go where we never thought we would go. But always, we have a chance to take a new turn, give life a fresh start. That's God's gift to us, and you should never throw away a gift. A new try at life, Miki. Think about it."

"I've really gotta go. I'm glad you're feeling better."

"Good-bye, Miki. Call me sometime."

Miki shook her head slightly and walked away, avoiding Grayson. She ignored Hunter's wave from his distant stance at the dock rail and headed toward the street, the set of her shoulders defying him to follow.

Hunter asked no questions when his grandmother pointed her cane in the direction of the wheelchair rather than continuing down the waterfront. When he had fetched the chair and helped her settle in it, he asked, "Are you happy you came, Granny Jen?"

"I'm at peace. I accomplished what I came for."

"Well, good."

"The harbor still smells the same, Hunter."

"Yeah, I guess it does. Pure Beaufort."

Grayson Tucker let Miki go without calling her back. He didn't think she would give him much of an answer today as to why she might have been at Gus's. Yet the very fact that she hadn't denied being there was an answer. Actually, Grayson was bluffing. Since her fingerprints weren't on record, he didn't know for sure whether they were on the tape recorder or at Gus's house. Her reaction told him more than fingerprints ever could, however. She was there, and she was hiding something. For Grayson, a page had just turned in this investigation. Grayson's gut had told him that there was more to be learned by sitting tight at the waterfront and keeping his eyes and ears open than by chasing after the big-time investigators and their leads. Let the SBI and the federal agents run forensic circles around town. Grayson knew more than anyone guessed. Today he had learned a little more. And if he could continue to play dumb just a little longer, he might get to the bottom of what was really going on in his harbor.

The fury in Miki's eyes was wild, and it matched the way her skin felt—on fire, as if she had been slapped a dozen times. "You told me no one knew I was with Bob Schneider," she said, her voice low and raspy. "You lied to me, Jack. You gave that tape recorder to Mr. Tucker, and then you told me no one knew." She wanted to hurt him, burn him with the fire of her betrayal.

"I like this Miki," he said calmly. "This is the woman I've been waiting to see. All that pitiful sniffling wasn't the real you."

"Answer me, Jack. Why did you give the tape recorder to him, and why did you lie to me?"

"I gave him the recorder because it's my job. I lied because what was on the tape had nothing to do with the man's death and shouldn't have brought the investigation back to you. I was trying to save you unnecessary worry. I apologize."

She glared at him, not ready to give up her fury.

"What exactly did Tucker say to you?"

"He said my fingerprints on the recorder matched those found at Gus's."

"Bull. You didn't go past Gus's door, and there were no clear prints on his door. Tucker's bluffing." He paused, eyes narrow. "You didn't touch anything else in the house that night, did you?"

"N-no."

"Hey, don't go sniffling again."

"God, I hate you."

"Good. There she is again." His eyes were still narrow, but a smile cut across his perfect face. "I'm glad you stayed, Miki. We're good together, and you know it."

"I don't know it."

"You do. We bring out the best in each other. Fire, anger, hatred. They're all signs of great passion. You enjoy this fury. It's a high, and it's honest, and it's powerful." His hands on her skin were insistent, and his kiss was violent and intense. She surrendered, not in weakness, but in a desperate need to feel something real, to dance with life one more time.

⁂

The Cat sharpened his knife. One way or the other, the end was near. His next execution would mean the end of his siege of Beaufort. More than that, to move on would mean the end of his identity by any name other than "The Cat," and the end of most ties to his network. With the exception of one trusted insider on whom he could call, The Cat would be working totally alone.

This final execution would be so bold that it carried the possibility of capture. His escape was carefully planned, but he was aware of the likelihood of an undesirable end. This could be his last execution, but even if it meant the end of him, it would still be a triumph. This one was personal.

TWENTY-FOUR

"Aunt Winnie, aren't you homesick for Uncle Paul?" Hunter asked as he peeled potatoes. "I mean, don't you need to be back in New Bern?"

Winnie chuckled. "Trying to get rid of me, are you?"

"Aunt Winnie." Hunter said in a reproving voice. "That's not what I meant."

"Of course I miss my husband. But I've decided to stay until you go back to school."

"Okay." Really, it wasn't okay. Winnie's particular ways could be annoying to Hunter. But Granny Jen was still weak, and she needed somebody around to help her. He ventured, "Then what will happen? She still needs help, doesn't she?"

"Mother and I have talked about it," Winnie said in her precise voice, "and she's going to try it with Eloise here in the mornings. And I'll come down every weekend."

Hunter suppressed a grin. Granny Jen was in good hands with Eloise, but poor Winnie would work herself to death every weekend, battling imagined dust. Finally, he commented, "Getting old sucks."

"I suppose that's one way to put it. But you know, Hunter, I think you're Mother's main reason to keep going these days." After a pause, Winnie added, "She's going to stay in this house as long as she can, you know."

Hunter was quiet as he put the pan on the stove and checked on his chicken in the oven. Finally, he spoke, not looking at her. "Uh, I've wanted to know something."

"What?"

"Did it make you mad when she gave me the apartment?"

"No. Why would you think that?"

"Well, it didn't seem fair. I mean, she has two other grand-children."

"Don't you worry about my girls. They've never loved it here like you do. And I know for a fact they've got their eyes on a few pieces of Mother's jewelry." She paused. "It's sad to say, but this house will probably wind up as a bed-and-breakfast some-day. Don't look so shocked. That's just reality, Hunter. That's the direction this town is headed. It's good for a piece of the property to stay in the Kittrell name. Mother knew what she was doing, as usual. Just don't ever sell it without giving someone in the family a chance to buy it, okay?"

"Sell it?" Hunter's voice implied she had lost her mind.

She chuckled, sounding exactly like Granny Jen. "I like you, Hunter. I know you don't quite know what to make of me, but I like you."

Fortunately, the back door opened just then, for Hunter had no reply to her statement. "Hey, Hunter," called Amy's friendly voice. "Want to try a little fishing tonight?"

"Shoot, yeah. This curfew has about dragged me down."

"You kids don't need to break curfew now," warned Winnie.

"Oh, we'll head out in the opposite direction from the harbor. Grayson will never know," said Hunter.

"It's dangerous anyway."

"Everybody's after my tail, not my throat," Hunter replied grimly. "I need a break. We'll be in early. Promise."

They met before eight, the sky mellow, the water voluptuously slick. "Do your parents know you're doing this?" asked Hunter as he swung off the dock into the boat.

"I told them I was going fishing with you. I didn't spell it out, but it seemed pretty obvious we would be out past curfew."

"Just so your dad doesn't come after me for kidnapping."

"I'm twenty-one. Good grief." They headed out, passing lovely old homes, comfortably large, their shaded lawns continuing across the street to the water's edge and ending in private docks. They glided past a stretch of practical cottages crowded along the strip of land between the road and the creek. A couple of sturdy ponies, scruffy from a lifetime of existing on the windswept shoal opposite the houses, stared at them as they passed. Several boats were coming in; theirs was the only one going out.

"Do you ever see Miki?" asked Amy.

"Every day. All she gives me is the back of her head, but I know he hasn't left with her. And she knows I'm here. That's all I can do."

"Why would he leave with her? Wouldn't he have to stay until this thing is solved?"

He shrugged. "What can I say? That's my fear, and I'm hangin' on to it." He made it sound like a joke, but his fear was genuine.

"What else scares you?" she asked lightly.

"Not being."

For once, Amy didn't ask another question. Hunter throttled up when they reached open water and motored on for several minutes to a familiar deep hole known to be a good spot for panfish. No other boats surrounded it tonight. Amy gave him an okay sign and went forward to drop anchor as Hunter cut the motor. Neither spoke as they clattered rods and jigs, rigging up.

Finally, Hunter continued the conversation. "Do people, like, expect you to be?"

"Like my dad wants me to work for him?"

"Not do. Be." When she just looked at him curiously, he sighed. "Maybe you can't understand. You probably already are what everybody thinks you should be."

She cast out and let her jig sink before reeling in, flipping the tip of the rod as she reeled. "Are you saying you're not at peace with who you are?"

He made an annoyed sound. "I'm saying people expect me to be something that I'm not, and that I don't know how to be, that I don't even know if I want to be."

"I think if it scares you, then it's a sign that you want to be." She cast again. "I, for one, like you better this summer than I have in, well, about three summers."

"Maybe you're the one who's changed."

She gave him a *get real* look, then yelled, "Aargh!" and gave her rod a jerk. "Missed. You broke my concentration, Hunter."

"You still fish like a girl is your problem. Let me show you how it's done." He dodged the ice cube she chunked at him and settled down to fish.

They had three spots and one flounder in the box before Hunter spoke again. "I should have called you last summer before I left for school. I should have told you good-bye."

"It's okay," said Amy, her eyes on her line. "You were mad at me."

"I was mad at myself," Hunter said quietly. "I thought I had lost my best friend in the world, and it was my fault."

She glanced quickly at his face and looked away. "I'm glad we're still friends," she said simply, and he nodded.

Night came earlier these days, the sky draining from yellow to gray. They fished in companionable silence until a cruiser approaching drew their attention. As the boat came closer, running lights glistening on the water, its bulk took form in the remaining light as a sleek thirty-six-foot Bayliner cabin cruiser.

"You know, I've seen that boat before when we were out," Amy commented.

Hunter shrugged.

"At least twice. I know I saw it the day you found the dead guy."

That got his attention.

"It passed me in a hurry going in as I was headed back to you."

The cruiser passed them, moving quickly in the channel, one hundred feet from their position in open water. Hunter was not yet burning his signal lights, and he sat still and eyed the boat carefully as it went by. "I saw a cruiser that day," he said. "Didn't think much about it at the time. This is creepy." He put his rod aside. "Pull up anchor."

"Huh?"

He started the motor. "I'm going to follow it."

"Are you nuts? What if it's the killer?"

"I don't think he saw us." He grabbed her rod and reeled in. "Navigate for me."

"He could run this boat down, Hunter."

"I'll keep my running lights off. Maybe he won't see us behind him."

"Bad idea."

"There's no one else on the water. Nobody will run into us."

"There's no one to see him if he decides to murder us."

Determined, Hunter fired his motor and followed at a distance. The cruiser led them straight toward Taylor's Creek and Beaufort, staying in the channel. Once the cruiser entered the creek, Hunter backed off, widening the distance. He had nowhere to hide now. The night had grown very dark, and Amy sat perfectly still, as if not moving would conceal them. They passed a public boat ramp, then private docks, some lighted. Hunter kept toward the far bank, away from the lights.

Suddenly, the cruiser disappeared. For one panicked second, Hunter was disoriented; then he realized the cruiser, too, was running with no lights in an unlit stretch of the creek. With a whispered curse, he killed the motor. Ahead, there was a distinct change in tone in the cruiser's engine from a running whine to a growling idle. Was it reversing direction? Hunter hesitated, hand on the switch. Any indication that they were about to be run down and he would plow straight for the Beaufort shore, where they could chance a sprint to the nearest house.

The engine noise quit suddenly, and they sat in silence, listening for the next sound. Amy shook her head slightly and pointed discreetly to the Beaufort shore. Hunter heard the muffled bump of a boat docking. Dimly, he could make out the dark form of the boat at an unlit private dock.

They drifted on the incoming tide until they were in the center of the channel, sitting ducks should the owner of the cruiser look their way. If he was the killer, this was not a safe place, and neither was the opposite bank. Carefully, afraid to make a sound, Hunter picked up the paddle and pushed them toward the closest dock, quiet splashes alerting Amy. Straining, she reached toward the approaching dock and grabbed a firm hold, stopping their progress. Hunter's long arm kept the skiff from bumping. And there they sat, staring into the darkness, trying to recognize the dim figure they could see mooring the cruiser, expecting him to leave the dock and head for a nearby house, hoping he wouldn't come toward them.

They waited. A long minute passed. Then they heard the unmistakable sound of a speedboat cranking up. Even in the darkness, Hunter could see terror in Amy's eyes. He cursed himself for putting her in danger against her better judgment.

There was a horrifying moment when the growl and gurgle of the speedboat seemed to come toward them, and then the noise distinctly moved away, on toward town and the city docks. They never even saw the boat. It was running without lights, and it must have been black.

Hunter didn't attempt to follow. The speedboat was traveling too fast for the blackness of the night. If the driver had seen them, he could have outrun them, passing by Beaufort toward the harbor and out to sea, or he could have turned and broken their little boat in two. Although it seemed important to see where it went, Hunter was afraid for Amy's sake.

"What was that all about?" Amy asked when the sound had died away.

"Somebody else breaking curfew?"

"Somebody going to a lot of trouble not to be seen. I'd sure like to know why."

"I feel like a fool saying this, but I guess we'd better tell Grayson," Hunter said. "Could be nothing, but it sure seemed like something."

"Yeah," Amy said. Then, she surprised him by saying, "Ease us in closer so we can get a look at that cruiser."

Hunter did not dare start his motor yet, and so they eased along by paddle and Amy's sure arm, pulling themselves from one dock to the next, pushing away from boats when necessary. Finally, they were beside the cruiser, and Hunter stood carefully and looked over the side.

The deck was trim—not a cooler, not a fishing rod in sight. No seashells, no sand, no beer cans—nothing to indicate the boat's purpose on the water.

Without telling Amy what he was doing, Hunter hoisted himself up and bellied over the side. Amy stood up.

"What? Are you crazy?" she demanded. "Get back here."

"He's not coming back," Hunter whispered.

"You are insane."

"I know," he answered. To his surprise, the cabin was not locked, and he ducked inside. A quick tour of the salon and galley yielded no food supplies of any kind. Very odd. A glance inside the tiny head revealed a bottle of men's cologne, no razor, no toothbrush. Inside the stateroom, he opened a locker. Identical sets of men's shirts and slacks hung neatly, apparently new. And inside a drawer were new boxers and socks, packaged.

Not sure what to make of it, Hunter decided to look for shoes. Dropping to his knees, he pulled out a drawer beneath the berth. "Oh, crap!" Flailing awkwardly, he scrambled backward, slamming the drawer with his foot and kicking the cabin door shut. He dropped over the side into his boat with a thud, cursing in a whisper.

"What?" asked Amy, startled.

"We're getting out of here now. Push off. Push off." He couldn't crank the boat fast enough, and Amy heaved mightily, shoving them away from the cruiser.

Once they were pointed toward home, she slid back to his seat. "What is it? Tell me."

"It's him. It's gotta be." He leaned close to speak privately above the noise of the motor. "Scuba gear in a drawer. Changes of clothes, all alike. Too weird, Amy."

"Maybe he's a diver."

"With no food, nothing to drink in the galley? I don't know what it means, but it freaked me out, and I'm calling Grayson."

They cut quickly through the water toward Hunter's dock.

Neither spoke. Hunter was watching the water. Just as he backed off the throttle, reducing the noise, he said, "I'm really sorry I got you into this, Amy."

"I'm glad," she responded. "Maybe you've actually found the killer. Maybe this will all be over tomorrow."

Hunter frowned as he bumped the boat against his own dock. He wasn't sure finding the harbor killer would mean it was all over for him unless the guy confessed to killing Doug Sanders. Reaching up to steady the boat, his hand came in contact with a man's shoe. Hunter looked up to see Amy's father frowning down at him. "Uh, hello, Mr. Goodwin," he said.

"You know, kids," said Mr. Goodwin as he caught the mooring line, "when you say you're going fishing in a town under siege, old folks like me picture you dropping a hook off the dock here. Thank God you're back all right. Don't you know you could have put my daughter in danger?"

Hunter looked at the mooring cleat as he secured the line, then he climbed out of the boat, faced Amy's father squarely, and said quietly, "Actually, I did."

"What happened?" Mr. Goodwin asked sternly.

"Something weird, a little scary. This stuff seems determined to follow me this summer." And Hunter launched into the story even as he strode toward the house. Amy and her dad had no choice but to keep pace with him. He finished the tale on Granny Jen's stoop, in a hurry to call Grayson.

"It looks like you're the one determined to follow," Mr. Goodwin said without malice. "And, darn it, if you're going to get involved, I wish you would have sense enough to leave Amy out of it."

"I do too, probably more than you," Hunter said candidly and opened the door.

"Hunter?" Amy squeezed past her father and gave him a quick hug. "I'm glad we both made it home okay."

⟶ ⟶ ⟶

Grayson Tucker sat on his porch well past midnight, thinking. He believed every word Hunter had told him. The two stealthy boats, the identical clothes, the scuba gear—it all fit in with the scenario he'd been piecing together for weeks. He'd observed the speedboat from his bench tonight when it had docked at the city docks, and he knew who had stepped off that boat.

He could make an arrest now, this dark night, and his gut told him he would be arresting the harbor killer. "The Kitty Killer," Jack Franklin had called him. But what good would an arrest be? Unless a search turned up a knife that could undeniably be proven to be the murder weapon, or unless the man's fingerprints were on the gun Grayson felt certain Hunter was hiding, he didn't have much to give the D.A. He had a lot of questions and a gut feeling, but it took some answers to go to trial. It took hard evidence to get a conviction. So far, Grayson had neither.

But he did have patience and a gambler's instinct. He believed with a little luck and a few more days, he'd have something more to go on. If his gut were right, he also knew the name of the next potential victim.

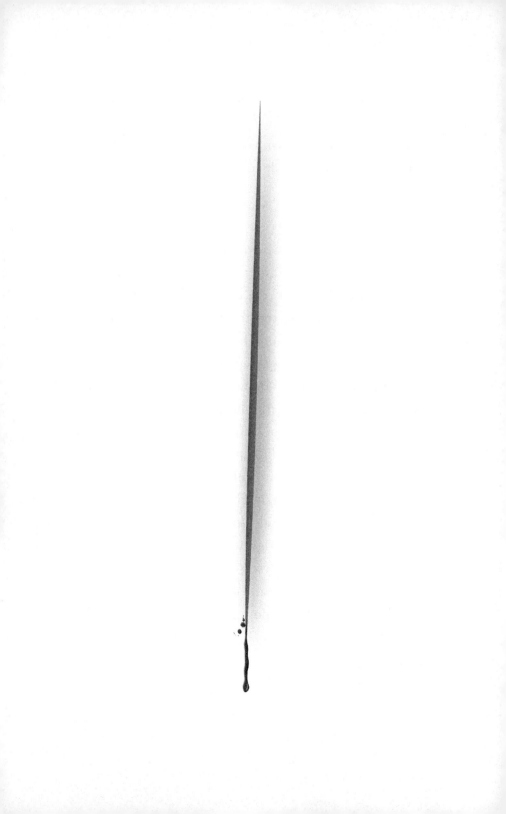

TWENTY-FIVE

"You've been working late on your drawings," Granny Jen commented to Hunter over breakfast the next day.

"Oh, man. I thought I had my music pretty low," he replied.

"You didn't disturb me," she chuckled. "I just couldn't sleep."

"Is something wrong?"

"A lot on my mind is all," Jen said. She chewed quietly, eyes closed, the morning breeze ruffling her white hair. Finally, she looked at Hunter and smiled. "What I want to know is, when is the unveiling?"

"Uh, I don't know. Haven't thought about it." He sat slouched in his chair, as nonchalant as ever, yet when he glanced up at his granny, he had the distinct feeling he no longer looked like a boy in her eyes.

"Well, I'd really like to see what you've been working on so hard," Granny Jen persisted.

"I guess it's about time to bring it out, if I'm ever going to." Hunter looked away and frowned. The work had kept him occupied, had kept his mind focused, but he was still not sure why someone had tried to frame him, nor why no further attempt had been made. And, for certain, he had no clue as to how to get Miki away from Jack Franklin. Never had the feeling that she was in danger left him.

"What did I say to bring on such brooding?" asked Granny Jen.

"Oh, sorry. I've got a lot on my mind. I'll go get my portfolio. You know," he said as he started out, "I've always dreaded leaving here, going back to school. I'm sort of anxious to get back this year."

"Why is that?" she asked encouragingly.

"I want my advisor to see these drawings. Whether he thinks they're great or not, it will show him that I'm really serious. It's hard enough to get a good internship without the entire department thinking you're about to bail out." With that, he left Granny Jen's porch and headed across the lawn toward his apartment.

He was halfway up his stairs when a car door slammed. Grayson Tucker came toward him, looking tired and strained.

"Hey, Mr. Tucker. How's it going?"

"Hunter, I need to talk to you."

"Come on up." Hunter led the way, somewhat resigned, somewhat curious. Once inside, he tried to sound casual. "Did you check out the cruiser?"

"We have it under surveillance."

"Damn. You ought to be searching that sucker. Taking fingerprints."

"It's your fingerprints I want today."

"What!"

Grayson held up a hand, halting the explosion. "I need the gun, Hunter. Today. And I need your fingerprints to help us sort out any other prints that might be on it."

"Mine are definitely on it. And if it turns out to be the gun that smoked that tourist-guy . . ."

"I know who the boats belong to," Grayson interrupted firmly.

"Well, I sure didn't read in the paper that you'd made an arrest!"

Grayson's voice was grim. "It's not a crime to act suspiciously or to own scuba gear. So far, I don't have enough to make an arrest."

"That's why you need to search. Don't you get it? It's probably where he keeps the knife, too."

"Maybe. Maybe not. Maybe we'll find a knife. Maybe we can prove it was used in those murders. Maybe not. There has to be something else that ties a suspect to a homicide. An arrest doesn't mean squat if you can't get a conviction."

"That's why you need to check those boats. Don't you watch TV? That dead tourist's . . ."

"Mr. Sanders?"

"Yeah. Well, his blood is somewhere besides that beach. You said so yourself. Clothing fibers. Hair. Stuff like that. Go find that on those boats, and then I'll give you the gun. I swear on my honor as a Southern gentleman."

Grayson almost smiled. "Those boats aren't going anywhere. We're watching them around the clock. And if I don't get my hands on something concrete, very soon, we will search those boats and just hope we turn up something besides scuba gear and new shirts. I'm gambling on another piece of evidence, Hunter.

And you may be sitting on it."

Hunter stared long into Grayson's brown eyes. "What happens to me," he finally said, "if mine are the only prints on the gun and the boat guy has no link to the dead tourist?"

"The tourist's name was Sanders."

"Okay. Maybe you can prove the guy on the cruiser iced those drug dealers, but what if I'm still your best suspect in the Sanders thing? What then? What happens to me?"

Grayson's voice remained quiet. "Maybe I have another link, Hunter."

"Tying the guy on the boat to Sanders?"

Grayson squinted slightly.

"Who owns the boats?"

"You know I can't tell you that. You're just going to have to trust my instincts on this. I know I'm gambling, but you're not expendable. I'll do everything I can to protect you. And that's my word as a Southern gentleman."

Hunter sighed and looked toward his blue window. "Oh, hell. I may as well get it over with." He walked to his kitchen and pulled out his only knife.

"Interesting," Grayson said.

"Not really. There used to be a whole box of these around here somewhere. I'm sure you've seen knives like this. Used to be a commercial fillet knife. I guess after it was sharpened a thousand times, it wound up this short and thin."

Hunter went to his closet and began to saw into the wall with the knife. He sat on the floor, one long leg stuck out into the room. Grayson studied him thoughtfully.

"You know, Mr. Tucker, I have a theory," Hunter said.

"What's that?"

"Well, it was weird how the noose was around my neck, and then it just lifted. Like evaporated." He sawed carefully. "If you had arrested me, then I would have taken credit for at least one murder. By proxy, sort of. Maybe all of them. Anyway, I think the guy wanted to get all the glory. Be famous or whatever. I don't know why he messed with me to start with, but I think that's why he left me alone."

"Don't touch the gun," was all Grayson said. He came forward with a gloved hand, lifted the gun out of the wall, and bagged it. He left without another word.

When he reached his car, Grayson sat still and breathed deeply, then grabbed a bottle of antacid. Hunter's theory was smart, and it fit his own theory of who the killer was. In fact, it fit so closely that he wanted to rush down to that boat and put every inch under a microscope. Not yet. Not yet, he told himself.

Hunter opened the passenger door and climbed in. Grayson wasn't really waiting for him, but he guessed he may as well go on and get the kid's fingerprints.

"My hands are shaking so hard, you probably can't get a print," Hunter said with a laugh.

Grayson smiled and didn't admit that his hands were shaking too badly to crank the car. He took a couple more deep breaths before doing so.

He had the gun.

He knew what type of knife he was looking for.

And he knew where Rob Kittrell was at this exact moment.

"No! No, no, no, no!" Grayson slammed the top of his desk with his fist with each exclamation. His secretary tiptoed to the door, looked in and found him sitting with his head in his hands, and then left without asking questions.

Grayson was not prepared for the lab report on Hunter's gun. Because this case took precedence over every other investigation in the state, he had his answer almost too quickly. Yes, the gun had been fired recently. Yes, a .32 caliber could have been used to kill Doug Sanders. Yes, there was another set of prints on the gun.

They were not the prints Grayson had wanted. They did not belong to the owner of the cruiser.

Grayson knew he had to make an arrest quickly, before the SBI went after Hunter Kittrell. The prints were the same as the second set on the tape recorder.

Most likely, they belonged to Miki Stone.

An hour later, Grayson had Miki Stone in custody. Grayson leaned back in the interrogation room's leather chair, its oak arms stained dark from decades of oil and sweat. The chair squeaked as he swiveled from side to side, a monotonous sound that continued for five minutes. Afternoon sunshine streamed in through a high window, heating up the room. In a calm, deep voice, Grayson drawled, "Young lady, I'm waiting for you to tell me something that makes some sense."

"Jack said you were bluffing before about the fingerprints." Miki's voice was icy.

"Maybe." Grayson pointed at her ink-stained fingers. "But very soon, I'll have proof that your prints are on that gun. Now would be a very good time for you to explain that."

"I don't have to say anything to you. I want a lawyer."

"Okay." Grayson did not make a move. His big hands were folded on the table, and he stared at her across the four feet of hard oak that separated them. It was very intimidating, and he knew it.

Defensively, Miki said, "I told Jack that I stole Hunter's gun and then lost it."

"Let me remind you that you have asked for a lawyer." Again Grayson made no move toward the telephone.

"I'm just telling you what you already know. Jack knew I had sneaked into Hunter's apartment, and so he asked me about the gun. I don't see what the big shock is that my fingerprints are on it." She narrowed her eyes, matching his intimidation. "Or have you been too busy bench-warming to read what's in your own reports?"

Grayson didn't flinch. Nothing in his eyes revealed that the reports Franklin had turned in didn't say anything about Miki having stolen Hunter's gun from his apartment. Instead, he said very calmly, "I'm not going to ask you any more questions until you have a lawyer. But there's nothing that says I can't make it very clear to you the trouble you are in. Doug Sanders took several photographs of you before he died. He seemed to have had an obsession with you, and he also seemed to think you were Vanessa Singer. He may have even thought he was going to see Vanessa the night he died."

Miki's hard facade was crumbling fast. Grayson continued, "You and I both know that you're hiding something about Gus York's murder. And the tape recorder proves that Bob Schneider thought he was talking to Vanessa Singer just before he died. Now you and your lawyer can figure out how you're going to answer that coincidence and see if you can explain how the gun with your fingerprints on it wound up back in Hunter's apartment after Doug Sanders' murder."

Miki stood abruptly, shaking, a trapped look on her face. "I'm getting out of here."

"You are not free to go. You are only free to call your lawyer." Grayson shoved the telephone toward her. She sat back down, and somewhere behind the tears and the terror, Grayson saw the college kid Hunter had brought with him to Beaufort.

Grayson did not look back as he walked out of the room. Maybe that kid would be grateful to know that she'd been a sacrifice. She had bought a few more days of freedom for Hunter. It wasn't likely another agency would arrest Hunter for the same murder for which Grayson had arrested Miki. Not just yet, anyway. And all Grayson needed was a little more time.

"You have no cause to hold her without bond." Jack Franklin's voice was loud, and it exploded through the hallways of the county courthouse.

"I have her prints on the probable murder weapon."

"You have Kittrell's too."

"It was his gun. His prints should have been on it, and he has an alibi. She has yet to explain why she had the gun or where she was the night Doug Sanders died."

"Let's hear you explain where you got the gun."

"You'll find out at the bond hearing Tuesday."

"You cannot hold that girl four days on such load-of-crap evidence."

"Wanna bet?"

"Yeah, I'll bet." Jack's face was contorted with rage. He was standing close, and he pushed at Grayson's chest with his knuckles. "I'll bet her daddy's big city lawyers will have her out of your dinky jail before the sun sets on this town." Grayson held his ground. "And I'll bet even your good old boy judge will throw you and your evidence out of court two seconds after you stumble in. And I'll bet the national news will call you the South's stupidest police chief while I arrest your cocky little Kittrell friend and, by God, his ass won't see daylight again until doomsday."

"You might not be so quick to bet," Grayson said in a carefully controlled voice, "if you knew how high the stakes really are." And then he turned slowly and walked away.

"You did what?" Hunter kicked the side of the police car and sliced the air with one fist. If Grayson had not been wearing a badge, Hunter would have dived through the open window for his throat, and Grayson knew it.

"I trusted you. I trusted *you!*" Hunter turned his back with a jerk. Grayson let the car roll forward. "Get in, Hunter," he said quietly.

Hunter stopped and stood for a defiant moment, back to the car, fists clenched. When he gave in, it was not without a scattering of gravel and a slam of the door.

Neither spoke as Grayson drove away from the curious eyes of onlookers. On a side street, he stopped the car and sat chewing a toothpick.

"You were supposed to go after the guy on that cruiser." There was resentment in Hunter's voice, disillusionment.

Grayson gave a sigh.

"Why did you arrest Miki?"

"Her fingerprints were on your gun."

"So? Big deal." Even as Hunter struggled to appear nonchalant, Grayson could tell the wheels were turning in his head. "You told me you need plenty of evidence to tie a person to a dead guy."

"That's right." There was finality in his voice.

"What was she doing with my gun? Did you ask her that? There has to be an explanation."

"Hunter, do you love her?"

"What kind of question is that?"

"Do you?"

"It doesn't matter. Don't you get it? I care what happens to her. I was—I was—." He slammed the dashboard with his fist. "Damn it! I was supposed to get her away from Jack Franklin. I didn't know she was in danger from you, too."

"She is away from Franklin," Grayson said. "You have to trust me, Hunter. I know what I'm doing, and I have the best interest of both of you at heart."

"Trust. Yeah, right." Hunter got out of the car, slammed the door, and stormed off without another word.

Back in his office, Grayson was ready to clobber the officer who stood before him. "No!" Grayson shouted. "This cannot have happened. Not in my town."

"I swear, it was just like I said," the officer insisted. "Her lawyers brought the magistrate with them. We had no choice but to let her go."

"That's not what I'm talking about." Grayson's voice was shaking with the effort to control his rage. "I told you—I gave you a direct order—to call me the minute her lawyer showed up."

"There were three of them, and it all happened so fast . . ."

"Nothing happens that fast. You didn't call me because you disagreed with me for holding the girl. You didn't think I knew what I was doing, and so you . . ."

"But the magistrate himself came down and set bond."

"And I said I wanted her held without bond. Where are those lawyers now?"

"I don't know. It's not my job to know."

Grayson turned his back and made for the nearest exit. It didn't matter now whether he talked to her lawyers or not. The damage was done. He had wanted a chance to suggest to them that she was safer in jail than anywhere else.

What he could not have told them or Hunter was that he knew something big was going down tomorrow. Maybe on the waterfront, maybe somewhere else. It would be between Jack Franklin and Rob Kittrell. And whatever Miki knew about the murders could get her caught in the middle.

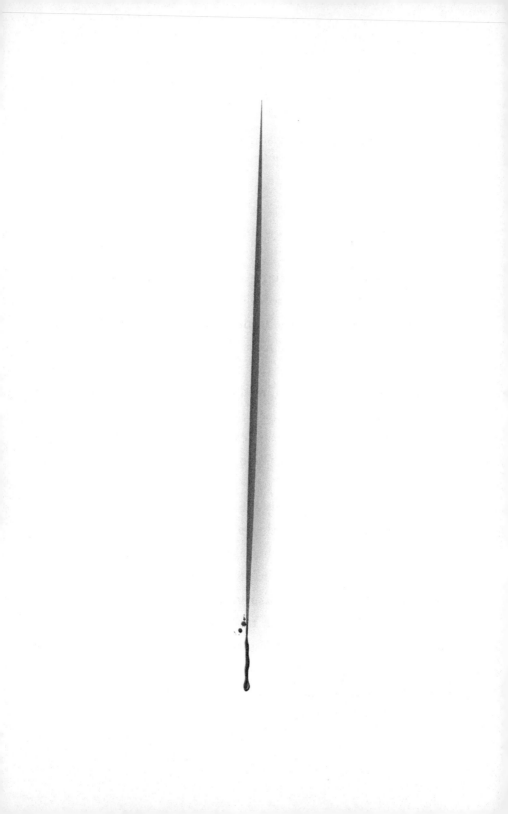

TWENTY-SIX

That night, the eve of Hunter's birthday, was heavy with August mist. Amy and Hunter sat on the end of his dock, their legs dangling. They were saying good-bye, sort of. Amy would be leaving for Chapel Hill in a couple of days. Hunter would be in Charlotte by this time next week. Neither said much.

"Best summer?" she asked, continuing a lifelong game.

"This one."

"Worst summer."

"This one."

She was quiet in understanding. When she spoke, her voice was small but frank. "We're not going to happen, are we?"

There was nothing indifferent in the way he looked at her. His face winced with genuine regret. "It's my fault," he said, and he looked back at the water.

"Mama says we're too much like brother and sister anyway," she said.

"Is that what you think?" He looked at her again, but she was staring intently at the water. He studied her curved lashes, her cheek where the dimple was hiding, the pretty turn of her mouth. He had kissed her last summer, her lips sweet and earnest, and it had not felt like kissing his sister.

When she didn't answer, he said, "You told me I need to decide who I am and what I want."

She smiled a little.

"I think I've figured out this summer who I'm not. I'm going to really try this semester to get my act together. And I know that my mind's still tangled up with Miki, and when I finally say good-bye to her, it's going to take some time to get her out of my system, but . . ." He swung his legs and looked away. "Granny Jen's invited me back for Thanksgiving." He saw Amy's legs begin to swing alongside his. "And I thought if you weren't seeing anybody by then, well, maybe we could, you know, get together."

When he looked at her, the dimple had come out of hiding. That was all the answer he needed.

When Hunter came home that night, barely an hour past curfew, Aunt Winnie was watching for him. "Hunter!" she called from the porch. "You're late."

He shrugged and started up his steps.

"Your grandmother is waiting up for you," said Winnie. "She's asked to see you in her room."

Hunter frowned in concern. It was not like Granny Jen to send Winnie after him. He nodded a greeting to the police officer Grayson kept constantly guarding Granny Jen's door and stepped into the house. Worried, he strode to his grandmother's room, knocked, and entered quietly. Granny Jen sat propped by pillows in bed, her hair combed neatly, wearing a silky blue robe.

"Bad day?" he asked, trying not to appear too concerned.

"It's a good day," she said. "And tomorrow will be even better. I'm just conserving my energy for your birthday."

"So," he said, trying to lighten the mood, "do I look like a man yet?"

She smiled and studied him approvingly. "You know, I think maybe you do. What do you plan to do on your birthday?"

"I guess go to work like I always do. I wish I had known this curfew was going to last so long; I might have found a morning job to make up for the hours I'm losing every night. And," he added with a careless shrug, "I don't know, maybe try to talk to Miki."

"What were you doing with your grandfather's gun, and why did she have it?" Jen asked abruptly.

He looked at her. How did she manage to know so much? "I'm ashamed to say what I was doing with it, and I have no idea why she had it. She didn't kill that tourist, though. You've got to believe me on that."

"I know she didn't. Surely, Grayson knows that. I keep thinking maybe he's trying to flush out the real killer. And your reason for having that gun brings me to my reason for wanting to see you. Forgiveness." She punctuated the word with a stately silence, and Hunter just stood and looked at her, almost afraid of what she might say. "It's time for you to begin to understand forgiveness. You have held on to your resentment against your father too long." When he frowned, she continued firmly, "Yes, it was a bad blow for a little boy, and it has made life hard for you. But you're a man now. It's time for you to let it go. You can choose to make what you want of your life from this day on, and you can choose how you will react when you see him again." When Hunter said nothing, she added, "Forgiveness is a choice, Hunter, an action. It's not an abstract feeling."

"My feelings toward my father haven't exactly been abstract."

"That's why I'm telling you this. You can't help how you feel, but you can choose how you act."

He sighed and took a step away.

"One more thing, Hunter." Her eyes twinkled. "Winnie doesn't think you should have to cook on your birthday. She's planned a delightful meal for the occasion."

Hunter left her room laughing, and some of the weight seemed to lift from his shoulders. It wasn't until he returned to his apartment that he wondered at her words, *when you see him again.*

Hunter's birthday dawned another easy Carolina day. The sun promised to be bright but not too hot, the wind just right. Showers were expected by late afternoon.

Hunter woke up early as he always did at Granny Jen's. Next week, he would be fighting the alarm clock to give him ten more minutes, but today he was glad to be awake, glad to see the sun stream blue through his window and glow happily on the coral wall. He surveyed his apartment. It belonged to him now, but it would be a few years before he would get to spend more than a few days at a time in it. He hoped to get started next summer in an internship program—if anyone would have him—and he would have to intern for several years after graduation before he could apply for a license and work as an architect on his own. One day in the not-too-distant future, though, this would be his home.

He stretched and thought about turning twenty-one. Until now, it had always seemed pretty cool. He could buy his own liquor. Nobody could tell him what to do. Now that he was twenty-one, it seemed a little scary. Nobody had to take him in if he fell flat on his face. He could screw up his life in a heartbeat, just by one bad move. He had to stop playing with life and start planning how to live.

And he would be living his life with memories of a dead guy and without Miki. It still made him sick to think about Sanders, and it still hurt to think about Miki. He no longer ached for her. He just wanted a chance to finish it, to get her safely away from Jack Franklin, to see her free of the murder charge. And when it was over, he wanted to kiss her good-bye.

As he swung out of bed and reached for a pair of shorts, a man's voice stopped him cold. "It's about time you were waking up."

Sweat broke out on the back of Hunter's neck and his gut twisted. He did not look toward the sofa. His movements deliberately slow and nonchalant, he pulled on the shorts and stood to his full height beside the bed. He preferred to face his father wearing pants and on his feet.

"How did you get in here?" he asked.

"I have ways." Rob Kittrell's native Carolina accent carried a West Coast twang. "You look good, kid."

Hunter did not take a step in the direction of his father. Chin lifted and jaw relaxed, he stared at the man he had both hated and longed for his entire life. He allowed nothing in his expression to reveal that his heart was banging his ribs with an awful commotion.

Rob Kittrell was sprawled on Hunter's sofa as if he were relaxing in his own living room, one foot propped on the wooden crate Hunter used as a coffee table, his body more lean and lanky than most men of forty-one. He was a good-looking man worn-down by life, the lines of his face deep, the glint in his eyes calculating.

Eighteen years of words and hatred and pretending not to care jammed inside Hunter's throat. He couldn't think of a single word to say.

"Got any coffee?" asked Rob.

"Uh, no. I do breakfast at Granny Jen's. Sorry." Hunter was relieved to have something easy to say. "Do you want to see her for breakfast? She's always up by now."

"Huh! You're planning on starting her day out with a heart attack, eh?"

"Actually, in some weird way, I think she's sort of expecting you." When Rob didn't respond, Hunter continued, "And Aunt Winnie's here."

"Well, hell. A family reunion." Rob looked toward the blue window, his eyes flat and dark, and made no move to stand. With a glance at his son, he said, "I've missed you, kid."

"Yeah, you missed all right." Hunter swiped the crate from beneath his father's foot without apology and sat on it, leaning forward intently. "You missed my basketball games; you missed my birthdays; you missed graduation—well, hell, what am I thinking?" Hunter bopped his forehead with the palm of his hand. "You missed my whole life."

No hint of regret crossed Rob's features. He smiled briefly at his son's humor. "You turned out okay," he said. "And thanks for the phone call."

"You don't know a damn thing about how I turned out." Hunter wanted something more from his father than he was getting: a fight, an apology, excuses, maybe a mushy outpouring of love that Hunter could stomp.

"Sure I do." Rob's shrug was careless, so much like his own that Hunter wanted to strangle him. Eyes narrow, Rob continued, "I've survived this long by being able to read a man's eyes. I can tell by yours that you've got it together."

Hunter stared him down. *Read this, man,* he thought. *I hate you and I wanted to kill you until I saw a real dead guy.* Rob blinked first. "Why are you here?" Hunter asked, continuing to stare down his father. "This whole town is under siege. I've got cops and reporters watching my place day and night, all of them looking for you. Not a good time for you to come sight-seeing."

Rob chuckled and pulled a pack of cigarettes from his shirt pocket.

"Not my brand," said Hunter when Rob offered him one. He sat on the crate and stared at his father lighting the cigarette, his guts in a knot, wishing the man cared half as much as he did. Damn it, he had always thought his father at least cared. "Why are you here?" he repeated

"Attending to some business," Rob said casually.

"For how long?" Hunter demanded.

Rob crossed his legs, long arm draped across his knee, and

took a drag of the cigarette.

Hunter leaned forward, his lips tight, and punched the air between them with one finger. "You know, after eighteen years of never hearing your name mentioned, I get hit with it everywhere I turn this summer," he said. "People are looking for you, people think they've seen you, people put your name in the same sentence with the harbor killings." Hunter sat back and waited for a response, an outburst. What he got was another chuckle.

"I haven't killed anybody lately, kid," Rob drawled slowly, his voice more Southern than it had been. He looked at his son sardonically over the cigarette, pleased with himself.

"The name's Hunter." Hunter stood up. "Hunter Kittrell. My mom wanted to change it to Barton, and I wouldn't let her, damn it." He kicked the side of the sofa.

"Good for you," Rob said calmly. "Keep your name, if it means something to you. Myself, I've changed names so many times I have a hard time keeping up with who I am."

His father's eyes were hard and shrewd, and Hunter turned his back and walked to the kitchen. Something inside him was shaking loose, hurting his chest, and he needed a break. Hunter pulled a carton of juice from the fridge and turned and stared at the back of Rob's head, the hair a little darker than his own, just touched with gray. *Forgive,* his grandmother had said. Forgive what? Forgive the man for not being who Hunter wanted him to be? Maybe he needed to forgive himself for caring so much all these years about a father who didn't care at all.

Hunter poured orange juice into a paper cup and returned to the sofa. This time he shoved the crate from beneath Rob's foot with his own foot and sat down once again. He drank from the carton and offered the cup to his father.

Rob took the juice, stubbed out the cigarette in a dish, and looked, in amusement, at Hunter sitting on the crate. "What happened to all the crap that was in here?" he asked.

Suddenly, Hunter was furious, so intensely furious that his hand shook and he had to set the carton down. This man had been gone for eighteen years, and he had not asked about his mother, his son, his sister, his former wife, where his father was buried, how his brother had died. The only thing he was curious about was the furniture.

Hunter struggled to keep his voice from shaking. "You've been gone a long time. And now you show up in the middle of a blood bath. I want to know why." Hunter leaned forward, hands on his knees, his body tense.

Rob didn't even twitch. He looked his son over. "You know, you're not at all like I pictured you. You've got this tension thing going on around you." He made a circle with one hand. "I thought you'd be more like me and less high-strung like your mom—"

"You leave my mom out of this!" Hunter sprang to his feet. He stood over his father, fists clenched, swallowing sobs of anger and hatred that sliced his heart. "What do you want?" he shouted.

Rob squinted up at him.

"I've waited a lifetime to talk to you." Hunter's voice was loud and shaky, but he didn't care. "If you don't have anything important to say now, just leave."

"I can't do that," Rob said. "I'm supposed to be here until eight o'clock. It's all part of the script." He smiled at the puzzled frown on Hunter's face, a slow, careless smile. "Did you read the letter I left in that chest?"

"No, I didn't read it," said Hunter, deriving some satisfaction from being able to say that. "I burned it."

If Rob was shocked or disappointed, he did not show it. He leaned his head on the back of the sofa and laughed, a flat, unnatural sound that sent a chill down Hunter's spine. The laughter stopped abruptly. "Maybe I left some of myself in you after all," he said.

Rob stood up, walked to the dining chest, and pulled out the drawer. "Always have a contingency plan, kid," he said. He removed the drawer and set it aside. Beneath the drawer space was a dust panel that Jack Franklin had removed the first time he searched Hunter's apartment. There was no secret compartment beneath that panel, Hunter knew. Hunter watched in fascination as Rob reached inside the drawer space, pushed against the under-side of the cabinet's top, and slid back a panel Hunter never knew existed. A piece of paper fell out.

Rob grinned at Hunter's dumbfounded expression. "This is the business end of that letter. You missed the part about how your beloved granny threw me out and forbid me to come back." Rob laughed again. "All this time, you thought I was the bad guy."

Hunter stood his ground. "Let's hear it. Let's hear your story. Or aren't you man enough to tell it to me face to face?"

"I'm not looking for a fight," Rob said. He waved the paper. "I'm just here to make a deal."

"Story first." Hunter rubbed his chest which was aching more by the minute. Granny Jen would be wondering where he was by now. Knowing she was thinking of him gave Hunter strength and a feeling of control he had never felt before.

"Short version then," Rob said, his eyes narrow. "She caught me selling and grabbed you away from me. Said she'd turn me in if I ever came back. She would have, too, stubborn old—" The fire in Hunter's eyes stopped Rob's tongue. "Anyway, you didn't have to grow up a poor fatherless kid. It was her choice."

Hunter rubbed his chest again. No longer was he at a loss for words. He had plenty of words ready to say to this man, but his new-found control told him to wait.

"Want to hear my deal?" asked Rob. Hunter didn't blink. "You're twenty-one today—happy birthday, by the way. According to the terms of my father's will, unless I got my ass back here by today, you would get my portion of his estate. And I couldn't get it unless I turned myself in. My inheritance. What a crock. Like it was going to do me a whole hell of a lot of good in jail. So you see what's kept me away all these years."

Hunter waited.

"But who should call me this summer but old Grayson Tucker offering me a sweet, sweet deal. Seems he can get me a reduced sentence if I'll just play a little game with him. I can have my inheritance after all and still have some life left after prison."

Hunter continued to wait. Things were shifting around in his chest. With every breath, anger and hatred seemed to be leaving his body, and the stronger forces of love and power were pumping in his heart. His mind, disciplined by hours of working out precise architectural details, was sharp and ready.

Rob waved the paper again. He smiled a charming, cocky smile that Hunter recognized as his own. "Here's my deal for you. I'll give you a fourth of this money today if you'll turn over the deed to this apartment." When Hunter didn't respond, Rob added, "I know it's yours. Donald told me before he died that Mama was going to give it to you this summer. It's a good deal. Enough money to get you through school and started on your big career. A chance to get rid of this dump." Rob looked around. "You'll never use it to its full potential, anyway."

Hunter didn't ask what Rob wanted with the apartment. He didn't care. He closed his eyes, breathed out the last hard chunk of hatred, and smiled, tears rolling down his cheeks. Forgiveness wielded a sharp blade, and his heart had taken a deeper cut today than he could have anticipated. But the blade had struck a healing blow and left no wound.

His Uncle Donald had been a smart man. He had known that this moment would come for Hunter. There was no doubt now in Hunter's mind that Donald had left him a sizeable inheritance. Donald had seen to it that Hunter could keep the things Rob would try to take away from him: a home, self-respect, even money. Hunter may have grown up longing for a father, but Rob Kittrell would have never been the daddy he wanted. Everybody who loved him knew that. Granny Jen had known it when she sent Rob away.

Hunter wiped the tears with the back of his hand, not caring what his father thought. Donald had asked Hunter whether he knew what his uncle valued most. As a matter of fact, Hunter did. It wasn't money. It was trust in God. It was belief that life was worthwhile. It was having people around who loved him and stuck by him no matter what. Those were the things that made him rich. Without them, a person groveled in poverty no matter how much money he inherited.

Hunter opened his eyes and squinted at his father. "You keep

the money," he said. "I'll figure out what to do with this dump."
He stepped back and looked at the words on his blue window.
The Lord shall preserve thy going out and thy coming in. The words
no longer mocked him. His father had gone out the wrong door
and had never come back. He was still gone as far as Hunter
was concerned. It wasn't God's fault, and there wasn't anything
Hunter could do to change it. He just had to make sure he stepped
through the right door himself.

"It's nearly eight o'clock," said Hunter. He felt strengthened
by forgiveness and a strong dose of growing up.

"Are you trying to get rid of me, kid?"

"No, sir. I'm just ready for breakfast. You're welcome to come."

Rob looked at his son curiously. "No hard feelings?"

"No way." Hunter stuck out his hand for a handshake and
smiled an easy, generous smile when Rob took his hand. "I wish
you the best. I honestly do."

A car pulled into the driveway. Rob turned to go. "That's my
ride." Just before he dashed down the steps, he said over his shoulder, "Get down to the waterfront in an hour. Grayson has a show
planned. A regular Broadway musical."

Hunter started down his steps with a lot on his mind. His
father said Grayson Tucker had called him this summer. Jack
Franklin was in Beaufort waiting for Rob Kittrell. People had
died all summer while Jack waited for Rob. Jack may have known
about the terms of his grandfather's will and the likelihood that
Rob would show up by Hunter's birthday, but Hunter's gut told

him Jack did not know Grayson had called Rob. *A sweet, sweet deal.* What had Rob meant?

A reporter jumped out of his car and started firing questions about the gun. Hunter stopped in his tracks and shut his eyes, thinking hard. Rob had put the letter in Hunter's apartment. Had he come back later and planted the gun? If so, that would make him the killer. But how could he have gotten it from Miki, and why would he have gone on a rampage of murder in Beaufort Harbor? Hunter shook his head. Rob seemed intent only on grabbing his inheritance. And Rob might have slipped by the federal agents watching Hunter's apartment this morning, but he never would have gotten by the officer guarding Granny Jen's door unless Grayson allowed it.

A sweet, sweet deal. Maybe the big question was, what connected Jack Franklin to Rob Kittrell? There had to be something Hunter was missing, some secret that went beyond a drug agent waiting for a dealer to return to his hometown. Hunter's eyes opened, and he jumped in place with a yell, startling the reporter and the officer guarding Granny Jen's back door.

Miki was in danger. His heart had told him so all summer, but now his head caught up. Jack Franklin wasn't just a federal agent looking for the harbor killer; he was the killer. He had to be. Who else could have taken the gun from Miki, killed Doug Sanders, and planted it in Hunter's apartment? And then he had gone after Hunter—why? Why had he done that? Shaking, Hunter started at a run toward his boat. He had to try once more to get Miki away from Jack. Whatever Grayson was planning, Miki would be caught in the middle.

TWENTY-SEVEN

Miki awoke to bright sunlight and a smoky, greasy odor. She could hear Jack moving around in the galley cooking breakfast. Her chest ached from the crushing weight of the burden within her. It was too great a weight to drag from the bed, and yet she did. Today she was blowing this place—one way or another.

She guessed Jack knew she was leaving; he barely tolerated her presence these days. The court only gave her two choices: stay in Beaufort or return to school. She was not allowed to be any other place until the Grand Jury convened in three weeks. Beaufort was not an option. She would put off until later today to decide whether to choose school or No Choice. No Choice would solve all her problems, forever.

Searching through several pockets, she found one upper and swallowed it with no water. She left behind the elegant silk dresses Jack had given her, packed only a few belongings in a knapsack, and left the stateroom in a long, shirred cotton skirt, her hair down.

"Traveling?" asked Jack.

"We've maxed this thing out."

"It was good while it lasted, though, wasn't it, sweetheart?" His smile could have been chiseled by a master sculptor. He looked just the way he had when she first saw him: a man ready for excitement.

"What is that smell?" she asked abruptly.

"Country ham and grits. The finest in the harbor." He extended a bubbling pot of grits for her observation.

"Undoubtedly because nobody else in the harbor would have it. I swear, Jack, you are Southern."

The glance he gave her was quick, but hard. "Have some anyway, before you leave, whether you like it or not. I won't send you out into the world on an empty stomach. Come on, sit down."

Reluctantly, she plunked down at his table. Her head was beginning to buzz, and she took the coffee he offered to boost the high.

"This will need to cook another minute." He passed a hand down his bare chest, a subtly appealing motion. She looked away. "I'm going to dress while we wait."

He slid the passageway door closed and left her sitting alone. She looked around, taking in the yacht's sleek appointments, waiting for the buzz in her head to lift the dead weight in her heart. It didn't. Quietly, keeping her mind blank, not yet facing the decision, she opened the drawer in Jack's table and pulled out the .38 pistol he kept there. She slipped it into her knapsack.

When Jack returned, he dished out two bowls of buttery grits and a plate of ham and sat beside her. She pushed the bowl away and leaned on the table, one hand covering her face.

"God, what now?"

"I'm sick, Jack. Just give me a minute and I'll get out of here."

"Sick? In what way?"

"Nauseated. Your cologne. It reminds me of the night Bob Schneider died. Just give me a minute."

"Lean your head all the way on the table."

"What?"

"Try it, it might work. No, not on your arms." Jack slipped to the seat beside her and took her arms in his hands. "Put your arms behind you." When Miki tried to pull away from him, he jerked her arms roughly behind her. "Put your arms . . ."

"Aiih! Jack, what are you doing? Jack!" She struggled to get away from him.

"Shut up, Miki."

"Jack, no. You're hurting me, Jack. What have I done?"

"You know too much," he answered, his voice smooth in her ear, his experienced hands pinning her arms behind her with a cord.

"I don't know anything. What's wrong with you?"

"Oh, you know, all right. My cologne? Think about it."

Her brain yielded up the memory in a flash: his cologne enveloping her the night Gus York died. He watched the recognition dawn in her face.

"Actually, I'm a little disappointed in you, Miki. I thought you might have caught on before now."

"I don't know what you're talking about. I don't know anything about your cologne except it makes me sick."

"Well now you do." He devoured his grits hungrily, taking the ham from the plate and crumbling it over the grits.

After watching him a minute, she said, "I wouldn't have if you hadn't overreacted. And it's not enough to go to the police with. For all I know, it's the cologne you wear when you're working a case. Now let me go."

"You just keep telling yourself that, sweetheart. Tell yourself that was a little man you saw in Gus York's kitchen. Tell yourself I didn't disappear for a while every single time someone died in the harbor. It might make the next few hours go a whole lot quicker."

"Why? What are you going to do with me? Tell me, Jack."

"It depends on whether or not I have a good day at work." His eyes mocked her.

"Don't play games with me."

"Oh, I won't. I take my work very seriously. Executing the scum of the earth is serious work. Why do you think I've remained a drug agent all these years? It allows me access to information on scores of names, including people who have been underground for years." He leaned toward her, and her breath caught over the nausea that rose once again. "If I have a good day, then it will mean that I have completed my finest execution yet. And I may be in such a good mood that I might consider untying you before I sink the boat. How long do you suppose it will take you to swim three miles?"

"You're the devil himself!"

He laughed. "You flatter me. And how does that make you feel, to think you might just have slept with the devil?"

Miki swallowed hard.

"You really should have eaten while you had the chance.

We won't talk about what will happen if I have a bad day, since you have developed this sudden aversion to me. But cheer up. I could have a really lousy day and die myself." He chuckled at the hope that came into her eyes. "No, no. You won't be on this boat. You will be awaiting today's outcome on another boat. My boat." He looked around. "I wasn't planning to make a run for it on a yacht owned by the government. I have an even nicer one waiting for me offshore. Aren't you going to beg me to take you with me, Miki? You've grown so fond of luxury."

She tried to spit on him.

"I get it. You think your Kittrell boy will search every boat up and down this creek until he finds you. Kind of makes you wish you hadn't turned your back on him so many times, doesn't it?"

She opened her mouth to speak, and a yell from the water interrupted. "Miki! Miki, I've got to talk to you." The voice resounded through the harbor. "I swear you've got to listen. Please, Miki!"

Jack covered her mouth. She tried to bite him. Hunter's shouts continued from the water.

"I can crush every bone in the side of your face with one blow," Jack whispered in her ear. "Your Kittrell boy can't help you, Miki." He lifted his hand from her mouth. "Don't make a sound. I'm warning you. Don't. I'll kill him, too, if I have to. Two Kittrells today or just one; it's all the same to me."

And she sat with her head bowed and tears streaming while Hunter shouted her name over and over.

"Miki, I'm coming back. It's my birthday, and you have to talk to me." Hunter was standing in his boat as he yelled, and he pulled away, shaking in desperation. He had less than an hour to get her away from Jack Franklin. He looked toward the boardwalk. Grayson was not sitting on his bench, but another officer was there and two more stood at opposite ends of the boardwalk. Surely Grayson knew Miki was in danger. Surely she was not expendable. Hunter felt helpless. He had to talk to Granny Jen. There was a piece of information he was missing. If anybody knew what it was, it was Granny Jen. "I'll be back in a few minutes, Miki." He spoke in a quiet voice, knowing she couldn't hear him. "I'll get you off that boat no matter what it takes." And he throttled up, ignoring the no wake zone, and headed for his own dock.

"Well, that was interesting," Jack said matter-of-factly when Hunter was gone. "I commend you for your self-control. You wanted to travel today, and so we will. Aren't you lucky? Here's what we're gonna do. We'll take a little ride to my cruiser, and we'll do it very quietly."

"I'm not going anywhere with you."

"Okay. Your choice." He walked into the galley and took his vegetable knife from a drawer. In one swift motion, he had it across her throat, the blade sharp against her skin. She could not even twitch. "I'd rather not kill you here in case someone finds you before I've completed my execution, but I will. It's your choice. Just remember, there's always the possibility I'll let you swim if I take you with me."

She breathed an "okay," and he released her. "Quickly and quietly. Don't even think about makin' a move."

"My bag."

"You're not going to need that."

"I need a tissue, Jack."

"Still spunky, are you, even in the face of death? Well, get it and come on." He kept her close, the knife in his jacket pressed against her side. They exited the starboard side, the bulk of the yacht hiding them from the boardwalk, and boarded his speedboat which was tied in the empty slip beside them. Jack forced her to lie down in the seat until they were out of sight of the boardwalk. All Miki could do was hug the knapsack and stare longingly at Hunter's house as they passed. His boat was docked, and she could see his Jeep in the driveway, but he was not in sight.

When they reached the dock where Jack's cruiser was moored, Miki tried to plot a quick escape. Kick. Scream. Grab the gun. Shoot. Run. Before her body could respond to her brain's commands, Jack pushed the knife through the fabric hard, the blade slicing her beneath her ribs. Miki screamed, her legs buckling.

"Shut up and get inside," Jack growled. He shoved her into the cruiser and forced her to sit in a swivel chair. Roughly, ignoring the blood flowing from her side, Jack jerked her arms behind the seat and tied her hands. He tied her legs to the pedestal that secured the chair to the floor.

The cabin was stifling and oppressively hot. Jack ripped the hem of her skirt with the knife and snapped the piece of cloth in front of her face.

"Don't put that in my mouth, Jack," Miki sobbed. "I can't

breathe. I'm about to throw up."

"Shut up." He forced the cloth into her mouth and tied it tightly. "Stop crying if you want to breathe. And I highly recommend that you not throw up. Drowning on your own vomit would be a stinking way to die."

Her eyes stared in horror at the red stain spreading across the front of her cotton shirt.

"That's not as bad as it looks. If you sit real still it'll quit. Of course, it might attract a few sharks later on, should I let you swim when I sink this boat."

He went to the locker and pulled out a shirt from the row of identical shirts. "This should have clued you in, if the cologne didn't. I always wore the same shirt to an execution. Shower, change, splash of cologne, and no one even knew I left the room. Too bad you weren't a little sharper."

Opening his jacket, he stashed the knife inside a holster. A hammer slammed against Miki's heart as she noticed the empty gun pocket. Would he miss the gun and return to kill her?

As he started to leave, he said, "By the way, have you noticed anything different about my accent the past few minutes? You were right about one thing. I am Southern."

★ ★ ★

"Granny Jen!" Hunter nearly stumbled into the house in his haste. "You've got to tell me something right now. It's very important."

"Your grandmother has a lot on her mind today," warned Aunt

Winnie. "Whatever it is can wait until a better day."

"Granny Jen," Hunter said more quietly, kneeling in front of her. "I have to ask you something. Miki is in danger. I think Jack Franklin is the harbor killer, and I think Grayson is about to force a showdown between him and my father in the harbor. But I don't get it. I need to know the connection between them."

Jen's smile was as sure and kind as ever, and she patted his hand and nodded for him to continue.

"The day my father left, we were—we were on the street or something," Hunter said. "I remember him waving good-bye. Was there someone else there? What happened after he left?"

"Yes, there was someone else there." Granny Jen's voice was strong, but Hunter noticed the tears in Winnie's eyes. She was afraid for her mother to relive that day.

He rubbed her hand lovingly. "Just tell me, Granny Jen. Then you can forget it forever."

"A drug deal went down right before my eyes, Hunter," said Jen. "Your father had you in the middle of it. The buyer was a friend of your dad's. I had met him a couple of times."

"So you talked to him before. Did he have a loud voice? Like maybe a Yankee accent? Like Franklin's?" Hunter asked.

"I don't remember anything unusual about his accent. He grew up in Wilmington, I think."

"Was he, like, really good-looking?"

"No more so than your father. About the same height and age." Jen frowned, trying to remember.

"What happened to him?"

"He went to prison. They arrested him the very next day."

Hunter looked helplessly at Winnie. "I can't make it fit. Someone with a drug record can't turn into a drug agent."

"Are you thinking Jack Franklin was your dad's friend?" Winnie asked.

"Yeah. And why would he want to kill my father? Just because he went to prison and Dad split? That doesn't make sense."

"Maybe he was a drug agent even then. I never actually saw the man Mother is talking about, but I do remember that no one ever heard from him again. Could be that supposedly being sent to prison was really his way of moving on undercover without anyone involved ever wondering about him."

Hunter gaped at his aunt with new respect. "And now, he's murdering . . ." He paused, a question in his voice.

"Dealers who slipped through his hands before? Slipped through the system?" Winnie shrugged. "Or, unfortunately, just got in his way."

"Oh, man, this is real. This is it." Hunter shuddered. "And a lot scarier than I even imagined. I almost punched the guy." Suddenly, he was in motion. "Aunt Winnie, call Grayson." He was out the door, running. "Tell him to meet me at the harbor. He's got to help me get Miki before it's too late!"

He ran the two blocks to the harbor with no plan, just a driving fear for Miki. In his brash desperation, he might not have stopped until he had both feet on Jack Franklin's yacht, but the scene in the harbor halted him.

The harbor was quiet, not a tourist in sight. With most of the yachts gone, the seagulls had even deserted the place. County deputies joined Grayson's police officers on the boardwalk, some keeping the camera crews pushed back toward the street, some staring nervously at the single yacht that was just docking. Even the reporters were subdued, eyes on the yacht. Hunter elbowed his way through the news crews and straight-armed a deputy aside to stand alone on the boardwalk. Cameras flashed as Grayson Tucker strode up and walked toward the yacht. An officer joined him and together they walked down the ramp. "This must be it," someone behind Hunter whispered. "The killer must be turning himself in."

✳ ✳ ✳

Jack Franklin sped toward the harbor. He was cutting his time close. Having to deal with Miki had distracted him. The Cat had lost his focus. He had left the yacht without his gun. He had only a few minutes to backtrack and get it.

Jack's plan was simple but brilliant. His sources had told him that Rob Kittrell would step off a boat today at nine o'clock and turn himself in. Rob wasn't fool enough to let a half-million-dollar inheritance go to his son. Jack knew Rob well. Rob Kittrell was Jack's first case as a drug agent.

Today, Rob would be Jack's last bust. Jack would arrest Rob on the boardwalk, watch the terror in Rob's eyes when he recognized him, smile for the cameras, and shoot Rob Kittrell through the heart. The first piece of scum ever to slip away from Jack finally executed in front of the news media. It was risky, but Jack had the element of surprise. He was sure he could pull it off and get away. And the world would know he was The Cat.

Jack came in sight of the harbor. Something was wrong. There were too many officers on the boardwalk. Rob Kittrell was just stepping off a yacht, and Grayson Tucker was there to meet him. Stupid Tucker! He probably thought he was arresting the harbor killer. Jack cursed himself for not grabbing his gun sooner and plowed toward the dock, nearly blind with fury.

Cameras snapped as Grayson led Rob Kittrell down the ramp in handcuffs. Reporters pressed forward, trying to push past the deputies, shouting questions. A smile spread across Rob's face when he saw Hunter standing in the center of the uproar. Hunter gave his father a slow salute.

"Tucker!" A speedboat blasted onto the scene and banged to a halt against the dock. Jack Franklin jumped out, and there was a murmur from the crowd. He looked like a man with authority—a man on a mission. "You fool. What do you think you're doing?"

Grayson kept his prisoner moving, but he put his big body between him and Jack.

"Answer me, Tucker. You're a damn fool, and everybody here can say they saw it. You arrested the wrong man. He's not the harbor killer."

Hunter stared at Jack's face, livid, twisted with hatred. He was a madman. What had he done with Miki?

At that moment, Grayson made a motion with his hand, and an officer dashed on board Jack's yacht. He disappeared inside the cabin and was back on deck in a second, shaking his head, *No*. Grayson released Rob to another officer and began to move toward the water in a hurry.

Cursing, Jack Franklin leaped into his speedboat and pulled

away, headed down the creek. In a second, Hunter was pushing through the crowd and running toward his own dock, long legs stretching his speed to match the boat's. "He was mine," Jack screamed. "I waited eighteen years. Your father was mine." And then the speedboat kicked into gear and pulled away. Hunter arrived at his own dock as Jack roared out of sight. He fumbled with the mooring ropes, finally pulled them loose, and jumped into his boat. By the time he cranked up, Jack was far ahead.

> > >

Miki was startled to hear Jack returning so soon. In his absence she had leaned forward, pressing the cut in her side against the edge of the table in front of her, trying to stop the bleeding. In doing so, she realized that the cord around her arms was not as secure as Jack had meant it to be. She had worked at the knot steadily in the hope that she would be free before he returned.

She did not want to die, not by his hand or her own. She had thought this morning that killing herself, ending all her problems, was a choice. Now that she was forced to face death, she craved life with more intensity than she thought possible. Despair and the desperate needs within her had driven her young heart to this moment. Now that there was nothing left but pure survival, instinct lifted her soul, making her see that life was worth grabbing.

Jack boarded the boat, frightening hate in his eyes. "Make up your mind," he growled as he started the boat. "I can slit your throat before I dump you overboard. Or you can feel the sharks eat you piece by piece." He screamed in laughter as he shoved the boat in gear and roared down the channel.

Dizzy from fear and loss of blood, Miki ducked down against the table. As her head cleared, she could picture exactly how to work the knot to free herself. Struggling, she twisted both wrists, maneuvering her hands so that two fingers could touch the knot. It did not loosen easily, but it did move, and she continued to work at it.

Jack let out a stream of curses, staring straight ahead, the cruiser still full throttle. Miki did not know that Hunter was behind them, his little boat bouncing wildly from wave to wave. She did not know that Grayson was behind Hunter in a police boat, blue light flashing. She could not see the row of patrol boats that were just ahead, blocking the channel, waiting for Jack Franklin. She did not know that Jack cursed because he knew he was trapped, and he had given himself away by running, in this boat, with a hostage. Grayson had tricked him. All she knew was that her hands were free and the boat was racing toward her death—and she had a gun. She tore the gag loose from her mouth and whispered hoarsely, "Jack." He turned and saw the gun pointed at his chest, the cruiser still speeding straight for the boats in the channel, and a terrible challenge came into his eyes. He reached for the knife in his holster.

She pulled the trigger.

Blood exploded from his chest, splattering her face. The percussion rang in her ears. The moment would forever divide her life—the instant she grabbed life by taking his. Never would she forget how his perfect features shattered into horrible evil, his face contorted by hatred, the awful blackness of his soul reflected in his eyes as he stared straight into hers as he died. He collapsed against the throttle and the boat slowed.

She was screaming hysterically, still holding the gun, when Hunter boarded the boat. "Miki. Miki. It's over. Give me the gun. Babe, he can't hurt you again. Give me the gun." He took it from her, both their hands shaking. "It's okay, now. It's okay." Miki was sobbing and coughing dryly as he reached across Jack's body and switched off the engine.

The gun was still in Hunter's hand when Grayson boarded the boat. Grayson, looking very sick, took the gun and surveyed the scene. He turned and barked to the men in the boats, "You! Flag down the paramedics and get up here. The rest of you stay put."

"I'll be fine," Miki said in a thin, strained voice. "Just get me off this boat."

Grayson stooped to untie her legs. "Young lady, I tried everything I could to get you to tell me what you knew about those murders. Anything that could have linked Jack Franklin to the killings. I put you in jail to try to protect you from this." His voice broke. He helped her to her feet and handed her a handkerchief to wipe Jack's blood from her face. "This officer will take you to the hospital and get that wound taken care of. Then I want you to come directly to the courthouse and give your statement to a judge. It won't take long and you'll be free to go."

She nodded, glanced at Hunter through her tears, and stumbled away with the officer.

Grayson and Hunter looked out. Six patrol boats surrounded the cruiser and news crews were just pulling up. Grayson sighed. "Hunter, you've managed to get in the middle of another killing."

"I know it," said Hunter.

"We've got a creek full of federal and state agents. None of them knows for sure who shot Franklin, and every one of them is going to want to ask you a hundred questions."

A reporter called out, "Chief Tucker! What happened here? Who is the harbor killer?"

"And I've about had my fill of that squawking," Grayson continued.

"Me, too," agreed Hunter.

"Ever play Monopoly?" asked Grayson.

Hunter smiled.

"Go straight to jail. Do not pass go. Do not collect two hundred questions." Grayson pulled out handcuffs. "I can get you out of here in a hurry. You can tell your story one time to a judge and be home in time for lunch."

"What are you going to say you're charging me with, Mr. Tucker?" Hunter asked as Grayson handcuffed him.

"I don't have to say anything, Hunter. Franklin is dead, you're in my custody, and that's all anybody has to know until the judge says it's all over."

TWENTY-EIGHT

Hunter and Miki stood alone in the anteroom of the court-room, waiting for the judge to see them.

"Why did you do it?" she asked.

He looked toward the window. The August sunlight appeared muddy in this room, caught as it was in the suspended dust.

"Why?" she asked again.

He shifted slightly and looked into her eyes, still blue, still lovely, now keen with pain. Before she could ask a third time, his mouth covered hers, savoring the warmth of her lips.

"What was that?" she asked, her voice shaking.

"That was good-bye," he whispered.

"I don't understand. You risked your life for me after the way I treated you. Why?"

He sighed and studied her face, pale from this morning's ordeal. Dark shadows beneath her eyes told him of the nightmares and sleepless nights she had suffered.

"I feel like I never really knew you, Hunter," Miki said. "And I will always regret that." After a pause, she added, "Nobody has ever thought I was worth dying for. I guess I'll never understand why you did it."

"I sure don't have all the answers," said Hunter, "but I know both of us have been asking the wrong questions. I can tell you for a fact that you're worthwhile to God. And I guess I did it because that's what people have always done for me—stuck by me no matter what I did."

Grayson walked in just then. "Sorry this took so long," he said. He looked at Miki's pale face with concern. "The judge is ready for you. It's just a formality. He'll ask you a few questions, I'll tell him you're not charged with anything, and that will be the end of it. Then I want you to get some food and some rest."

Tears began to roll down Miki's cheeks. "I don't have anywhere to go," she whispered.

"Sure you do," said Hunter lightly. He took her by the arm and stepped forward in an exaggerated motion. "Just take a step and you're in a brand new life." He dropped her arm and looked into her eyes. "That's all I want for you, Miki. I just want you to be okay."

She nodded and cocked her head at him. "Is Amy one of those people who stuck by you?" she asked.

A slow smile spread across his face.

"You're in love with her, aren't you?"

"Yeah, well, I guess maybe I am." Hunter winked at Grayson and held the door open for Miki. She squared her shoulders, took one long step, and strode past him into the courtroom, her long skirt flowing gracefully.

AUTHOR

Sheri grew up in Mt. Airy, NC, and still lives thereabouts with her husband and a pup named Cercie. Together, they've made a living running a couple of small business, and made a life doing the things they enjoy—traveling, hiking, camping, kayaking. Sheri loves music and yoga, inventing gourmet meals from random ingredients, laughing with friends, and most especially spending time with her daughter. A graduate of High Point University, she has burned more pages than most people will ever write, and is currently scribbling a third novel, which may or may not survive the flames.

Here are what reviewers are saying about
A Higher Voice by Sheri Wren Haymore

"If you can only buy one book this month . . . Buy this one! It will take you places you can only imagine and you'll believe in happy endings again."

"Thank you Ms. Haymore for giving us a book we can read again and again and never tire of. In the spirit of such books as 'Gone With the Wind' and 'Sense and Sensibility,' this book is timeless."

—**Melanie Adkins**, reviewer for "Have You Heard Reviews"

"Haymore has a deft touch with dialogue, and has created complex characters, an intricate plot, and protagonists you root for all the way. It's a classic mystery thriller with a twist. Satisfying echoes of Mary Higgins Clark. I look forward to Haymore's next book."

—**Beth Westmark**, published essayist for "The Broiler: A Journal of New Literature" and "Emerald Coast Review"

"A Higher Voice is a sprawling novel filled with well-defined characters, excellent descriptions, and a gripping story of romance and suspense . . . Readers, no matter what they believe, will be caught up in the dramatic story and find themselves hoping the appealing characters will succeed in overcoming their difficulties."

—**Jane Tesh**, author of the Madeline Maclin Mysteries and The Grace Street Series

"A Higher Voice *is such a wonderfully engrossing tale."*

"The author is able to pull the reader into the story so deeply, the outside world ceases to exist . . . Haymore is an author to watch."

—**Michelle Willms**, editor and journalist

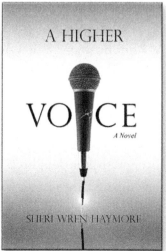

Available at

www.amazon.com
www.sheriwrenhaymore.com
www.wisdomhousebooks.com